what they're saying about
THE NIGHT EAGLES SOARED

The Night Eagles Soared by Steve Newman pulls the reader into the life of the United States military's men and women. The sacrifices, training, and dedication of these individuals are astounding. I always knew that their mission was dangerous. Reading about some of them in detail brought a face and heart into the picture. As a civilian, I urge you to read this book to gain more appreciation for the price paid for our freedom and protection.

—Elaine Littau,
author of *Nan's Journey* and *Elk's Resolve*

The Night Eagles Soared by Steve Newman is a book that speaks to the military reader. Authentic descriptions of ordnance and weapons effects are an integral part of the story and keep it real. I appreciated the technical details and the nod given to Homestead Air Reserve Base's Mako Squadron. As a member of the Armed Forces, I encourage everyone to read this book; it most certainly rings true.

—Col. Ross "Rosco" Anderson,
482d Operations Group Commander, Homestead ARB, FL

06 Sept. 2013
SBN

THE NIGHT EAGLES SOARED

To MSgt. Cobb

Fortune favors the bold!

De oppresso Liber

S. B. Newman

THE NIGHT EAGLES SOARED

S. B. NEWMAN

TATE PUBLISHING & Enterprises

Published by Tate Publishing & Enterprises, LLC
127 E. Trade Center Terrace | Mustang, Oklahoma 73064 USA
1.888.361.9473 | www.tatepublishing.com

Tate Publishing is committed to excellence in the publishing industry. The company reflects the philosophy established by the founders, based on Psalm 68:11,
"The Lord gave the word and great was the company of those who published it."

Published in the United States of America

ISBN: 978-1-61663-616-6
1. Fiction / War & Military   2. Fiction / Action & Adventure
10.07.08

DEDICATION

I want to dedicate this book to my wife, Brig. I love you more than you will ever know. It has been your undying love and faith in me that has kept me going day in and day out. I will never forget the day you told me to change the direction of my life, to focus on writing. You have stayed awake nights, reading what I have written, giving me opinions, editing my work. You are the love of my life, my best friend, my chief editor, and my partner for life. You are absolutely wonderful, and I love you.

To my children: Austin, Georgia, and John. I love all of you with all my heart. May God's blessings and mercy follow you all the days of your life.

ACKNOWLEDGMENTS

First and foremost, I would like to take this opportunity to thank each and every one of our troops who are currently serving this great nation in its time of need. My prayer is, "Father, give our men and women of the armed forces the courage and strength to do that which they must. And Father, please help them all make it home safely. Amen."

The Night Eagles Soared has been a work in progress for many years; and it was my mother, Lois Forbus, from Hugo, Oklahoma, who inspired me, God bless her soul. She was an English teacher and author, and it was her love of language and ability to teach that gave me not only the desire to write, but the ability. May her legacy live on forever.

I would also like to thank my sisters-in-law, Michelle and Amy; my father-in-law, Steve Thompson; and my wife, Brig, for their enthusiastic and positive support during a time in my life when I needed it the most. You guys made all the difference in the world.

To my earthly father: you have supported me in so many ways, and I love you for being strong and for setting such a positive example for me to emulate throughout my entire life. I hear your words and quote them to others on a daily basis. As far as this project, you would say, "Only time will tell."

To my stepmother, Judy, who, although she may not realize it, encouraged me tremendously, and always loved hearing my stories: thank you.

To my sister, Shannon. You are a person who has always faced life's trials and tribulations in faith. You have raised your two sons alone with the strength of two parents. Always loving, you are a great mother, a great sister, and an incredible teacher. I love you.

To my brother, Clayton, and sister-in-law, Rita. You guys are the shining example of what we should all strive to become. Don't ever stop being yourselves, and may the light of heaven shine upon your lives forever.

I would also like to thank the Christian staff at Tate Publishing for their insight and willingness to consider my work. There were so many. Thank you, Jennifer Shelton, Melissa Huffer, Nancy Meyers, Krista Motley, Rachael Sweeden, Jordan Bradford, Stefanie Rane, Stephanie Woloszyn and Dr. Richard Tate for having faith in not only God but also in me. I would also like to thank all the other unsung heroes at Tate Publishing who have worked so diligently to bring this project to fruition. Your efforts have not gone unnoticed; and for all of you, I am forever grateful. Thank you for doing what you do so well! "The Lord gave the Word; great was the company that published it," (Psalm 68:11).

I would also like to give a special thanks to Elaine Littau, another Tate Publishing author. She has been a tremendous asset to me throughout the entire production process and I appreciate all that she has done and continues to do through her writing ministry. Thanks Elaine!

Of course, it almost goes without saying, but it must be said: "Thank you, Lord, for answering my prayers, for bestowing upon me and everybody in my life your immeasurable favor. Thank you for giving me the courage to survive, the mettle to succeed, and the opportunity to be the person you intended me to be. Amen."

THE BEGINNING

An Air Force C-17 is an enormous aircraft, especially when the only cargo being loaded is a single Special Forces team preparing for a high altitude, low opening (HALO) parachute operation. Tonight's operation was different though, and the team had the entire aircraft to itself as they stood behind the behemoth plane, looking into it through the open tail section. The sound of the jet-powered generators onboard was deafening, and each man listened attentively as their company commander congratulated them upon being the first team selected for such a prestigious mission. He wished them luck and shook their hands, hugging each of them in such a way that made them all believe he truly cared about them as human beings.

They were beginning their journey into combat, into Afghanistan, the first team to get a mission; and this time, there would be no turning back. The night air in Germany was chilly in late September, to say the least; but the men didn't notice. It had been less than a month since Al Qaeda had attacked the United States by flying commercial jets loaded with innocent civilians into the World Trade Center in New York, the Pentagon in Washington DC, and into the ground out in Pennsylvania. These were the chosen few to be the first as they stood there, shaking hands with the brass, each general and colonel giving the soldiers a congratulatory pat on the back as they moved down the line, all of them wishing that they could be on this team.

Mike, the team sergeant was anxious; he didn't have time for such pleasantries. He had a lot on his mind, a lot to remember; and this sort of farewell did not suit his nature. Short in stature, standing only five feet nine inches tall, most of his men stood a head taller than him, but they respected him a great deal. Mike wasn't a small man; he weighed at least two hundred pounds and only had about 2 percent body fat. He was muscular, with strength greater than most men. He could out run everybody on his team, despite the fact that he was at least ten years older than all of them.

His strength didn't come from his muscles; it came from his character, his knowledge, his experience—years of having served on various teams, having conducted numerous operations throughout the world. Mike had earned the reputation of being one of the best; and for that reason, his team was selected to be the first one into Afghanistan, to link up with the resistance forces fighting against the Taliban; to train, equip, and advise them; to lead them into combat; to hunt down and kill Osama Bin Laden; to do what they could. Others would follow, but he and his team were the first as the generals lined up to shake their hands before the men boarded the plane.

The tarmac was well lit, but the fog that surrounded the plane kept the light muffled downward as the crew worked feverishly to get the aircraft ready for takeoff. The pilots were walking around, doing their preflight checks, as the load master and crew chief set up the oxygen console along with the oxygen tech, who would supervise the pre-breathing operations the period of unpressurized flight and the subsequent HALO jump would require.

The soldiers had already loaded all their gear onto the tailgate of the aircraft along with their parachutes, weapons, and ammunition, among other things. This flight would take at least ten hours, and the team would be required to pre-breathe pure oxygen for at least sixty minutes before the jump. Pre-breathing oxygen is the technique they would use to get the nitrogen out of their bodies before jumping from altitude and into the greater atmospheric pressure they would encounter closer to the ground. Just like scuba divers use dive tables to control their ascents to the surface in order to avoid the bends, these military freefall parachutists would breathe in pure oxygen prior to the jump in order to avoid getting the bends as they plummeted for over two minutes at terminal velocity, with all their equipment strapped to their bodies, toward the earth and even greater atmospheric pressures.

A light mist began to cover the men as the last of the brass had made his way past them in their parade of stars and stripes. Mike gestured with a final salute to the company commander and signaled for the men to follow him on board. Behind them, the load master and crew chief began closing up the paratroop doors at the back and on each side of the plane as the men moved toward the forward section of the aircraft directly behind and below the cockpit. Their plan was to conduct in-flight rigging of equipment, execute the pre-breathing of oxygen for an hour, and jump. It was simple really; nothing to it. They had done it many times in practice. Now they were doing it for real. Their mood was somber though, not having slept much over the last few days. *The rigors of mission planning can really zap your strength,* Mike thought to himself as the sound of the aircraft's engines being cranked up made him feel a bit sleepy. He knew they had a few hours and that it would be best to use the time getting some rest, so he shouted over the roar of the engines, "Get some sleep! I'll wake you up when it's time to put 'em on!"

With that, Mike sat down and looked at his watch, making a mental note: *Should take about ten hours till we are over target. Plenty of time to get some sleep.* The high-pitched winding of the aircraft's huge jet engines escalated as the crew continued closing the ramp and doing their chores at the rear of the aircraft. The team's equipment, to include their parachutes, was stacked up neatly, in a line two feet wide and about waist high in the center of the cargo hull floor. A bright yellow cargo strap stretched over the line of equipment from end to end, holding it all in place, the weapons box in the middle. In it, the team's weapons were secured: 5.56mm, M-4 Carbines, with advanced high tech gear like the Aim Point and Laser Target Designator attached to them. Two each, M-4 Carbines had M-203, 40mm grenade launchers attached under the barrel. There were also Beretta 9mm pistols, 7.62mm M-240B machine guns, 5.56mm M-249 Squad Automatic Weapons, and a couple sniper rifles all packed nicely away.

Each member of the team had a basic load of ammunition, and they relaxed with the comfort of knowing they had already packed a resupply bundle with enough ammunition to keep them in business for some time. In that bundle, they had also placed two 50 caliber sniper rifles; some 81mm mortar tubes and ammo; and, to top things off, a few hundred pounds of C-4 explosives.

Mike felt comfort in knowing that they had all they needed and national level support should they require anything else. He knew that with all these weapons and ammunition, they would be formidable—especially when you consider their level of training and the fact that they had an air force tactical air controller or TAC-P with them. He could call in air strikes—not just fast movers but the big guys, the B-52's with their massive payloads.

The team seated, he began to relax as the aircraft taxied from its chalked position on the tarmac and headed out under the fog-dampened lights. The plane rolled out toward the runway. On the flight deck, the pilot, co-pilot, and navigator were completing their preflight checks and communicating with the control tower as the air crew busily prepared for takeoff, finding their seats and strapping themselves in. The aircraft shook a little as it rolled over the cement and onto the asphalt taxiway.

For Mike, this was the beginning of the end. He knew that his time in the Army was almost over. It was a matter of age, and this was a young man's business. Mike knew that being selected to lead this team, on this mission, was the pinnacle moment of his career and although his time in the Army was coming to an end, he knew that this was the beginning of the rest of his life. It was the ultimate honor for him and his team to be selected for this and he wondered how he had done it. How had he been able to arrive at this position at this moment in time, at this incredible moment in history? *This is an incredible moment,* Mike thought to himself. *How did I get here?*

I*remember my first day in the Army. It was a cold December morning when I had reported to the recruiter's office for the ride to the city in order to sign up. I hadn't thought much about what I wanted to do with my life. I just knew that I had to get out of this town. Having completed high school a few years earlier, things weren't going that well. I had been working construction, roofing houses. It was hot, dirty work that proved to be fruitless even if you could find a job.*

A few years had already gone by since the Iranians had taken American hostages in Tehran, Ronald Reagan was in office, and my small town was closing in on me. I wanted to see the world, to experience something, anything other than just working like a dog for next to nothing. So I had joined the Army on the delayed entry program, right off the street, straight into Special Forces, jump school, and training as a radio operator. It was the day I was to leave for basic, Fort Leonard Wood Missouri, more commonly known as Fort Lost in the Woods.

The ride to the city was dark at first. And then we came to the outskirts of town, and I could see the high rises as the highway widened to six lanes and was lit up by the night lights on both sides of the road. We rode along in an old Plymouth Reliant, one with U.S. government plates on the front and back. My recruiter drove along, smoking cigarettes, Marlboros, with the windows rolled up. And I could barely breathe, but he was a sergeant and I was just a new recruit, so what was I going to say? He kept rambling on about how he was going to show those bastards at the reception station since he was wearing his khakis with all his medals pinned on. He kept talking about how proud he was that he had signed somebody up for the airborne, but I just zoned out, looking out the window as he continued the conversation without me.

The city lights flickered by, one after the other, reflecting off the dirty glass of the window as we continued down Interstate 35 toward downtown Oklahoma City. I hadn't been in the city much, having grown up just south of there, south of Norman on my family's farm, just south of the University of Oklahoma. There were many nights of fun in my little town, chasing college girls down on Campus Corner. But you needed a bit of money to do that—and time. I had neither.

We pulled off the freeway, and the sergeant continued his conversation as we drove down deserted streets under the city lights. It had rained earlier, making everything shiny wet as the car splashed its way toward the in-processing center downtown. We had been there back in September, when I had joined under the delayed entry program. I had wanted to leave right away, but they wanted me to wait a few months so that the timing would be right to get me into basic training, advanced individual training, and jump school on my way to Special Forces training without too much down time. Hell, I didn't even know what I had gotten myself into at that point. I just knew that I was getting out of my small town and was on the road to a different life. I hadn't known then that it would be twenty-five years before I would return to Oklahoma for good.

The drone of the C-17's engines continued their high-pitched spinning as the aircraft continued on its way, bouncing a bit from left to right on toward the end of the taxiway, turning onto the runway and coming to a halt. The brakes squealed loudly as the weight of the aircraft lifted from the rear toward the front; and the pilot brought the engines up, preparing for takeoff. The aircraft shook violently as the pilot brought the engines up to full power, holding the brakes, preventing the aircraft from moving. He released the brakes; and with a sudden jolt, the aircraft leaped forward and began slowly gaining speed as it rambled down the runway. Even with earplugs, the noise was deafening; but the experience of tactical takeoffs wasn't something new to Mike or his team.

This was a common practice, one that the Air Force used regularly to get their large cargo aircraft up into the air as quickly as possible.

Mike thought to himself, *this isn't the same as that day I flew out of Oklahoma City on my way to basic training. It was a nice flight, with Coke and a comfortable seat. Although it was the first time I had ever flown before. I didn't know about clearing your ears when you land. And man, my head hurt. I couldn't seem to get the pain to go away. It was like I had dove into the bottom of a swimming pool, on the deep end. The pain was killing me. I lit a smoke and tried to forget about it. But that just didn't work, so I popped a stick of gum in my mouth and began to chew it a bit. It would take several hours for it to subside, despite my best efforts.*

When we walked off the plane in St. Louis, the first thing I saw was a group of Hare Krishnas with their garb and tambourines. Hands filled with some sort of literature, one of the young Krishnas tried to get my attention and followed me through the terminal as I followed the signs down to the baggage claim area. I had never seen people like this before, so I curiously asked for one of their brochures. And they asked what I was doing in the airport. I proudly proclaimed that I was going into the Army. And with that, they began to beg me not to as some of them began to bang their tambourines and chant. It was at that moment when we moved down the escalator into the baggage claim area that a larger than life sergeant wearing his dress green uniform came out of nowhere and asked me if I was heading for Ft. Leonard Wood. I replied, "Yes." He grabbed me by the arm and pulled me away from the Krishnas, shouting at them to get the hell out of there. He took me over to the baggage claim area and told me to retrieve my gear and to get on the Greyhound bus that was parked just outside the terminal's exit.

It was December 7, 1982, ironically the date that would live in infamy as proclaimed by Roosevelt four decades earlier. It was the day I was inducted into the Army. What a day! The bus ride through the Missouri countryside was uneventful and dark. Completely full, the bus hadn't left the airport until late that evening. I sat there in the airport for at least eight hours, waiting for it to leave. Every now and then, another plane would land and a few more kids would show up and get ready to board the bus—kids from Chicago, New Orleans, backwater Mississippi, or Georgia, New York, and California, kids from all over the country, but I was the only one from Oklahoma. And I was older than most. Most were barely eighteen.

The engines of the bus groaned as the driver shifted gears, turning off the highway and into the front gate. There was a large tank that was set up as a memorial there at the entryway as the guards waved us through and we passed the parade field and the bowling alley. I couldn't tell which direction we were going, but it seemed as though the driver didn't either. We drove around the base a couple times before he came to a stop in front of a large brick building three stories high and several hundred yards long, a large stairway in front. We began to offload the bus as the drill sergeants started screaming at everybody for no reason at all. They had singled out this one Puerto Rican kid who couldn't speak English. He kept saying, "No hablo Inglais," as the drill sergeant, an average-sized black man with a high and tight haircut, nineteen fifty's-style dark sunglasses, and a smoky the bear hat on his head kept screaming at him to tell him his name. He shouted, "Well, hell, recruit; we'll just call you alphabet for now!"

We lined up, not knowing how to create a formation, as the drill sergeants ran around, hazing the crowd. Apparently, we were all a bunch of numb nuts for not knowing what to do. There seemed to be no method to their madness. As the sun began to come up, they all went inside the building, leaving us standing there, wondering how long we would be there.

A few minutes passed, and a black, '69 Z-28 Camaro came around the corner, burning rubber, and screeched to a halt. A tall man wearing civilian clothes and a cowboy hat got out, staggering up to the front steps. He turned and yelled out, "Smoke 'em if you got 'em!" and then went inside. So we did. Everybody lit a smoke and started milling around a bit, talking. The Puerto Rican kid was standing next to me. I gave him a smoke and lit it for him. He smiled. And as I was pulling another smoke out of my pack, the cowboy came back out and yelled, "Put 'em out!" Well, the Puerto Rican kid was just a little too slow. As he was blowing out his puff, the cowboy came off the stairs in two large leaps; lunged forward;

and slugged the Puerto Rican kid in the face, knocking him to the ground. Standing over him, the cowboy began to shout, "When I say put 'em out, I mean put 'em out!" It was at that moment that an older black man with all kinds of stripes on his sleeve came around the corner and shouted at the cowboy. The cowboy's faced turned red as the black sergeant berated him for abusing, and I quote, "My troops!" We never saw the cowboy again, but the black NCO turned out to be the battalion sergeant major.

We spent the entire morning drawing equipment, boots, and uniforms at the central issue facility, a long, one-story wooden building that had an aisle along the outer wall, marked by a counter that ran the length of it. There were different stations for each piece of equipment and an individual there designated to issue a particular item. Each of them had something to say. Most were men, veterans that had all been through this themselves. They seemed to revel in the pleasure of messing with us as we passed each station. I don't think I've ever been yelled at more than I was that day. All the equipment fit nicely into the one duffle bag, and we moved outside through a large double door after having signed for everything.

There was a sergeant—not a drill sergeant, perhaps one that was in training—waiting for us as we came out of the building. He was a skinny young man, perhaps six feet tall with a toothy smile that made you wonder. He had us form up into a formation, a task we had not yet mastered, and then he announced that we would be going down to the barber shop for haircuts.

Sitting in the barber's chair, facing the mirror, I could see my long, blonde hair, feathered back in the style of the day. I always considered myself to be a tough guy. And then the barber said, "Okay, Andy Gibb, how would you like it?" Before I could say a word, he cut a stripe right down the middle of my head. Then he held the strand of hair in front of my face and said, "That's the last you'll see of this." Laughing, he tossed my hair on the floor. And in less than a minute, he had shaved my entire head. Then he removed the smock and shouted, "Next man!"

I walked out the door, and onto the landing as a drop of water dripped off the roof and onto my head, soaking it. The guys that hadn't gotten their haircuts yet were standing there, laughing. I didn't say anything. I just walked down the steps and took my place back in formation.

A sudden jolt snapped Mike out of his daydream as the aircraft bounced from side to side. Rubbing his face, he sat up straight and looked around. Everybody had settled in for the long flight. The captain was reading a book, and the rest had gone to sleep. The sound of the aircraft seemed extraordinarily quiet as Mike realized that they were just experiencing normal turbulence. He stood up and walked back to the back of the aircraft, found one of the port windows, and looked out into the night sky.

A full moon lit up the white clouds below with a black night-glow that was comforting yet reminded Mike of skydiving out in Washington State. They had gone out there and spent two weeks doing all different types of military freefall operations out in the Yakama training center. They had conducted night, full combat equipment, high altitude, and high opening parachute operations with a twenty-five-mile standoff from the designated drop zone. Mount Saint Helens was covered in snow that last night. From altitude, it looked like a pimple ready to pop.

His thoughts drifted as he remembered all the different freefall jumps he had made over the years. Night, full combat equipment operations all over the country, daytime chopper blasts just for fun on Sicily, Normandy, Rhine Luzon and other drop zones around Fort Bragg. He had even jumped into El Salvador to link up with the troops he would lead into combat. Chuckling to himself, he remembered how scared he had been that day at Fort Benning, that day he had made his first jump. He had finished basic training at Fort Leonard Wood, Missouri; and then he had gone to Fort Gordon, Georgia to learn how to be a radio operator. Then he went to Fort Benning to attend jump school on his way to Fort Bragg and Special Forces training to earn the Green Beret.

It was hot in Fort Benning. By the end of April, It is already hot, I thought to myself as we did our flutter kicks in the gig pit under the shadow of the jump towers that made Fort Benning famous. Home of the Airborne. Then why are we always crawling around in this dirt?

The black hats were running the line, making corrections, as troops failed inspection. The black hats had them move into the gig pit, where they all eventually ended up anyway.

The gig pit is a rectangular-shaped area a hundred feet long and fifty feet wide, that is surrounded by a two-foot wall of green-colored sandbags. The entire area was filled with sawdust a foot deep, dry and dusty. The black hats loved to make us roll around in it, do push-ups, sit-ups, flutter kicks, hello dollies, grass drills, so forth and so on. The sawdust penetrated everything. And you didn't get to leave until you were completely covered in sweat, sawdust, and dirt. That is how you spent the rest of the day "filthy, dirty leg" the black hats would say. These guys were twice as bad as our drill sergeants in basic training.

That is how we started each day at jump school—getting inspected, rolling in the gig pit. Well, that is after PT and breakfast. There were more than a few occasions that I thought for sure my breakfast was going to come up but it never did.

I was part of a unique group of young soldiers called Sierras, troops that had already been identified for Special Forces training. They called us Sierras because we had a capital S along with our student number written on a piece of hundred-mile-an-hour tape pasted to the front and back of our steel pots.

A steel pot is the WWII vintage helmet that we still wore in those days. They were not as comfortable as they seemed to be when the TV heroes I'd grown up watching wore them. Having the definition of a Sierra didn't seem to bring us any privileges other than being singled out from nearly five hundred other troops that could just blend in. As a Sierra, the sixteen or so of us were given some very unique and special attention, especially during our morning inspections. In hindsight, the extra physical training probably helped more than it hurt. But at the time, it seemed as though it would kill us.

That was the day we would be making our first jump from an actual aircraft, "while in flight!" the black hats would emphasize. I remember having a good laugh about it with some of my roommates the night before. Shoot. What do they expect us to do, jump out before we even take off? The thought had occurred to me as we lay there in the gig pit, covered in sawdust. Up 'till now, things had been pretty easy, other than the constant exercising. We had gone through all the training. We had learned how to don our parachutes and everything else that goes with making an airborne operation.

We had also run around the airfield and across the Chattahoochee River several times. The bridge over the old river would bounce as we ran across it, five hundred or so soldiers, men and women, all running in cadence, singing songs. When we crossed the bridge, it would sway under our weight, making it hard to keep your balance. I thought for sure we would all end up in the river one day.

We had also been through the swing landing trainer and had been dropped from the mock aircraft on the thirty-six-foot tower and we had been through the two-hundred-and-fifty-foot jump tower. What a ride—better than Disney.

Up 'till now, it had been fun, even the gig pit. But today was going to be our first jump, and silence had fallen over our group as we went through the paces trying to survive the black hats' wrath for one more day, one more week, and five airborne operations.

After the gig pit, it was already lunchtime, so we marched over to the chow hall, where there was already a group waiting at the door, chanting, "Hit the hole pole man. Hit the hole!" while they stomped their feet and moved forward in groups of five up the stairway and into the dining facility. The chant was reminiscent of tower week, as teams of jumpers would rig parachutes to the assembly that held them in place as it pulled the parachute and the jumper attached to it up into the air. In the center of the ring, there was an attachment point designed to catch the loop at the apex of the parachute. One paratrooper would have a pole in his hands, and it was his job to attach the apex of the parachute to the apparatus. We would all chant, "Hit the hole pole man. Hit the hole!" as he would make his attempts. If he missed, the black hats would be on his ass like white on rice. Nobody wanted to be the pole man.

The chant had become our mantra for jump week. Now, "Hit the hole," had a different meaning. It represented the door of the aircraft. We had been practicing our exits in the barracks the night before, just in case one of us was chosen to be the first jumper to stand in the door. We didn't want to freeze up.

"Hit the hole pole man. Hit the hole!" We entered the dining facility, black hats on our asses. "Hurry up. You ain't got time to eat, airborne. Get a move on. Get the hell out of my chow line!"

In about thirty seconds flat, I went through the chow line, getting a little bit of everything served onto my plate: green beans, corned beef, mashed potatoes, brown gravy, Jell-o, wheat bread, and a coke. I found a seat and started eating my meal as a black hat saw my Sierra designator that was taped over my name tag. "What the hell, Sierra? You don't need to eat. Get the hell out of my chow hall!" I just kept eating as fast as I could. And before he could yell, "Get the hell out of my chow hall!" for a third time, I was on my feet, moving toward the tray turn-in point, eating as I went, the black hat on my ass. I downed the rest of my soda with the glass in one hand as I placed the tray on the conveyor belt. Then I set the glass down onto the tray and threw the silverware into an awaiting bucket of hot water. The black hat was still yelling. I just ignored it as I ran out the door and disappeared around the corner of our barracks building. I only had a few minutes to make it back to formation. We were set to run down to green ramp, down to the airfield, and get ready for our first jump.

In the battalion area, between the large, three-story barracks buildings, we formed up as a faceless NCO brought the formation to attention and announced, "Men, we are going to make our first jump later this afternoon, so get your minds right!"

The sergeants faced the formation toward the street, to the north, and out we marched onto the avenue. We began to do the airborne shuffle, a modified run that was neither a full-blown jog nor a fast walk. "Stand up, hook up, shuffle to the door. Jump right out and count to four," We all sang as we continued the shuffle down to the airfield. "If my main don't open wide, I gotta reserve by my side!" My main better open, I thought to myself. "If that one should fail me too, look out, ground! I'm a comin' through!"

Once inside the riggers' shed, we were issued our parachutes and reserves and began to prepare for the jump as the black hats made their rounds, giving last-minute instructions and answering questions.

I didn't dare look one in the eye, much less ask a question. There was too much water under the bridge at this point to bring more attention upon oneself. A cloud of dust, combined with the smell of cigarettes, created an unmistakably pungent odor that lingered throughout.

After receiving the primary jumpmaster's operational briefing, we all started putting our parachutes on. Having already adjusted the harness to fit, I donned the T-10 main parachute, pulling the leg straps up and through the carrying handle of the aviators' kit bag that was issued with the gear. Then I snapped the leg straps into the center ring, making sure the kit bag was pulled out between the leg straps in order to protect my private parts from the opening shock that would translate its force upward through the leg straps.

Pulling the shoulder straps taught, I snapped them into the O-ring harness and stood erect; testing to make sure it was secure. Then I had my jump buddy, the guy next to me, hand me my reserve parachute, another T-10 packed into a reserve pack tray that was designed to snap onto a pair of D-rings on the front of the harness. There was a belly band that came around from the right that threaded through two cloth loops on the back of the pack tray and then connected to the harness under the left arm. We left a quick release in the belly band connector so that the jumper could undo his harness once on the ground. The weight of the rig wasn't that bad, although the harness dug into my shoulders and thighs. Other than that, it was reasonably lightweight and comfortable.

Following suit, I helped my jump buddy don his equipment, and we retrieved our helmets, placing them onto our heads. We checked each other's paratroop shock pads, a rubber pad located on the inside back of the helmet, and chin straps to ensure we had put them on correctly. It was at that moment that a black hat, all of whom were jumpmasters, stood to my front, and I sounded off. "Right door, Jumpmaster!" He retrieved the yellow static line from the back of my parachute, routed it over my left shoulder, and snapped the anchor line snap hook onto the carrying handle, a loop of one-inch tubular nylon, on the top of the reserve pack tray. With my legs spread shoulder width apart, hands on top of my helmet, I stood ready for the inspection as the black hat covered every part of the parachute harness and reserve, touching them with his fingers and visually inspecting everything, making absolutely positive that I had put the equipment on correctly and that there were no material defects that *may cause an unsafe situation. The entire process—the way the equipment was issued, the briefings, the inspections—made us all feel a little better about the prospect of leaping out of a perfectly good aircraft.*

Today, we were going to do a daylight, Hollywood, static line, mass tactical airborne operations using two C-141 Star Lifter aircraft. This big jet had been in service as the mainstay airlift aircraft for the U.S. military since 1965. With its high-mounted, swept-back wings and four huge jet engines, the Star Lifter had earned its reputation as the work horse of the Air Force. It had a ninety-three-foot-long cargo bay that could carry one hundred and sixty eight paratroopers. Today, we were going to load both of them to capacity.

In four lines, we all moved out of the rigger shed onto the tarmac, walking a bit bowlegged up to the awaiting tailgate of these incredible aircraft. I had only flown once before, and that was the civilian flight I had taken on my way to basic. Now I was going to jump out of this huge aircraft.

We entered the back of the plane, leaning forward as we walked up the ramp. The tail section reached high into the sky and on both sides of the plane the black hats—now wearing Air Force emergency bail-out parachutes, static line parachutes, or aircrew harnesses—all loitered near the rear doors, along with the load master and crew chief. I noticed the anchor line cables overhead, the cables we would use to connect our static lines to, when we stood up, ready to jump. We continued to move forward, packing in tight on both rows of seats on each side and down the center of the aircraft. The seats ran the length of the fuselage. We sat sideways to the direction of takeoff, facing each other.

I was to be part of the first stick, seated inboard; about twenty feet back from the paratroop door on the port side of the aircraft. It was the port side of the aircraft, but we called it the right side door since we would be facing to the rear and the door would be to our right. The yellow static line hung over our left shoulders so that it would be to the inboard side of the aircraft. Most everybody was wide-eyed, silent as the load master walked across the top of our legs and conducted one last check of the anchor line cable. The cable was attached to the aircraft frame directly behind the cockpit and ran the length of the fuselage through a guide that hung from the ceiling and then to an anchor point at the rear of the plane. Near the paratroop door, there were several sets of lights designed to allow the pilot or navigator to signal the jumpmasters that it was clear to jump. Red lights on, the pilot began to wind up the turbofan jet engines. Slowly, he brought them up to full power while the flight crew raised the rear ramp, and closed the paratroop doors, sealing the entire tail section. With a slight increase in power, the pilot allowed the aircraft to break free from its chocked position. We started to bounce across the tarmac, turning toward the runway.

Our aircraft would be the second one in this flight of two, which would make rapid turnarounds in order to minimize flight time. We would be jumping from twelve hundred and fifty feet above ground level (AGL). The aircraft continued to taxi out onto the runway, as the roar of the first aircraft taking off almost completely drowned out the noise of our own aircraft. Suddenly, the first aircraft bolted down the runway, engines on full power, as our aircraft made the turn and the pilot brought the engines up to full power after having momentarily applied the brake, bringing us to a complete halt. The thrust of the four engines made the aircraft bounce up and down as the pilot held the brake until the moment that he was ready; and then, with a sudden jolt to the rear, we were all leaning toward the back of the aircraft now as the C-141 lunged down the runway for what seemed like an eternity. Then the front of the plane lifted; and with what felt like a downward push, the rear wheels lifted off the ground. The hydraulic pumps for the landing gear strained as they lifted the massive wheels and tucked them neatly away. Then, suddenly, the aircraft leveled off; and the overwhelming noise from the engines subsided as the pilot powered them down.

With a hand gesture, the crew chief let the primary jumpmaster, in his bailout chute; know that it was his aircraft. With that, he signaled both of the assistant jumpmasters; and they stood up and hooked their static lines to the anchor line cable, making sure the safety wire was in place. In unison, they handed their yellow static lines to the jumpmaster safeties standing behind them. The jumpmaster safeties were wearing aircrew harnesses over their battle dress uniforms. The harness allowed them to use a three-inch nylon strap to tether them to the aircraft. They had adjusted the strap so that *it would be impossible for them to exit the door. Their primary function was to assist the jumpmaster and ensure his safety.*

The paratrooper signal lights, positioned on both sides of the doors, were lit up red as the jumpmasters, in unison, turned to face the jumpers. In rehearsed unity, they both stomped their right foot onto the floor of the aircraft and shouted, "Twenty minutes!" as they pumped their arms twice, forward from their chests toward all of us, their fingers extended and spread. With that, they turned toward the skin of the aircraft and waited while the flight crew members opened the doors. As the doors opened, the sound of the wind rushing in overtook the roar created by the huge jet engines as the pilot powered them down a bit more.

The jumpmasters ran their hands around the door, from the bottom of the trailing edge upward across the top and then down the leading edge. Once satisfied that the edges of the doors were smooth, not offering a cutting edge that may destroy a static line, they began stomping on the floor, around the doors' openings. They stomped to the left and then right; and then, with authority, they stomped to the center. They had each gained a firm hand grip on the frame of the door about waist high as they pushed through the wind barrier and hung out the door with their knees in the breeze.

They checked the flaps that should have been at thirty degrees, indicating that we were flying at the correct air speed. Then they looked up, down, and to the rear, making sure that there were no other aircraft in our way. Feeling a tap on their shoulders from the flight crew members, they had just spotted the first navigation check point. Each of them pulled back into the aircraft and turned toward the group of jumpers, each of us waiting with nervous anticipation.

With the same rehearsed unity, they signaled, "Ten Minutes," although the time signals at this point were really just a formality, as the aircraft would be doing race tracks around the drop zone, allowing us to make a drop every five minutes or so. The pace was quick as the jumpmasters each stomped on the floor again, pointing with their palms facing up, fingers extended and joined toward the row of jumpers along the skin of the plane. "Outboard personnel stand up!" Giving the troops about thirty seconds to get to their feet, the jumpmasters stomped the floor again and pointed to the center line. "Inboard personnel stand up. Hook up!" they shouted, making a hook sign with their index fingers as they raised their hands over their heads. Stomping on the floor, they waved their arms from below their waists, palms up, fingers extended and joined. They waived their arms, bringing their fingertips up to touch their chests as they shouted, "Check equipment!"

The plane bounced a bit as it slowly turned, coming around on jump run. With another stomp, the jumpmasters shouted, "Three minutes!" The plane leveled off. The anchor line cable bounced up and down as the nervous jumpers pulled, unaware that they were leaning on their static lines to stand. Again, the jumpmasters stomped on the floor, cupping their hands behind their ears, "Sound off for equipment check!"

From behind me, in rhythm, I could hear the other jumpers sound off as the signal, "All okay!" came down the line one by one until I felt the man behind me smack the back of my thigh and yell, "All okay!" and I passed it along. The first jumper pointed with the knife edge of his hand at the jumpmaster and shouted "All okay, jumpmaster!"

The aircraft waffled left and then right, tilting on its center line as the wing tips dipped slightly to each side, making the line of jumpers stager a little to each side and then forward two or three steps. The jumpmaster shouted and pointed at the first jumper. "Stand by!" And then he leaned back out the door. Suddenly, he came back inside, stood facing the first jumper, and said, "Stand in the door." The paratroop lights still red, the nervous first jumper assumed his position in the doorway.

I kept thinking to myself, There is no way I can do this. I couldn't breathe. The fear was almost overwhelming. The jumpmaster was looking out, his head underneath the right arm of the first jumper as he again pulled back into the aircraft, pointed at the paratroop lights, and shouted, "Green light, go!" simultaneously slapping the thigh of the lead jumper, who disappeared into the blue.

With that, the line of jumpers slowly began to move forward, each man stomping on the floor, doing the airborne shuffle toward the door, the jumpmaster gathered static lines and pushed them to the rear as each jumper exited the aircraft. One by one, on each side of the plane, we jumped the momentum of the line building until, suddenly, I was in the door.

I leapt, keeping my feet and knees together, eyes closed in fear. I felt *the static line break away from the parachute pack tray; and the aircraft roared off, leaving me there in silence, falling, counting.* One thousand, two thousand, three thousand. Ah, come on, you son of a gun. Open up. Four thousand. *And with that, my parachute filled with air, snapping open, bringing my body to what felt like a screeching halt.*

I looked up to see my risers all twisted up, so I reached as high as I could, grabbing hold; and then, with an instinctual knowledge, having been through this before during our training, I started to make a bicycling motion with my legs, slowly bringing myself around, untangling the twisted lines as the parachute continued to control my descent softly toward the earth.

The lines came untwisted, and I noticed the other jumpers in the air all around me. There was nowhere to turn. I looked down and could see a line of yellow smoke blowing from in front of me toward my back. Luckily, I was already facing into the wind as I noticed the ground coming up really fast.

"Look over the horizon. Look over the horizon," I remembered the jumpmasters instructing us to do so that we wouldn't reach for the ground with our legs and hit stiff-legged and break a bone. I tried to anticipate the direction of my fall to no avail. I hit so hard that it knocked my breath out of my lungs as a noise of agony escaped from my mouth. Stunned, I laid there for a second, watching as my parachute continued to collapse over my head; but it didn't go away nicely. It filled with air, and the wind began to drag me along the ground, unwillingly. Realizing what had happened, I reached up and grabbed hold and opened the quick release, pulling on the O-ring, freeing my left riser. The riser flung away from my body with a ringing noise as the tension was let loose. Softly, the parachute collapsed to the ground and it was over.

Ears popping, I realized that I hadn't broken any bones; and the flight of two came back overhead, dropping its precious cargo once more. I realized then just how close to the ground we had jumped and felt exhilarated that it was over—that is at least the first one was over. Only four more to go, and then I would be on my way, on my way to Fort Bragg. Just like today, I had no idea what I had gotten myself into that day I had signed up to join the Army to become a Paratrooper and to go through Special Forces training.

RAPE, KILL, PILLAGE, AND BURN

On an early summer evening, I arrived to the in-processing center at Fort Bragg, North Carolina. The reception center wasn't much to look at, an overly-used World War II vintage, two-story, wooden building that had been originally designed as a platoon barracks. It had been painted white with black trim around the windows; but the paint was faded and peeling and the floors were worn and dusty—no shine on them at all. Support posts separated the first floor into sections, and on each post hung a coffee can that had been painted red. On the can, it said "Butts," and I knew that meant cigarette butts because of the wet ashtray smell that dominated the senses.

This isn't as nice as Fort Benning, I thought to myself. *Must be a rag bag running this place.* Rag bag was the term my drill sergeants had used to classify somebody that didn't measure up to the Army standard. The Army standard, I had learned, was different everywhere you went, so I had already decided that the Army standard for me would be how I defined it for myself, not how somebody else defined it for me. In the long run, this would turn out to be one of my strongest attributes and a source of success.

"Private, what in the hell is your major malfunction? Airborne!" somebody yelled; and there were so many privates that I didn't realize the yelling was directed at me.

Across the counter was a scrawny little black sergeant who had one really big right eye. I swear it looked like it was about to pop out. In fact, it was so big that, for a moment, I didn't even notice that his left eye was swollen shut. He must have gotten into a fight because surely he couldn't always look like that. Just the sight of him scared the hell out of me; and as he began to yell again, I jumped back a little.

"Write the date, Private, in block sixteen. Put today's date on it, now!"

I looked at my watch and realized that it was already 2:00 a.m. Sounding out for everyone else to hear, I wrote, "Fifteen May, nineteen eighty-three."

"Those of you going to the 82nd, move your gear upstairs and rack out," said the scrawny NCO. "And the rest of you, where you going?"

"Eighteenth Airborne Corp."

"You guys can take a seat. It'll be awhile before they get down here from Garrison to pick you up."

"Special Forces."

"What the hell? Who the hell is going to Special Forces?" he barked.

I thought, *Oh boy. I'm the only one.*

Then a few other guys stepped forward; and in perfect harmony and deep monotone, they said, "We are, Sergeant."

I didn't say a word.

Then he shouted, "You dirtballs wait outside. They'll be here in a minute to get you!"

I picked up my gear and walked back out the way we had entered, past the latrine and the stairs and out the door, back into the street.

A tall, lanky kid followed me out of the building with his duffle bag strewn over one shoulder. He laid it down on the street next to my gear and said, "Hello. I'm Doug, from Kansas."

"Is that right? Well, it is a small world. I'm from Oklahoma. Chew?"

"Sure. I was supposed to quit, but I'm thinking of starting up again."

We sat there for a couple hours, enjoying our Copenhagen and waiting for a ride to where, neither of us knew. They had already picked up the ones going to Eighteenth Airborne Corp, and the guys going to the 82nd were soundly asleep.

We were wondering what the hell was going on when, suddenly, an old Ford pickup, probably a '69 model, came burning rubber from around the corner. It was a light puke green color; and on the side of the doors, it had "U.S. Army." As the truck pulled directly in front of us, it screeched loudly to a halt. Obviously, it needed a new set of brakes; and I could smell oil burning as a light cloud of smoke quickly engulfed the pickup and everything within ten meters of it. A square-shouldered NCO jumped out of the passenger side, and the driver sat there and lit a smoke. As he stepped up onto the curb, he put his green beret on, making him seem larger than life. A white patch of cloth on the front of his beret stood out in the light glowing dimly from above the reception center door.

"Those of you going to Special Forces, get on the truck."

We all hesitated for a second. Surely this couldn't be what they sent to pick us up. There were seven of us with all of our gear.

"I said get on the truck!"

And with that, we piled all of our gear into the bed of the truck; and one by one, we climbed on top. I looked at my watch, and it was already 4:00 a.m. We headed out, rear wheels rubbing on the inside of the truck's fenders. We all held on for dear life as the driver popped the clutch, jerking the truck into motion. I was sure we wouldn't make it more than a mile; but after only a few minutes, we pulled off the road and onto a sidewalk and stopped in front of a three-story brick building, our barracks. The sign out front was dangling from only one chain, hanging off-kilter at a forty-five-degree angle. It said, "Company A. John F. Kennedy Special Warfare Center and Institute for Military Assistance."

"You guys move into the transient rooms on the first floor and get some sleep. Be in the day room at 0800 hours for a briefing. The next course has already been selected, so you guys will have at least two months of prephase before you start your training."

I didn't know what prephase was; and at the moment, I was so tired I didn't really care. I just wanted to get some sleep. Doug and I moved into the first room we found, grabbed a rack, and immediately went to sleep.

At 7:30 a.m., I was abruptly awakened by the noise of boots stomping up and down the hallway outside my door. I could hear the muffled conversation of what sounded like at least twenty men. Peeking out the door, I saw that there was at least that many, soaking wet, boots covered in mud.

One of the guys in my room said, "Those are the prephase guys coming in from a land navigation exercise. They've been in the field about five days now."

They looked beat. Most were limping, and they were filthy. I had never seen soldiers that looked so bad.

Then another roomie said, "They've been in prephase for over a month now, and they are getting ready to start phase training in a few days."

I closed the door and wondered what the hell I had gotten myself into. These guys looked like death warmed over, and they hadn't even started the training yet. It didn't really matter though. I had orders to be here, and I couldn't just go home. I had volunteered for this, not really knowing what I had gotten myself into. It didn't matter. I was going to stick it out, no matter what. My orders stated that should I fail, I would be assigned based upon the needs of the Army; and I figured that that would mean permanent kitchen patrol

(KP). I had done enough KP during basic to know that I would do anything to stay off that detail. Of course, I was naïve. I didn't know that being assigned within the needs of the Army probably meant the infantry since I was already a radio operator and an airborne-qualified paratrooper that probably meant the 82nd. Ironically, years later, I worked with the men from Bravo Company, 1st Battalion of the 504th Parachute Infantry Regiment of the 82nd Airborne Division—one of the best infantry companies in the world. They call it the "All-American Division." Most of the troops I met were Latino. Many had joined to get their citizenship. The rest were probably poor white trash from places like West Virginia or Oklahoma, like me; or they were inner-city blacks with an attitude and an aptitude that suited the infantry. All of the lieutenants were fresh out of ROTC, baby-faced and impressionable but eager as hell. I didn't know that I would go there if I had failed Special Forces training. I thought I would end up peeling potatoes for the next four years; so I decided that no matter what, I was going to make it or die trying.

A few minutes before 8:00 a.m., we walked into the day room and stood around for awhile. Most of us were raw recruits, fresh out of jump school. Many had just completed infantry basic and had the confident demeanor of that experience under their belt. We were all in extraordinary physical condition, but I was a great deal smaller than most—at least that is how I perceived myself to be. Some were playing pool on an old pool table that dominated the main entrance while others sat and watched television. It was strange that so many men could be so engulfed in soap operas. The need to have something, anything to do, just to pass time was still not a concept that I had come to embrace but would eventually come to understand and also long for. Before I had joined the Army, I had listened to my uncles talk about their time in the military. All had been veterans of WWII, but they didn't talk about combat. Instead, they cracked jokes like, "Hurry up and wait," and until now, I hadn't truly known what they had meant by that; but the concept of it would become a well-known concept to all of us.

"Everybody out front. Fall in formation now!" barked an NCO

from the door of the day room. I turned around, and people were running toward the door; so I followed suit and ran out of the day room, turned left, and headed out the door, down the steps, and onto the sidewalk that ran parallel to the front of the barracks.

There were several NCOs wearing green berets with white flashes lined up on the side-walk. There was a space between each—about thirty feet. Apparently, they were there in order to designate specific locations for everybody to line up. There were already about two hundred men in formation behind the sidewalk. They were the prephase candidates. They didn't look any better than the group that had come in earlier.

The NCOs that were lined up began to shout, "Weapons fall in here. Medics, fall in over here. Engineers over here. Radio operators fall in over here!"

I breathlessly fell in with the radio operators as people scrambled to find a place in line.

Once the movement began to subside, the first sergeant stepped out onto the porch in front of the barracks above the steps and stood there, looking us over, hands on his hips. He was a short, stocky man; and he looked as though his youth had been stolen. His face, round and sunburned, was sternly studying the group.

He shouted with a slight Southern drawl, "Fall in!"

Several hundred boots made a single, unified stomp on the cement as we came to the position of attention.

He shouted. "Report!"

The NCOs up front each turned in unison and from left to right sounded off.

"Weapons. Forty-four present!"

"Demo. Thirty-two present!"

"Medics. Eighteen present!"

"Commo. Twenty present!"

"Prephase. All present!"

Each NCO saluted, and the first sergeant returned it as they reported. A nervous young aide handed the first sergeant a clip board and stepped back into the barracks, disappearing into the shadows. We stood at attention as the first sergeant announced, "The following personnel will fall out and fall into the day room as I call your name." He began calling out names; and as he would call out a name, that person would sound off with the last four numbers of his social security number and then run out and around the formation; up the stairs, past the first sergeant; and disappear into the shadowy entrance of the barracks. He kept calling names for almost ten minutes, and I noticed that they were all from the prephase section of the formation. When he was done, there were only about fifty or so of the prephase troops still standing there. He shouted, "All of you prephase students still standing in formation will start the Q course on the eighteenth. Your next formation will be tomorrow morning at 0800 hours. Go get cleaned up and get some rest!"

They let out a loud rebel yell and bolted from the formation and ran into the barracks.

Then he said, "All weapons and demo, you start prephase today. Next formation is at 0600 hours tomorrow. Uniform is what you're wearing now, along with your rucksack and LBE (load-bearing equipment). Get your gear together for the rest of the day, and be out here tomorrow morning at zero six hundred hours, ready to go. Fall out."

They all shouted, "Hooah!" and bolted up the steps past the first sergeant and into the barracks.

As they cleared past him, he said, "Okay. All you radio operators and medics; this is your lucky day. All those idiots in the day room just got cut from the course because we caught 'em cheatin' on land nav. Therefore, you've got a choice. You can start prephase in the morning, or you can start the Q course on the eighteenth. Those of you who want to start the Q course stand fast. Those of you, who want to start prephase, take two steps to the rear."

Slowly, most everybody started stepping back, out of the formation. I looked around, and realized I was the only one in my rank that wasn't moving.

Just then, the first sergeant shouted, "Fall in!"

Snapping to attention, I stood there, looking ahead, but noticed that there were only five or six of us left in the formation.

The first sergeant shouted, "All of you who took two steps to the rear, you start prephase in the morning. Formation will be at zero six hundred hours, rucksack and LBE. Fall out!"

They sounded off and ran up the steps, past the first sergeant, and into the barracks.

As they cleared past him, he shouted, "The rest of you fall in on me up here in front of the steps. Move!"

So the rest of us, not more than twenty-five, formed up in front of the steps below him as he stood there looking down on us with a curious glint in his eye. Then he said, "Okay. Look. You've got two days to get your gear together. You'll have a formation each day at 0800, but other than that, the rest of the time is yours. Get a copy of the packing list for phase one from my orderly, and make sure you have everything on it. Make sure Sergeant Atwater gets your names before you go anywhere, and I'll see you guys out at Camp Mackall on Wednesday. Good luck."

He turned and walked back into the barracks, into the day room; and from where we stood, you could hear as he started yelling at the guys in there. I thought to myself, *Man, those guys are in for it*. It still hadn't dawned on me what an extraordinary stroke of luck this had been.

On the morning of the eighteenth, I woke up at four o'clock and my gear was packed and ready; but I had not been able to open a bank account, so I still had about three thousand dollars in paychecks and about ninety dollars in cash. The packing list said we could bring no more than forty dollars, but I figured they would never find out. So I packed the checks and my money away in my duffle bag, hiding them in a sock. No one would ever know.

I took a shower and got dressed, putting on my brand-new jungle boots. They were a little tight but very lightweight. Some of the sergeants were looking at me strangely when I walked out of my room into the hall wearing my new boots and brand-new olive green OG-107 uniform.

One commented, "Well, at least he isn't wearing starch and spit shines."

As they enjoyed a laugh at my expense, I smiled, not getting the joke. Everything I had was practically brand-new. I had just been issued all of this gear and had only been in the Army little more than five months. With my duffle bag on my shoulders, I carried my rucksack in my right hand. The night before, I had rigged it for the jump we would make into Camp Mackall later that day.

We all slowly walked out of the barracks and formed up on the sidewalk. The first sergeant came out with a big mug of coffee in his hand. He shouted, "Fall in!" and then took the report from the NCOs, the same ones that had been there earlier in the week. Later, we addressed them as our TACs, trainee counselors; but they weren't really counselors. They were more like drill sergeants on steroids. Once he had received the report, he told us to get on the eighty pax trucks. My drill sergeant in basic said that after we had graduated, we would never have to ride on an eighty pax truck ever again; but that was obviously not true. An eighty pax truck is a tractor-trailer, with the trailer designed to carry about eighty passengers when seated. We packed at least one hundred and twenty-five people, along with our gear, onto each of the four trucks and then departed for Mackall.

Camp Mackall had been a glider training center during WWII and was now where the Special Forces conducted most of its initial field training. We rode along for almost an hour, and I had been lucky enough to be standing next to a window on the right hand side of the trailer. We were packed in like sardines as some smoked, others held quiet conversations, and others quietly contemplated the future. I stood there, looking out the window, as we passed the rifle ranges that lined Chicken Road and then St. Mere Eglise drop zone. We left Fort Bragg out the back gate and continued on a blacktop road for a short while until we entered the cantonment area known as Camp Mackall. The forest was much denser than the civilian-owned land nearby as we passed over the swampy black water that ebbed, steadily churning. A sign read "Drowning

Creek." Then we turned right at a T intersection, past a sign—"Big Muddy" (an arrow pointed to the left) and "Camp Mackall" (an arrow pointed to the right). We passed a depression in the ground filled with water. It was stagnant and oil-black. It looked as if it had been there forever. Turtles were sunning themselves on motionless logs that provided floating platforms and safety.

The entire camp was surrounded by an eight-foot chain link fence that had a single strand of razor wire on top of it. At the far end, there was a rappel tower. About a half dozen white rabbits were running free around a series of old wooden shacks covered with black tar paper, and there was another row of silver tin buildings that resembled the barns farmers kept their hay in back home. As we came around the far side of the camp, we pulled into the main gate and parked in front of two large silver tin buildings. A sign in front of each indicated that one was a classroom and the other was the camp headquarters.

As the trucks came to a stop, the doors on the trailer flung open; and there stood one of the TACs with his Green Beret and white flash perfectly placed upon his head. He started screaming for everybody to get off the truck and to form up in front of the headquarters building.

As we started shuffling around, trying to get to our gear, he decided that we weren't moving fast enough; and he snatched the first man off the trailer, throwing him to the ground.

In an angry voice, he shouted, "Drop and give me twenty!" As the man who had been thrown to the ground started counting off the repetitions, the sergeant began taunting him. "You want to quit, don't you?"

"No, Sergeant."

"I know you want to quit, you piece of trash. Quit. Quit now before I have to scrape your sorry butt off this road. Quit!"

I stepped off the truck and around them as he continued the hazing. I noticed that the same scene was being played out at the doorways on each of the trailers.

The first sergeant was standing at attention in front of the headquarters building and shouting, "Fall in on me!" so we all ran into formation and came to the position of attention. I heard somebody back over by the trucks say, "to heck with this." But I didn't look around to see what was going on. The hazing by the trucks continued for only five minutes; then suddenly, it was so quiet I could hear crows cawing in the distance as they sounded their alarms of impending danger. The TACs moved a group of troops to the headquarters building and lined them up, single file, their duffle bags still in hand and their rucksacks still on their backs.

The first sergeant announced, "Look at these posers behind me. They are quitters. I think we have a new record: twenty-three. All of them quit before they even got off the trucks."

The quitters all stood there with their heads down, looking at the dirt as the TACs hovered menacingly around them.

"Okay, men. There are a few rules you must follow while you are here. You will not walk. You will run at all times while you are in this camp. You will carry your weapon with you at all times. It is never to be more than an arm's reach away from you. You will wear your LBE at all times. Do not leave the barracks without either. On the command of, 'Fall out,' you will fall into a barracks, secure yourself a bunk, put your duffle bag on top of it, secure the rest of your gear, and be back here in formation in one minute. Fall out!"

In a mad dash, everybody bolted toward the silver tin buildings. I ran as hard as I could and luckily found a bunk in the first building of the entire row. Not taking any time to look around, I threw my duffle bag onto a cot, turned, and ran out of the building. The TACs were lined up, indicating positions for the formation in front of the first sergeant. Each was calling out a barracks number and ordering us to fall in, according to the barracks we had selected. I fell in with the first platoon, fourth squad, last man in the file. Our TAC, Sergeant Ford, explained that this was how we would fall in from now on.

We marched around the camp and back out the way we had entered and turned off the hard ball road onto a dirt lane. "Route step march," was given; and we walked slowly down the trail. After a short distance, maybe one kilometer (click), we crested over a hill; and below us was a triangle-shaped airfield. We were on the back side, across the way from several support buildings; and there were several two-and-a-half-ton canvas-covered trucks waiting for us. Deuce-and-a-halfs are what we called them. Each truck was filled with parachutes; and as we lined up, we were each given one, along with a reserve. We continued single file around the trucks, onto an area that had been recently mowed; and someone shouted, "Get 'em on!"

After sitting in the hot sun for over an hour, with the parachute on, it was finally time to board the aircraft. There had been a National Guard C-130 Hercules taking lift after lift of paratroopers up to jump the entire time, but it was finally our chance to go. I followed in line, like ducks waddling behind their mother. We stumbled clumsily up the ramp, our rucksacks hanging upside down from our parachute harness—upside down and between our legs. We walked up the ramps, straddling our rucks, into the back of the aircraft. The engines were running; the exhaust fumes were hot, burning my eyes, nose, and throat. So I held my breath for a moment. It was difficult to breathe, and I was sweating profusely. We found our seats. As the aircraft rumbled against its brakes, bouncing a bit, the flight crew looked professionally cool, with their flight helmets and tinted visors. They walked around, obviously in charge of their aircraft; but as we took off, the jumpmasters began to move around and take charge. The aircrew stood behind them on the upwardly sloping ramp in the back of the plane. They stood there idly, waiting for their next chore.

"Twenty minutes!" shouted the jumpmaster as he stomped forward onto the floor of the aircraft with his right foot, knees bent. He held out both of his hands, palms opened and fingers extended and spread. Then he closed his fists, pulled his arms into his chest, and then protruded them outwardly once again with his fingers extended and spread, indicating with hand signals that which he had just moments earlier announced so authoritatively. My knees were shaking a bit; and I prayed, as I did every other time I jumped out of a perfectly good aircraft, "Father, give me the courage and strength to do that which I must. And, Father, please help us all make it without getting hurt. Amen!"

The aircrew started moving around as the jumpmaster turned to us, stomping his right foot forward and giving the hand signal. He shouted, 'Ten minutes!'

The clamshell on the back of the aircraft began to open, and I could hear a loud roaring sound over the drone of the aircraft's engines. Then the load master began to lower the ramp, and sunlight beamed into the rear of the plane. Over the edge of the ramp, the ground could be seen. The aircraft made a sharp, right-hand turn. The ramp floated up and down at an angle, making the earth appear as if it was spinning out and away from us. The sight made my stomach a little queasy for a moment, so I looked out and up at the sky.

The jumpmaster kneeled down, his back toward us, his rucksack splayed out in front of him. He was looking out and down for the drop zone. Soon, he stood up and turned toward us and stomped his foot, signaling with his hand as he shouted, "Three minutes!" With both of his hands, index and middle fingers extended and joined, he pointed to the skin of the aircraft and shouted, "Outboard personnel stand up!" as he motioned upward over his head with his hands and fingers. The earth continued spinning out of control behind him.

The sergeant, acting as the jumpmaster's safety, stood, holding the yellow static line, keeping it from getting tangled. The roar of the wind rushing past the opening was deafening. It completely drowned the sound of the C-130's powerful prop engines. The jumpmaster signaled, "One minute!" I noticed that the jump command lights in the aircraft were already green, which was a standard procedure for a jumpmaster release. It also meant that this was it; it was time, and we were going to do it.

My rucksack hung upside down in front of me, attached to the D-rings of my parachute, which were also used to connect the leg straps of the parachute harness around the buttocks and thighs. With a quick thumb press, I checked them as the Jumpmaster gave the command, "Check equipment! Sound off for equipment check!"

I checked my chinstrap and the paratroop shock pad in the back of the helmet of the man in front of me. Giving a quick glance at his static line, I could see that it was not tangled; and I felt the man behind me slap my right thigh as he shouted, "All okay!" I repeated the gesture on the thigh of the man in front of me and shouted the same and listened to each of the soldiers in front of me sound off.

At that moment, the jumpmaster shouted, "Standby!" and I could feel the aircraft level off as the earth seemed to be rocking back and forth underneath our feet outside the tailgate.

I focused on the horizon and the jumpmaster as he turned toward the rear of the aircraft. He was still looking down to his right as he signaled with his thumb and index finger, ten seconds. He was making a sort of pinching motion with his thumb and finger; then suddenly, with his left arm swinging around, palm out, fingers extended and joined, he pointed to the rear of the aircraft and shouted, "Follow me!" and disappeared off the ramp.

This was my first jump, right out of jump school, a tailgate, C-130 day blast into Camp Mackall to start Special Forces training. Following the jumpmaster out, the troops in front of me began to do the airborne shuffle to the edge of the ramp. I felt a nudge from the man behind me. He was as anxious as anybody. The sound of the aircraft was deafening, but I could still hear the metallic sound of the static line snap hooks running down the anchor line cable and the sound of the pack trays opening; and suddenly, I was in midair. "One thousand, two thousand," I counted, keeping my feet and knees together, eyes closed. "Three thousand, four thousand. Come on. Open up, you son of a gun! Oh, thank God!"

Hanging there quietly, I could see the aircraft as it trailed off black exhaust into the distance. A silent breeze filled the nylon of my canopy. Drifting slowly toward the ground, heart pounding, the adrenaline rush subsided and I realized that I had several twists in my risers. I was also running with the wind, so I began to make a bicycling motion with my feet while reaching up to grab the risers above my head. I pulled them apart and made a bicycle motion with my legs. Spinning out of the twists, I gained control of the parachute. I was running with the wind, so I looked around and didn't see any other canopies in my way. So I pulled down hard on the right toggle; and that brought me around, facing into the wind. I could feel the canopy drop a little air and then regain it.

Looking down, I could see that I was out over the middle of the triangle-shaped airfield; and I noticed the yellow smoke blowing directly toward me—a good sign. I was doing it right. As I approached the ground, I had to force myself to look at the horizon. Looking down made it seem as the though the ground was rushing up very fast. Looking out over the tops of the pine trees, I tried to keep my feet together, knees bent. Suddenly, I could hear someone yelling, "Drop your rucksack! Drop your rucksack!" I reached down, found the yellow pull tab on my lowering line, pulled it, and my rucksack fell away, downward, and then suddenly came to the end of its tether, jerking me around to the left a bit. I countered by pulling on the right toggle slightly, and I heard my ruck hit the ground.

I looked down just in time to see my feet hit the ground; and I crumbled to the earth, and the wind blew my canopy over onto the ground behind me. Still filled with air, my canopy began dragging me across the ground like a sled. I reached up to my right shoulder and pulled out the quick release snap and felt for the canopy release assembly. Finding the cable ring, I shouted, "Riser!" and pulled it as hard as I could. It made a distinct ringing sound as the riser on my right shoulder was released from the parachute harness. The canopy collapsed to the ground.

I laid there for a second, eyes closed, trying to collect my senses. One of the instructors began yelling, "Get the hell off my drop zone, Airborne!" And the C-130 swooped in, landing as it screamed past me only a hundred feet away. The roar of its engines was amplified as the sound reflected off of the tall pines that surrounded the airfield. The plane spun around, lowering its ramp, ready for another load.

My platoon was forming up. The sergeant gained accountability as we turned in our parachutes and reported back. Once we were all together, we marched back to the camp, singing slowly in a low baritone voice, keeping rhythm with our steps. The sun slowly sank behind us, below the trees, as we marched through the dust and into the shadows.

The heart of a soldier is the soul of a man. He is a knight without armor in a war-torn land. A fast gun for hire is an SF soldier. SF soldier, SF soldier, where have you been? Around the world and back again!

Our first day in the Special Forces was almost over as we marched in the darkness down the hill and into the camp. There were lights on in the large classroom; and the mercury light on the telephone pole outside the camp headquarters was already on, lighting up the gravel parking lot but blocking out visibility of anything beyond that.

We formed up, dropping our rucksacks in front of us; and then we stood at ease as the platoon sergeant discussed the following events with one of the instructors, along with the other platoon leaders. When he returned, he informed us that we would be getting a class on edible plants and animals as part of our survival training. So we began to file into the classroom. The flimsy plywood floor bounced as we stomped into place along wooden benches. We stood there as the entire class filed in. There were about four hundred of us still there at this point. A tall blonde sergeant with a square jaw named Luke stood next to me. He began to get frustrated as we waited, so he slowly started pounding his rifle butt onto the floor and in a low voice he began to chant, "We're gonna rape, kill, pillage, and burn, We're gonna rape, kill, pillage, and burn. Hey! Hey! Hey!"

A few of us near him started picking up on his chant; and soon, there were thirty, then a hundred—and then all of us were pounding our rifles on the floor and chanting. The entire building shook. The tables moved as our chant grew stronger and stronger.

Soon, the instructors came in and sounded off, "Take seats!"

And all at once, we sat as a group, waiting silently.

We sat through class that first night, learning about edible plants and snakes; but the anticipation of what might be coming in our near future through this training weighed heavily on our minds. I don't think any of us realized just what we had gotten ourselves into. I sure didn't. That night, the cadre ran us out of our barracks only a few minutes after we had bunked down, and I learned my first big lesson as a Special Forces soldier: don't go to bed in your underwear, without your boots. They ran us out of the barracks before I could get dressed; and we spent the next two hours in the rain, learning how to do right hand falls and left hand falls as part of our hand-to-hand training. The hand-to-hand pit was something that we would all become used to over the next several weeks; but that night, I was out there in the sawdust in my underwear, getting rained on and being chastised by everyone of the cadre. When it was over, I took a shower, got cleaned up, and dressed; then I went back to sleep in my fart sack on my cot with my boots and uniform on.

The next thirty-two days went by so fast that it seems as if it was a blur now. We did our survival training, hand-to-hand, land navigation; and then we did the patrolling field training exercise. We went through the rappel tower and then the slide for life. The slide for life was a moment to live for. The day before, while I was rappelling for the first time in my life, I had accidentally spit out my chewing gum onto the rappelling instructor's glove. It stuck all over everything; in his anger, he put a boot to my head as I was in the ready position to rappel off the chopper skid with a seventy-pound rucksack on my back.

That same instructor was the slide for life master, giving the class and then running the training. There must have been twenty of the cadre there that day, all watching with excitement as we all climbed the tower. I was in the first group, perhaps the fifth or sixth man to make the ascent to the top of the tower—a narrow, metal tower that supported one end of the cable that was used for the slide.

I could hear the guys in front of me sound off with their name and social security number as I continued to make the climb. Then the captain who was in front of me sounded off; and I saw the instructor wave his flags, the signal to go. When the captain went, he slipped. You see, the cable had recently been greased, and the metal triangle handles we used to connect to the slide were covered in it.

The captain went; but when he did, he lost his grip and fell past me, a few inches in front of my face. I watched as he pumped his arms, trying to keep his balance, as he yelled all the way down until his right foot caught the cargo net, flipping him upside down, sending him face first into the knots that tied the net together in six-inch squares. Screams of agony came from deep within his gut as blood gushed from his face across his brow. His leg was tangled and broken in the nets as the medic tried to climb up and get to him.

I was next in line. My whole body shook with fear as I reached the top of the tower. An instructor there told me, "Take your mind off that, and get in the game!" I hooked my triangle to the cable and looked down at the primary instructor, who was standing along the edge of Drowning Creek, watching me. I sounded off my last name and then my social security number and he waved his flags for me to go. I kept my body position exactly the way they had taught us: feet and knees together, pointing parallel to the cable, watching over my right shoulder for the signal to drop. Suddenly, he waved his flags; and I let go, flying, waving my arms in a counterclockwise motion over my head and around again as I dropped toward the water. Later, one of the instructors told me that he had waved me off too soon, that I had dropped from too high, but that the primary instructor was anticipating that I wouldn't let go at all after what we had all just witnessed. Landing on the water, my body flat as a pancake, I skipped as if I were a stone once and then twice, my legs flying into the air; and then I entered the water headfirst. I could feel the rush of the current flowing by. Debris from the bottom had been kicked up by the last few jumpers. I was disoriented for a moment, not knowing which way was up or down; so I reached, looking for air, or the bottom and I found the latter. The current had carried me downstream about twenty yards before I could get oriented and put my feet onto the bottom. But I found it, and then I was able to stand. The water was only five feet deep.

I guess I had been underwater for some time because the now-nervous cadre had reacted. Four of five of them had jumped into the water to save me. They must have thought that I had been knocked unconscious from that enormous fall, and so there I was, standing chest-deep in the dark water of Drowning Creek, about twenty yards downstream as each of them came up from below, heads shaking, shouting, "We can't find him!" The rest of the students, seated in the bleachers that were parallel to the creek, burst out in laughter. For that, I was given the chance to elevate my feet on a rock and do pushups with my face going into the water each time I would count a repetition.

That was the start of survival training. That afternoon, we slaughtered a goat and cooked it over a campfire. Little did I know that for the next few days, that would be the only meal we would be provided. After that, it was up to us to find a meal as they spread us all out over an area of more than twenty thousand acres, forbidding us to have any contact with other students. We were to forge our way around a twenty-acre area and find our own food and water for the next three days. For me, it was a lot of fun. For others, it turned out to be a disaster. One guy got scared at night. I guess he got scared being all alone. So he set off his parachute flare, the signal we were given if an emergency would arise. The problem was that nobody saw it; and so the flare caught the woods on fire around the guy's camp and burnt everything he had, including his rifle. I was nowhere near this area when it happened, but the next morning, one of the cadre pulled into my AO and took my parachute flare away from me while telling me what had happened.

Over the next few weeks, I lost about forty pounds, to the point that I was skinny as hell; but I wasn't the only one. Most of us had lost a lot of weight, along with a lot of buddies. We had started out with over four hundred men; and now, as we lined up for the last road march of phase one, there were only seventy-five or eighty of us left.

That day is one I will never forget, having made it through the entire first phase of Special Forces training. The only thing we had to do was make it through a twelve-mile individual road march. To this point, we had walked hundreds of miles, perhaps enough to have crossed the entire continent; and today, it would be over. We had done our last hand-to-hand session the night before, having perfected the sleeper hold as a group. We were now ready for what might lie ahead. I thought for sure that everybody would make it through that day, but it turned out to be too much for some; and when we loaded the eighty passenger trailers that afternoon, there were only sixty-two of us left out of a class of four hundred and eighty men. We had arrived at training riding on over ten of these eighty passenger trailers. Now we all climbed into just one and we had room to spare. I stood, looking out the window. A cool breeze gave comfort as we passed Big Muddy Lake and Drowning Creek and exited the cantonment area that had been our home for over a month. Somebody in the front of the trailer started singing "Ballad of the Green Berets," as we continued down the road; and soon, everybody joined in.

THE AMBUSH

It was a typically warm summer night for Central America, but my soldiers were freezing to death. They weren't accustomed to temperatures below seventy-five degrees and the air at this altitude was a great deal cooler than what they liked. For that reason, they had their field jackets on with the collars turned up and the inside flaps of their patrol caps pulled down over their ears. They walked with a slow, lanky gait, braced against the coolness with their shoulders hunkered in a way that made them look like a band of old men walking in the night. There had been snow on the ground when I left North Carolina, and I was accustomed to the cooler weather. Now I was profusely sweating, so I had stripped off my uniform top and was wearing only a brown t-shirt underneath my gear. That must have seemed strange to those little Latin troops, but I was comfortable.

The men, about a hundred and twenty of them, were from the

4th Infantry Brigade that was located near La Ceiba, a small fishing village that catered to the tourist trade along the Central American, northern coast of Honduras. Since Ronald Reagan had become president, I had learned to love Central America. At the age of twenty-six, I had spent the majority of my adult life living, traveling, and working throughout the region, fighting against the communist threat that the president felt was knocking on our doorstep back home. I didn't mind. Since making it through the Q course, I had decided that the more time I could spend away from Fort Bragg the better. Doing these little missions was better than waiting around at Bragg for something to happen, better than getting drunk down on Hayes Street, spending Friday nights bar hopping from one mama san hustle joint to the next.

That's why they called it Fayettenam. All along Hayes Street, there stood a little oriental girl in the doorway of each club, the youngest ones the clubs could muster; and inside were the older, more experienced veterans from back in the day. The smell of cigarettes, beer, and hand lotion permeated everything in those little bars. When you walked out, you could still smell it for awhile. It would soak into your pores. The majority of the girls were not Vietnamese though. Most were Korean or Thai; the younger ones were all Korean. The GIs inadvertently had created their own little piece of down range heaven right there in North Carolina by getting married overseas and by getting divorced once they came back. The girls, many of them, turned to the only occupation they had ever known.

Fort Bragg was a distant memory for the moment. My troops and I were no longer on the coastal plain of the Northern Caribbean coast; and as I was in a foreign land, so were these men. Though they were still in their own country, they were away from their homes, and they were a little nervous about it.

The lieutenant with whom I was working was a bit older than I, and he had a great deal of practical field experience. He was a good man, an unusual commander for a Latin Army—mostly because he gave me the impression that he cared a great deal about his men.

Despite his apparent concern for his men, he was extremely harsh at times and would order them to be beaten for almost any reason. It didn't take much to set him off. I never actually saw him do it himself. He didn't need to; he had some very capable sergeants who were well versed in the manners of corporal punishment. The U.S. Army would probably consider what I had been witnessing to be human rights violations; and at times, I felt as though I should report what was going on, but I couldn't. I understood how these men did business, and the strict discipline they displayed was a necessity to keep this conscript unit together. I didn't turn a blind eye to it. I would often speak with the lieutenant about how I saw things and made recommendations on how to resolve the disciplinary problems within the unit without resorting to such drastic measures. I was having some success, but change comes slowly in Latin America.

"Why are we stopped?"

"*Sargento*, we must conduct a recon now. *Vamonos.*"

We had been working along a twenty-kilometer stretch of the border with El Salvador for over two weeks, setting up observation posts during the day and moving into ambush positions at night. We were trying to keep the El Sal Guerillas (G's) out of Honduras. They had been infiltrating across the border to escape the pursuit of the Salvadoran Army and air force. Once they were in Honduras, they would move into Red Cross camps or small villages for a little R and R. The Hondurans probably couldn't have cared less about the El Salvadoran government's problems; but these G's had to finance their operations, so they would collect food and money from the peasants who etched out a living growing coffee and raising a few cows high in the mountainous area along the border. If the peasants couldn't pay up, then the G's would hack off a big toe, a finger, or an ear; and sometimes they would kidnap the large *hacienda* owner's children and demand a ransom. It was for this reason that the Honduran government took an interest in what was going on in the country next door. Since the Soccer War of '69, the two countries had maintained a great deal of animosity toward each other; and of course, each blamed the other for all their problems.

The lieutenant and I moved along a rocky trail lined with an ancient rock wall. Both were just below the crest of the ridge. This trail and rock wall allowed us to move undetected, along with our security detail, into the position that we would use as an objective rally point (O.R.P.). The area the lieutenant had chosen was a good, defendable position, densely forested with planted plantain, banana, and mango trees. The entire area was fairly flat and surrounded with large boulders that were oddly round, like boulders you would see in river beds. The boulders looked like they had been placed there in a slightly symmetrical pattern. They were perfect, slightly scattered, offering considerable cover from small arms fire. In the distance, a dog was barking; and with a quick hand gesture and a single nod to his men, the lieutenant dropped off a security team as we quietly continued to move down the ridgeline. We moved along the rock wall, past a small patch of coffee plants, corn, and beans all growing together. I couldn't help thinking that this was incredibly ingenious of the *campesino* to make such productive use of the land. Farming in a place like this must have been unbelievably hard.

We were close to the place the lieutenant had selected to establish the ambush position; and as he was setting in the rear security team, I made a mental note of my pace count, checked my map, and wrote a note in my little green book about how well the lieutenant had established sectors of fire for the rear security team. He gave them special instructions to avoid firing in the direction of the team we had left behind to secure the O.R.P. I always carried a small note pad to write on in order to keep track of positive and negative teaching points or lessons learned during these operations. It helped me remember what to say when we would conduct after-action reviews. Sometimes, rather serious arguments would break out during these sessions—especially if somebody had messed up and someone else had gotten hurt. Oftentimes, my notes were beneficial to finding a solution to problems that had arisen while we were out. I used my own version of shorthand in order to keep them brief; and of course, I never wrote down specifics that could be used against me, should I become a POW. In this scenario, becoming a POW was very unlikely; but I always tried to make it a habit to do the right things.

In the distance, a thundercloud was brewing; off in the darkness, the storm was making its presence known. It gave its unmistakable warning as the cloud sparked and thundered softly, lighting itself up and then sounding off. The huge thunderhead was flashing like a neon light, highlighting the distinct outline of the mountains around us; and it seemed to be saying, "Look out. It's going to rain tonight."

The flickering light of a candle dimly shined its yellow glow from the window of a *campesino's* mud hut about five hundred meters to the west of our position. Smoke lazily drifted from his chimney; and the smell of tortillas mixed nicely with that of beans cooking and coffee being brewed gently, blending into a familiar aroma that was punctuated by the smell of the smoke that was generated from the smoldering charcoals of the fire.

A pair of donkeys just out of view could be heard grazing nearby as they snorted the dust from their nostrils and chewed contentedly, reassuringly undisturbed by our presence. "*Sargento,*" the lieutenant quietly whispered in my right ear, "*vamonos.*" We walked softly, slow down the trail, toward the position he had selected; and as we approached, I noticed that it was perfect. We could move the entire company into this position without being detected. We were downwind from the *campesino's* hut; and the trail along the ridge-line with the rock wall and coffee fields covered our entire route. I would recommend to him that he send a small security element forward of the company, up along the ridge, just to make sure we weren't ourselves walking into an ambush.

We got down and low-crawled about fifty meters to a position along the edge of a low cliff that gave us a tactical advantage over anybody that might be moving along the gently flowing stream down below. The *campesino* had leveled off a number of small fields; and he had stacked the rocks up, forming small walls that surrounded each plot. This would provide cover to anybody in the kill zone, so I made a mental note to make sure we had a few men ready to toss hand grenades. The cliff followed the creek bed that made a sharp curve to the left, away from where we were at. We both knew that this would be a perfect position for an L-shaped ambush. I nodded to the lieutenant in agreement and made a gesture using my index finger, drawing the letter *L* on his hand. He gave me a thumbs-up; and we moved back, crawling on our stomachs and then on our knees until we had moved back enough to stand up.

I waited at the rear security position as the lieutenant moved and set up the left and right security teams. Each position was manned with an M-60 machine gun crew of three men—two for the gun and one for security. They also had two M-16s, hand grenades, and a couple of Claymore anti-personnel mines. The Claymore was a particularly useful weapon, a command-detonated shape charge made out of C-4 explosive that was embedded with metal balls like buckshot that, when set off, would fan out into a deadly one-hundred-and-eighty-degree semicircle. The lieutenant had to make sure the men at each position knew exactly what their sectors of responsibility were and what to do. It took him awhile, so I made a radio check with the team and gave them the code word for all okay.

"Buckshot zero six, this is Gunny. California one one break, two zero zero meters west of checkpoint zero three. Over."

"Gunny, this is Buckshot zero six. Roger copy. California one one break, two zero zero meters west of checkpoint zero three."

I checked the map again and then took my right boot off and dumped a small rock out that had been digging into the side of my ankle for several hours. It had worn a hot spot (the start of a blister) onto the side of my foot. It was no big deal. Blisters on your feet are something you get used to in this business. Avoiding blisters was imperative, but it was something that you could not completely prevent.

The lieutenant returned from setting in the left and right security positions and sat next to me under the cluster of banana trees I had been using for a little concealment.

"*Sargento,* are you ready?"

I replied that I was and recommended that he plan on putting a couple machine gunners into position at the apex of the L in order to improve his interlocking sectors of fire and how, by doing this, he would greatly enhance his ability to execute the ambush from there. I also mentioned the idea of sending a small recon element ahead of the company, up along the ridgeline, just to make sure there wasn't anybody up there that could compromise our mission. He made a facial expression that gave me the impression he had not thought of sending the recon team up along the ridge but he agreed that it would be a good idea. He also decided that we would position ourselves, along with two machine guns, at the apex of the L and use those weapons, along with a Claymore, to initiate the ambush. We would also throw a few hand grenades ourselves.

We left the men in the security positions with instructions to return to the patrol base, should the lieutenant and I not return within a couple hours. Slowly, we moved into the O.R.P. and linked up with the security team; and the lieutenant queried them. He wanted to know if they had seen anything, and they responded that they had not. It had been quiet, so he gave them some last-minute instructions and let them know that we would be bringing the company in to occupy the O.R.P. within the next hour or so. They were instructed to be ready for the company and to give directions to the platoon leaders as they entered in order to facilitate the company as it occupied the position. As we moved out, the lieutenant told me that he intended to leave two squads from third platoon along with the mortar section at the O.R.P. and that he would occupy the ambush site with the remainder of the company. For the ambush, we had two weapons squads from third platoon, first platoon, and second platoon. The two weapons squads from third platoon would provide left, right, and rear security, to include the machine gunners at our position. First platoon would occupy the bottom half of the L, and second platoon would occupy the top half of the L.

As we were moving back to link up with the rest of the company, the squelch on my radio began to crackle; and I heard the comforting sound of a pilot's voice beckoning my call sign.

"Gunny, this is Night Raider one five over."

It was an Air Force special ops AC-130 Spectre gunship. Having them on station was part of our pre-mission planning. I keyed my handset; and in a voice just above a whisper, I replied, "Night Raider one five, this is Gunny. Go ahead. Over."

"Gunny, we are on station. Mark your position." I pulled an infrared chemical light out of my load-bearing vest (LBE). I had tied a piece of gutted parachute cord to it, and then I had connected it to my vest prior to departing base camp. Placing my night vision goggles up to my face, I cracked the glass vile that was inside the plastic tube. The chemicals began to mix, and the infrared light invisible to the naked eye gradually gained in its intensity. I wrapped the end of the parachute cord around my right index finger and began to sling the chem light around on the end of it, making a circle of infrared light about six feet in diameter over the top of my head. The pilot confirmed to me that he had identified my position; and I informed him that we had men in position, securing the ambush site. He confirmed to me all four positions, a pair of donkeys, and the *campesino's* mud hut. He then announced that since the area around my position appeared to be all clear, he would return to the standby position and loiter there.

When we arrived at the company's location, the platoon leaders were waiting attentively for the lieutenant to brief them on the changes to the plan. When he was done, he gave them twenty minutes to get ready to move out and then turned to me and asked me what I thought. I recommended that he quickly get something to eat and drink because we probably wouldn't have another opportunity for awhile. It was now time for the platoon leaders to do their jobs. He had done his part; now he had a few minutes for a much-deserved break. I pulled a bottle of water out of my rucksack and handed it to him. Then I retrieved a bag of beef jerky, and we shared it. As we sat there, blankly chewing on the jerky, the thundercloud in the distance was noticeably closer; and I hoped that it would not disrupt our close air support.

There was a slight breeze now. I hadn't noticed it while we were moving; but now I did, and it felt refreshingly cool. I welcomed it. The soldiers seemed to hunker down as if they were in a blizzard. I couldn't blame them. They had never lived in an environment that got below seventy degrees, and to be faced with temperatures in the fifties was a dramatic difference for them. I went ahead and put my shirt back on, having broken a bit of a sweat, making the skin on my arms shine in the night light, despite the fact that the illumination was quickly getting darker.

The lieutenant was snoring slightly as the platoon leaders approached our position. I couldn't blame him, since I knew he hadn't slept much over the last two weeks. We had been having a rough time of it, constantly on the move, from one position to the next, trying to avoid contact with the civilians, working our way along *la frontera*. I nudged him, and he awoke as the platoon leaders squatted in a semicircle around the two of us. Their heads were just below our feet because of the slope of the hill, and this inadvertently placed them into a physically subordinate position to ours. I recognized all of them and could see the exhaustion in their faces. This would be our last mission—hopefully. Then we could go back to *La Ceiba* for a break. I suddenly felt sorry for them in a way. I realized that I would be going back to the States soon but they would still be down here, etching out their soldierly existence. Being a soldier in one of the poorest countries on the planet was not the most glamorous of lifestyles.

These men had a smell about them, the kind of smell only an infantry man would recognize: a mixture of body odor and wet clothing that reeked with the smell of cheap tobacco. You grew accustomed to it after awhile, but I imagined that the smell of the entire company would be something that could give it away. That is if the G's could smell it over their particular odors. With a quick nod from the lieutenant, he gave the command to move out; and without a word, the platoon leaders stood up and moved out. We looked at each other, our faces just inches apart; and without a word, we recovered our gear and fell into position, as the troops had already formed up and were moving down the trail.

The thundercloud that was in the distance had grown into a super cell by now, and the inevitable rain was on its way. What illumination we had from the stars was now gone, making the night so pitch black that you couldn't see your hand in front of your face. If not for the occasional bolt of lightning or flash of thunder that lit up the night like the flash bulb from a thousand cameras, there would be no light at all. Of course, I had my night vision goggles; so I would put them up to my face from time to time and take a look around. These poor men, in the cover of darkness, through the night vision goggles, appeared green and beaten. Their shoulders were hunkered over under the weight of their gear, and they stared blankly at the ground. The movement that the lieutenant and I had made in less than an hour would take at least two hours with this many men. It was best to move slowly, keep the noise down, and not lose any troops. It would be easy for any one of our elements to get separated from the company in this darkness.

The squelch on my radio began to break.

"Gunny, this is Night Raider one five. We are coming off station due to weather."

This was bad news but not totally unexpected; the weather had taken a turn for the worse and apparently, it was not going to get any better. "Roger that, Night Raider. Thanks for your help. Keep a cold one saved for me."

He replied with the classic breaking of squelch twice to acknowledge.

Well, that was that—no close air support for the rest of the night. I couldn't blame these guys. They were professionals and always willing to work with us, even when others wouldn't consider it. It had been comforting to know that they were on station, and it was better to have them and not need them than to not have them at all. Unfortunately, we still hadn't completed our mission for the night; and not having them on station would be a disadvantage.

It didn't really matter though. We still had a lot of combat power with our mortars, machine guns, and over a hundred M-16s. I felt safe but, as usual, slightly alone. Being the only American for miles around makes you feel isolated even though you're surrounded by an entire company of infantrymen.

I sat against a rock, behind the machine gunners, in our position at the apex of the L, and waited for the lieutenant to finish his checks. He would be along in a few minutes and ask me if I wanted to inspect the line. This time, I decided to just watch him through my night vision goggles and let it ride. He knew what he was doing. My job was almost finished here. One more ambush position, one more sunrise, one more hump back to base camp, and one more deuce-and-a-half ride back to *La Ceiba*.

I would be on my way home, back to Fort Bragg, home of the Airborne; back to the barracks; back to running in the matta mile. We called it that because it was said that, "If you don't mind, it don't matta." The matta mile was actually area G on Fort Bragg, part of a small greenbelt that was kept that way to allow wildlife a way to pass from north to south between Fayetteville and the post.

When I had been in training group, we would hump our rucksacks all over area G, sounding off, "Rucksack, hit it!" At that, you had to be able to touch the rucksack of the man in front of you. But when we sounded off with, "Hit it!" each man would slam the rucksack of the man in front with an open palm in a manner that tended to push him a little harder. Inevitably, someone would fall down and cause a massive crash. There would be big dog pile of troops all tangled; and of course, there was always the unlucky fool that would get hurt. Once, out at Camp Mackall, I fell on the pavement and scraped all the skin off the back of my hands, foolishly trying to keep my rifle from hitting the ground. My buddies were trying to help me up but only succeeded in dragging me for twenty feet or so with my hands pinned beneath me and my rifle. It almost cost me a shot at my beret, but the medic in my training platoon took good care of me; and unlike some who were medically terminated, I didn't get an infection.

My attention was suddenly drawn back into the present as the lieutenant exhaled and began to low-crawl forward, like a lion stalking its prey. He moved slowly forward. He turned his head sideways, straining to stay as flat to the ground as he could. He moved forward, his hand stretched out, reaching shakily for the clacker of the Claymore. I sat there motionless, without feeling, numbed by the surrealness of it all as I looked through my night vision goggles. I could see that half a dozen G's were silently, cautiously moving forward through our kill zone. They scanned with their heads and rifles in perfect unison from left to right, looking for the death we were going to rain down upon them. Their leader held up two fingers, and every other man took a step to the right. The lieutenant let go, and the Claymores exploded with a devastating blast that ripped through their formation with bone-shattering devastation. *Bam!* The sixty gunners let loose; and tracers began to ricochet up and away from down below, across the gully from left, right, and center. I tossed a hand grenade, and more Claymores exploded with such violence that I was taken by surprise. First and second platoon had opened up with all they could; the noise was deafening. After only thirty seconds or so, the men started changing magazines; and the machine gunners were getting low on ammo, and the lieutenant blew on his whistle. The left and right machine gunners lifted their fires, shifting outwardly away from the kill zone; and the lieutenant fired a flare into the air. At that moment, the men from first and second platoon let out a yell that could curdle the blood of a vampire and sprang down into the kill zone, taking no prisoners. A shot rang out, and one of our men collapsed into the shallow water. Somehow, one of the G's had survived the ambush and was able to get off a single shot before he was beaten to death by the wounded man's squad.

My heart was pounding, and I didn't even notice the ringing in my ears as first and second platoon came rushing up out of the ravine, yelling, "*Fuego en el oyó. Fuego* in the hole! Fire in the hole!" A bright flash of light, and then *bam!* The satchel charge exploded, destroying the weapons and other gear the G's had been carrying.

The lieutenant yelled out, "*Quinientos metros a las síes.*" (Five hundred meters, six o'clock.) It had only taken a couple of minutes; and now we were on the run, moving to the O.R.P. and falling in behind a few of the troops, we ran with our weapons in our hands. We ran back towards the O.R.P. I hadn't known it, but the lieutenant had coordinated for the mortar section to execute an automatic covering fire as we pulled off the ambush site. I heard the distinct sound of mortars leaving their tubes—*shuuuunk, shuuunk, shuunk*—from in front of us; then, a few seconds later, I heard, *kah-wom, kah-wom, kah-wom,* as the rounds exploded to our rear. Five minutes after the ambush, we arrived back at the O.R.P., breathlessly heaving for air.

We didn't stick around for long. The company continued to move as the weapons section recovered its gear. We moved back to where we had established the initial security position and stopped. There, the lieutenant decided to conduct a security halt to watch and listen for any threats. The night air was still; and in the distance, smoke from the ambush was climbing into the night air. It had stopped raining, and I hadn't even noticed when it had started. I felt sleepy as the adrenalin rush from the ambush began to settle.

The lieutenant said to me, "We sleep here for now and move out when the sun comes up."

I couldn't sleep just yet. Out of habit, I had to check the perimeter one more time.

I moved from position to position, checking on the men, having them point out to me their sectors of responsibility. A few had gathered around the solider that had been hit during the ambush. They had brought him to the center for the medic to work on him, but to no avail. The man was dead. We would evacuate him in the morning, when the host nation rotary wing aircraft could get into the landing zone.

"Buckshot zero six, this is Gunny. Over."

"Gunny, this is Buckshot zero six. Go ahead. Over."

"This is Gunny. Break. California one one. Break. Security halt 150 meters west of checkpoint one. Break. Enemy KIA: six. Friendly

KIA: one. Break. Request rotary wing extraction for friendly KIA at first light. How copy? Over."

"Roger copy, Gunny. Rotary wing extraction at zero six hundred on landing zone Bravo one. How copy? Over."

"Good copy Buckshot zero six, this is Gunny. Out."

In the morning, we would put our soldier that had been killed on a helicopter. I could fly out on the chopper, but wouldn't, because it would send a bad signal to the men. I would walk out with them. We would walk out together, ten clicks or so down to the main highway, where the battalion would have trucks waiting for us. From there, we would make the long drive back to *La Ceiba* and start all over again.

JUST CAUSE

Rain, downpouring rain, comes and goes as fast as you can walk across the street as the smoldering heat from the tropical Panamanian sun soaks you with sweat anyway. It was always hot, never let up. Every day, you woke up and knew that today, it was going to be hot; and perhaps, if you were lucky, it would rain. And of course, during the wet season, it did, like clockwork, every day around two.

A train, an engine and a passenger car, clamored by, *clankity, clankity, clankity clank,* chugging along through the rain on the dilapidated tracks of the Panama Canal rail that in its heyday, when the Americans were running it, was the pride and joy of the republic. Now it was an eyesore, an old, dilapidated system that no longer provided the people with enough confidence to actually ride on it. I stood there at the urinal of our barracks latrine, looking out through the third floor screen window that had no glass, across the ball field at Ft. Davis, at the train that slowly made its way toward the port town of Colon, past our little base, chugging along.

Still wearing my sweaty physical training (PT) uniform, a white T-shirt with my name stenciled with black shoe polish on the front, a pair of yellow shorts, white socks, and a crappy pair of Adidas running shoes with holes, I stood there, urinating, looking out the window at the train as it derailed across the main road. "Man that would take some time to clear up. Folks from Ft. Sherman wouldn't make it back to work on time. That's for sure."

Sweat was still pouring down my face from the five-mile run we had just finished—up to Tank Top Hill and down to dock forty-five and back to the barracks. It was eighty-five degrees at six o'clock in the morning when we had started and at least ninety-five degrees by the time we finished, but that didn't stop us from doing a good half hour of calisthenics: flutter kicks, sit-ups, hello dollies, frog kicks, mountain climbers, squat thrusts, pushups, chin-ups, and wind sprints. It was a daily routine. Sometimes we would rucksack six miles, swim a kilometer or two, and then do flutter kicks just for fun. Every day. But that was just to get started. Then we went to the range: the rifle range, the demo range, the close quarters combat range—you name it. We went to Range 37, Battery Pratt, Battery McKenzie, and Range 2, so forth and so on. We trained day in and day out. We trained hard because we knew it was coming. We knew that we were going to have to take down Noriega, but we didn't know when.

This morning, we had done PT like animals; and I was worn out as I stood under the hot shower, hands against the wall, water draining over my head, steam rising up over me as I tried to regain my senses. I could hear the giggle of two Colombian girls behind me. One of the guys had brought them in from Colon. Prostitutes from Bogotá, they were barely eighteen; but I paid them no mind. It was a common sight in our barracks. They would walk back down to the main gate and kiss the MPs as they waited for the Chiva bus to come pick them up. There were always a few of them around in the morning. We all shared the only latrine on the third floor—the troops and usually one or two women that somebody had brought in the night before.

I shaved in the shower; washed my head, under my arms, my crotch, and feet; and turned the water to cold and then stood there, trying to cool off, trying to bring my body temperature down to a tolerable level. I was hungry and needed to eat. The two young women stood in front of a sink, looking at themselves in the mirror as they put their lipstick on. They stood there naked, as they applied their makeup. I brushed my teeth and combed what little hair I had. In this heat, we kept our hair very short—high and tight in fact. A friend of mine named Billy came in and moved in behind the two young girls, putting his hands around their hips; and looking at me with a smile, he said, "Hello, ladies," and winked. I smiled and walked away with my towel around my waist as I went down the hall to my room to get dressed.

A few days earlier, we had conducted a fifty-mile road march, all on pavement. Many of the guys on my team had blisters so bad that they had missed PT that morning as they began to shuffle into the team room. Russ, one of the senior guys on the team, was on crutches and wearing only socks. Of course, they were dripping wet as he sat down at his desk; and taking them off, he complained about the rain. "Doc," he said, "look at my feet, they are all ate up," holding up both feet for all to see. Russ had no skin on the bottom of either foot. It had peeled completely off. He had been in so much pain that we had carried his gear and him for the last three miles of the road march that last night. Doc had given him some sort of pills that had made him a bit loopy, so he had started singing Hank Williams's "A Family Tradition" as we carried him to the finish point. That morning, while I was in the shower, he had hobbled in with his crutches to show me his feet and asked how mine were. I showed him, commenting, "Not a single blister!"

"You lucky dog," he said.

Our team room was on the second floor of the same building that housed our entire battalion, the barracks on the third floor, with the company headquarters for all three companies and their team rooms on the second floor while the battalion headquarters and the chow hall were on the first floor—a pretty nice set up if you ask me.

Most of the married guys on accompanied tours lived on base within walking distance to the battalion while others lived on old Fort Espinar, which had been renamed Fort Gullick since everything but the housing areas had been turned over to the Panamanian government. Others lived on Ft. Sherman, home of the jungle warfare training center, which was on the west side of the canal along with Gatun drop zone.

As Russ carried on about his poor, pathetic feet, I sat there, looking out the rain-soaked window as the deluge of tropical rain drained off the awning above the window like small rivers perfectly separated two inches apart, making it seem as if the view was through a waterfall of prison bars.

Across the sidewalk, which was at least twenty-five feet wide, stood a row of enormous mango trees that lined the entire front of our building. I loved those mango trees for the shade they provided and the fresh mangos that I would gather. Often, I would eat mangos to save money. My financial situation left me with only enough money to buy two meals a day in the chow hall; but if I needed anything else, I would have to go without food. So I would pick mangos and have them for dinner most every day. They were plentiful and delicious, large, yellow and red, succulent fruit that satisfied your hunger with their sweet, smooth texture.

Today, however, there were none, as the rain made the branches sag and the leaves hang, drenched. The branches were motionless, and the mossy mold that was growing on the windows blurred the view. It wasn't actually mold. It was more like a type of moss that grew in the jungle; and since Fort Davis would be closing soon, there was no concern to keep it cleaned off.

Everything was soaked. It had been raining since before we had finished physical training. Now the parade field in front of the barracks was covered with water. You couldn't see the building on the other side of the square. The rain continued pouring as if the heavens had flooded.

Today, there was too much rain and we wouldn't be going to the range, announced our team sergeant. "Today, we are going to conduct medical cross training. Doc will be setting up in the back for you guys to practice giving intravenous injections, and you will practice putting on a splint. As soon as he is ready to start, he will let you know." I sat there, listening to the Panamanian radio station that was playing American rock and roll when, suddenly, it began to broadcast a tone similar to the tone radio and TV stations in the States make when there is a test of the emergency broadcast system. It was an annoying tone; it captured our attention, as an announcer came on and stated that the president of the republic would be making an address to the nation momentarily. We all looked at each other in a way that expressed our disinterest; and somebody commented, "Not again."

Manuel Noriega was the dictator of Panama. There were even pictures of him hanging in the hallway of our company area from when our unit had participated in parachuting competitions with the Panamanian military; but over the last few months, the Panamanian defense forces or PDF had been executing a campaign of harassment against the Americans living and working in the Canal Zone. Two or three weeks earlier, a friend of mine had been pulled over by a group of PDF soldiers wearing their green fatigues and black baseball caps at what we called checkpoint Charlie, along the trans-isthmian highway between Colon and Panama City. He had his wife with him, and she was eight months pregnant. The soldiers, thinking that he couldn't understand their Spanish, had taken him out of the car and had him spread-eagle over the hood. Then they began commenting to each other that they were going to kill him and rape his wife. Thinking quickly, he pulled a twenty-dollar bill out of his pocket and offered it to them, acting as if he couldn't speak Spanish. Perhaps it had caught them off guard or something; but they quickly decided to let him go, his wife never knowing how close they had come to becoming another statistic.

For months, we had been collecting data on a pattern of intimidation against the Americans conducted by the PDF; and we had been running reconnaissance patrols around the bases to include Howard Air Force Base. There had been several incidents of PDF troops infiltrating U.S. bases, but no violence had ensued. I had personally conducted reconnaissance patrols between Fort Davis and Fort Gullick, picking up signs and tracking PDF Special Forces troops who were being trained by Cuban operatives. We conducted infiltrations around the bases using Black Hawk helicopters and a new technique called fast roping to penetrate into small landing zones that couldn't ordinarily be used. A fast rope is a thick rope about the size of a fireman's pole. And using the same concept, it is hooked onto the ceiling of the aircraft; and the soldiers slide down it, holding on just like a firefighter would on a pole at the fire station. The big difference being that as soldiers, we carried our rucksacks, load-bearing equipment, and weapons with us—at least eighty pounds of gear, sometimes more; and as we practiced, the machismo of doing it from as high as possible went out the window as people got hurt, sometimes badly.

The gray skies continued to pour down heavily upon our little base with a vengeance as Noriega began to speak. We sat there, not believing our ears, as he declared a physical and psychological war against the Americans, who were holding up the progress of the republic by not turning over the canal fast enough to suit his desires, I suppose. There had been a treaty negotiated between the United States and the Republic of Panama that guaranteed that the canal would be turned over in its entirety to Panama. This treaty was to be implemented in phases and included the withdrawal of all American troops from the republic on December 31, 1999, still ten years off.

Most Panamanians didn't believe the United States would ever honor the treaty; and in the end, they would wish that the United States had stayed. The old saying, "Hindsight is twenty-twenty," would eventually play itself out in '99; but today, the president of Panama had just declared war on the United States.

For months, we had lived under constant changes in personnel movement limitations, which were code letters that would communicate the threat outside the base and identify movement limitations on all American military personnel and their families living within the Canal Zone. We had been at PML "Delta" for several weeks now. This meant no unofficial travel off post if at all possible. Then, suddenly, that day, they lowered the PML to "Alpha," or unrestricted. We all thought that was unusual, but we all decided to go into Colon for the evening after work and have a few beers and mess with the Colombian girls at the Olympia.

It had been some time since any America GI's had been in Colon. We had been busy, very busy, keeping tabs on what Noriega and his goons were up to. The Panamanian Defense Forces were not efficient military men, but they were very efficient at controlling the population of that small Central American country. They were experts at corruption, harassment, and intimidation. They thrived on squeezing money out of everybody, especially the poor workers that had to transit the nation's highways. They had checkpoints set up about every twenty miles or so along every major avenue leading into and out of Panama City and every other small town along the Pan-American Highway that traversed the entire country coming out of Costa Rica and dead ending about thirty five kilometers from the border with Colombia. Movement was difficult and counterproductive. The requirement to pay bribes at every checkpoint could become very expensive; and if you were a foreigner, especially American, you were expected to pay more. Now, they didn't stop everyone; but if an individual showed any outward sign of being well off, then they would definitely be stopped and harassed just like my buddy and his wife. If you were American these days, you were putting your life into your own hands to travel outside of a U.S. installation.

Noriega's propaganda against the Americans had gotten so bad that the once loving population had begun to turn against the United States and take out their anger against the only targets they had available to them: the U.S. service men and women, along with civilians that lived in the Panama Canal zone. An American civilian amateur radio operator who lived in Panama City had been jailed some months earlier for speaking out against the regime. Noriega claimed that Panama had a right to control its own airwaves. Many

Americans had been beaten, or harassed at check points, or pulled over by Panamanian Defense Force members and ordered to pay bribes in exchange for not being arrested on any one of a thousand trumped up charges. I remember witnessing the spectacle of national elections in which the winners marched in Panama City in order to claim their victory only to be turned away by thugs who beat them with rubber hoses. Later, I was able to prove the presence of PDF members at that event; but nothing was ever done. Besides all the hell we had been put through, we were now going to PML "Alpha." I distinctly remember hearing someone say, "Waahoo!"

There were several bars in downtown Colon, and none of them would meet any reasonable standard of cleanliness in the U.S.; but they had one thing that all the GI's wanted: beautiful, young, light-skinned, Columbian girls who would do anything for a few bucks. The fun was mostly in messing around, hanging out. Of course, the girls loved us because we could speak Spanish. There was one old lady, whom we called the sergeant major; and for tips, she would watch our backs, set us up with a new girl, and generally take care of us all as we pounded back beers and enjoyed ourselves.

That night, we had occupied a big, round table that was located along the outer wall of the Olympia, with both outside exits in our view. The table gave us a perfect view of the entire bar so we could cover each other's backs and still have quick access to the rear door and an exit that was down the hall. There was a bar with red vinyl stools running the length of the interior wall, and the girls staged themselves at strategic points along its length. There must have been thirty-five girls there that night, and only a few GI's.

The sergeant major had escorted us to the booth as she summoned up five or six girls; and she promised to be back if we needed anything. The girls started bringing up beers, Cerveza Panamá, my favorite, as we began to settle in. A few Japanese sailors walked in, and all the girls jumped up and ran over to them and began to play with their hair and smothered them with attention. You should have seen the look of satisfaction on those sailors' faces.

A few hours passed. Most everybody had tied on a pretty good buzz; and suddenly, the sergeant major burst in through the side door, her deeply wrinkled face contorted with concern, her eyes wide, full of fear. She came straight to our table and breathlessly exclaimed, "Something terrible has happened! All the PDF are acting very strange. They are causing trouble for the Americans." With that, she turned and went back out the way she came in. We sat there, looking at each other, confused, wondering what had happened. Somebody commented, "Well, it can't be that bad. Our beepers haven't gone off yet. About thirty minutes passed; and then, suddenly, she came back in through the front door and hustled past the doorman, the Japanese sailors, and the girls, and came straight to our table. In Spanish and with a detectable note of fear in her voice, she said, "The PDF killed a gringo (a Navy lieutenant) in front of the *comandancia* just a few minutes ago. Apparently, he was taking pictures of the entrance, and they shot him on the spot. The entire PDF has gone on alert!" At that very moment, all of our beepers went off with the message, "Personnel Movement Limitation Echo is in effect." Without a word, we all bolted to the doors, found our cars, and raced back to Fort Davis.

Beer still on my breath, I entered the company area; it was a madhouse. People were starting to arrive, and questions echoed down the hall. "What the hell is going on?" somebody exclaimed. And over the noise, I heard somebody yell out, "Get your act together! We are going to Panama City tonight!" Of course, we already had everything packed and ready to go, in footlockers, in our rucksacks, in our wall lockers. I retrieved a uniform and put it on: a faded pair of Olive Green 107, rip-stop fatigues. I retrieved my load-bearing equipment, which already had enough water, food, medical supplies, and ammunition to support me for at least a few days if need be. I pulled my night vision goggles out of the top flap of my rucksack and checked them to make sure they worked. Then I checked the contents of my ruck, and I thought to myself, *Oh man! A hundred pounds of nothing but radio gear.* Then I checked my blowout lockers, one full of ammunition, hand grenades, and Claymore antipersonnel mines, along with prepared time fuses with blasting caps, all set depending on the situation. The second footlocker carried extra batteries and electronic gear. Everything was already packed, checked and double-checked. I stacked the two lockers up, set my rucksack and LBE down on top of them, and went down to the arms room to draw my rifle and pistol, an M-16 A2 and a Beretta. Not the best combination of weapons but the best we had at the time. The M-16 would only fire on semi-auto or three-round burst mode. I would have preferred a full auto rifle. The A2 was a residual effect of the post Vietnam-era military planning that put saving ammunition ahead of combat power of the individual soldier; and as with any war, this one was come as you are. This was the gear we had.

My buzz was starting to wear off as three Chinook CH-47 helicopters started making their approach to land on the open field behind the battalion headquarters, behind my barracks room, below my coveted latrine window. One of the other companies was already lined up out there, ready to go, as the helicopters landed. They didn't power down the engines as the troops loaded quickly; and just as quickly, the aircraft took off.

Somebody shouted, "Hurry up! We've only got a thirty-minute turnaround before they get back. And then it's our turn."

The grass on the landing zone was still heavy with moisture as the Chinooks returned, flying along the Panama Canal; around Tank Top Hill; over the old French Cut; and turning right, toward the waiting group of soldiers. Fully blacked out, the choppers were barely visible as they approached, hovered, and then turned to the right 180 degrees, dropping their tailgates as the pilots plopped them onto the ground in a perfect line to our front, spreading from left to right. The *wop, wop, wop,* sound of the rotor blades slowed just a bit as we jumped up and carried our gear toward the awaiting openings. The loadmasters of each aircraft exited to starboard, off the ramp, and conducted a visual inspection of the engines and rotors as we waddled through the muddy grass, braced against the rotor wash as the overwhelming smell of hot JP-5 exhaust took our breath away. I thought to myself, *Just get to the ramp. You'll be able to breathe then.*

One of our guys fell as he stepped onto the ramp, his boots covered in mud. He fell on his face, busting his nose wide open; and blood gushed out. His buddies drug him aboard. I took my seat, rucksack at my feet; and the aircraft lifted in a lunge, straight up two hundred feet, and then tilted forward as the remainder of the flight followed in suit and lined up behind us. The loadmaster left the tailgate down as we passed over dock forty-five. The enormous Gatun locks lit up the night sky, and then Gatun dam and locks came into view and soon faded as we flew just over the top of the water, directly over the canal and into Culebra Cut.

The jungle on both sides of the canal was dark, and the moonlit night reflected off of the water vapor that hung just over the tops of the trees like a soft, white, undisturbed blanket. The jungle had always felt safe to me, like home; but I knew that this time, if we were going to be in combat, it wouldn't be in the jungle. It would be in the city. We would fight for control over urban terrain. The days of fighting in the jungles were probably over. Now the battle would be to control cities and populations. Ear plugs in, the sound of the aircraft was muffled. Only the high-pitched whining of the rear turbine penetrated; and of course, the thumping rotor blades vibrated the chassis and everything within it.

Suddenly, the flight lifted nose high and to the left. We flew out over Fort Clayton and across Albrook Air Force base as the choppers landed in front of the hangars that still stood on the south side of the base next to what was left of the original airfield.

There was a road that curved from the entrance of the airbase, past the hangars, and around down by the *comandancia;* and then it curved back over the Bridge of the Americas, back to Howard Air Force Base. It was the Panama American highway that led all the way back to the United States.

The choppers hovered in line to the front of the hangars, turned ninety degrees to the left, and dropped tailgates as we landed. The loadmasters exited the aircraft, tethered by coaxial communications cable, and stood starboard, watching, inspecting their aircraft as we exited, one by one, toward the awaiting hangars to our front. The doors to the hangars were closed, huge doors, painted deep red. We made our way to an opening in the center, an open doorway that looked incredibly small in comparison to the hangar doors that loomed overhead. A large tractor was off loading sea land containers to our left, stacking them in front of the hangar doors in rows three high and two wide as we moved forward into our new home: Task Force Black.

The eighteenth of December, 1989, I thought to myself. *Another Christmas on alert, another Christmas away from home, and for what?* I found a cot and put it together next to the man who was in front of me. We slept that night, and all was quiet. We slept soundly, still feeling the effects of our beer buzz, recalling the smell of the Colombian girls. It seemed like an eternity had passed. We slept.

Morning came without incident. The sun, hot by now, seemed high in the sky; but it was only 0800 hours. We gathered and were given a ride to the base dining facility. Grits, eggs, ham, sliced toast, orange juice—we ate, not knowing what to expect. Briefings were scheduled and then rescheduled. We sat on our cots, sharpening knives, cleaning gear, cleaning our rifles. We waited, sweating through our t-shirts in the hangar. We waited for something to happen.

Around 2:30 p.m., my buddy, Stan, came down from the command center. He had a large book in his hand, and he gathered the radio operators together. He said, "Jake, you're senior man, so you're in charge."

But Jake said, "No. Mike has more experience. He is in charge."

I thought to myself, *"What a piece of work!"* Jake outranked me by over two years; but he didn't want to step up, so I did.

Stan and I sat down on a bunk, the rest standing around; and we went over the communications electronics instructions and procedure for our part of Operation Just Cause. We were going to take down *Cerro Azul*, the mountaintop that supported the Panamanian television repeater site, TV 2, Noriega's primary means of communications with the population. We would shut it down without destroying it and then, on order, turn it back on so that the department of defense could transmit messages to the Panamanian people.

We had been in mission planning for months. The biggest worry were the guy wires that held up the antenna, huge cables that surrounded the mountaintop. They would be invisible to the pilots of our aircraft. Our plan was to air land on an LZ on the southern slope that was covered with Kuna grass, estimated to be no more than three feet tall this time of year. The slope of the mountain should pose no problem. The top, where the guy wires were, had been somewhat flattened out during the construction of the tower, making it an easy landing zone for the new MH-60 Black Hawk helicopters that were to be our infiltration platform.

Romeo eight-eight would be my call sign for the duration of the mission, until the instructions changed. We committed the call signs to memory and programmed the frequencies into our different radio packages. Our mission was rather simple really, no more difficult than any of our training missions—actually easier. It was cut and dried: take the hill and turn off the repeater site; then on order, turn it on. Then all we had to do was hold in place until relieved.

To help us with the technical aspects of turning the repeater site on and off, we were given two technicians from the local armed forces television and radio service. Neither had flown in a helicopter, and neither had ever fast roped. Fast roping was our alternative infill method, so they had to learn; and we taught them.

We went to the dining facility for our dinner meal: chicken, mashed potatoes, baked beans, soda pop, white sheet cake, and coffee. Not bad. My belly was full, so we decided to walk back to the hangars. The stroll was only a half-mile or so, but we were supposed to stay out of sight. The sun had started going down, so we felt that it was okay. It was December 19, 1989.

We walked back into the hangar, stepping over the metal frame of the small pedestrian door. There was a distinct note of activity as everybody was checking their gear and putting camouflage on their faces. The word spread: "H-hour is tonight, and we are going in at 0100 hours. Get ready, and try to rest up a bit. We've only got a few hours left." The other radio operators and I checked our frequencies, learned each other's call signs, and memorized the operational codes we would use to abbreviate our messages. We still had time, so we packed extra ammunition into thirty-round magazines for our rifles and placed them into an aviator's kit bag. We would take this along and kick it out of the chopper as we were inbound to the target, a self-resupply if we needed it.

One of the Intel guys came down and updated the team on the situation. Apparently, the PDF had moved a platoon into position on top of our little hill; and they were supposed to have a .50-caliber heavy machine gun. *Great,* we thought to ourselves. *Just what we need.* But the truth was that between our gunships and the mini guns on the Black Hawks, we wouldn't have too many problems getting on the ground. We would be outnumbered though, and that was cause for some concern; but we were so pumped and ready to go that it didn't matter. Someone exclaimed out loud, "To heck with them!" and we all nervously chuckled.

There were several different task groups of sixteen to twenty-four men in the hangar. One group was going to the Pacora River Bridge to conduct a halting action to prevent the Battalion *Dos Mill* from entering the city. They were the premier infantry unit designated to reinforce Panama City in times of trouble, and they had a tough reputation as a special operations unit. The truth was that they were basically a gang of thugs that Noriega would use to squelch demonstrations in the city. Nevertheless, they were formidable, with their armored personnel carriers and light infantry operational capability. The element going up against them, should they respond to the city, was a group of only seventeen or so men. The Pacora River Bridge was a choke point for the enemies' movement into the city, but destroying the bridge was out of the question. It would cut off the entire eastern half of the country from resupply and create a huge humanitarian disaster. Cutting the battalion off at the bridge and holding it was the only real option. The men going there wouldn't be alone; they would have a Spectre gunship on station and fast movers if needed.

There had been some other teams in the hangar, small, four-to-twelve-man teams; but they were set up to conduct reconnaissance, and well, they were already on the ground somewhere throughout the country. Our objective was to keep Noriega from escaping, capturing him so that he could be brought to justice. In his speech, he had made a statement; one that made us think the PDF would stand and fight. The mantra they had taken up was, "*Nunca hamas, ni un paso atrás!*" Roughly translated, that meant, "Never again, not one step back!"

Two Black Hawks were parked behind the hangar across the cement road on the grass. They were parked facing north, parallel to the road, waiting for us. There was a banyan tree directly behind one of them, between it and the hangar; and to the south, there was a small creek that cut through double culverts under the road that ran the circumference of the mountainous area called Quarry Heights. There was a huge set of metal bars on the base side of the culverts to prevent people from walking onto the base, but the culverts were large enough for a man to stand upright inside of them. On the opposite side of the road was a strand of triple canopy jungle. Between the choppers and the culvert, there was an open field and a narrow shelf or mound perhaps two feet high along the slight ridgeline that ran from the hangars to the west, toward the main gate of the airbase. Its function was to collect water from the open field and guide it toward the culvert and into a creek that ran out all the way into the ocean.

Inside the hangar, we were energetic, unable to relax much. The colonel in charge of the task force came down from the headquarters section that was upstairs and called us all together. His speech was short but exciting as he confirmed that H-hour for the direct action missions would be 0100 hours and that we should all get some rest if we were able. He talked about making history and the significance of our effort this night.

"Men, we have a mission. It is real, and we are going to execute at H-hour without fail, without hesitation. Our role is significant in the big picture, and one day, you will look back on this as a great day to be a soldier in the United States Army Special Forces. Godspeed!"

It was dark outside. I looked at my watch. It was almost 10:30 pm; and we had time to relax, to think things over. Lying down on my cot, I fell asleep.

I was awakened abruptly as somebody kicked one of the legs on my cot; and a voice from across the room shouted, "H-hour has been moved up! We launch now!"

Looking at my watch, I realized that an hour and fifteen minutes had passed. The sound of gunfire from the west penetrated our collective consciousness. Somewhere close, just outside the hangar's western doors, the distinct sound of two M-60 machineguns responded to that of AK-47's, which were firing in simultaneous bursts.

Grabbing my rucksack, LBE, and rifle, I followed my teammates to the waiting Black Hawks. The pilots were already firing up the turbines as the gunfire subsided slightly; and then, suddenly, over the sound of the aircrafts engines, a heavier thud of several .50-cal M-2 heavy-barreled machine guns reported their presence as I cleared the doorway and crossed the street to the helicopters, their blades slowly beginning to turn as the pitch of the turbines steadily increased.

The Black Hawks, with their swept-back rotors, are an incredible aircraft, smooth and powerful. I jumped into my position in the doorway, next to the loadmaster's seat, my feet hanging out, just behind the front, starboard side wheel.

Russ was standing between the seats of the crew, just behind the cockpit, getting a head count. Then he tapped my helmet. "Hey, take your buddy and go back to get the resupply ammunition. We left it at the door!" Sitting next to me was the Air Force combat controller, a young kid, tall and lanky. "Come with me!" I yelled; and with our rucksacks on, we ran back through the hangar door and bent to pick up the ammunition that we had loaded in magazines and placed into an aviator's kit bag earlier.

We both realized that it was heavy, very heavy, especially since we were both still wearing our rucksacks. The kid, said, "Let's run." I said, "No. It's too heavy. Let's walk." I walked backward out the door, picking the bag up over the rail that ran across the bottom, and pulled as the kid followed and came around parallel to me. We set the bag down for a second and adjusted our grips. From the corner of my eye, I noticed that the quick reaction force was running, single file out of the other hangar to our south as tracer rounds ricocheted off the street between the two of us and the helicopters, green tracers from an AK; so, without a word, we bolted to our chopper, lifted the bag with ease deep inside, and leapt into our positions.

Instantly the aircraft lunged into the air, straight up. The impact of the takeoff forced me to look down, and I could see red and green tracers streaking across the ground from north to south directly below and where the aircraft had been.

The pilots lifted us up away from the hangar. The tracers did not follow. Then we arched forward, the tail of the aircraft lifting; and I could see a trail of M-113 armored personnel carriers traveling down the road between the hangars and what I assumed was a PDF infantry squad that had taken up firing positions along the road, near the culverts. The APC's opened up on them with their .50-caliber machine guns as we flew north over the airbase, across Fort Clayton and over the mountains. I recognized the trans-isthmian highway and a high school, the name of which I couldn't recall, as we turned east and flew toward our objective: *Cerro Azul.*

From my position in the doorway, the distinct, brilliantly lit outline of Panama City was in full view. I looked down, through my feet, at the rusty tin roofs of mountaintop homes as we continued to fly a couple hundred feet above them, straight for our objective.

A bright flash of light highlighted the outline of an AC-130 Gunship as it opened up with its Howitzer onto the Panamanian *comandancia,* where the Navy lieutenant had been killed just a few days earlier. All around the area, tracer rounds ricocheted into the air as fire fights broke out near the *modelo* and the *comandancia.*

As the mission approached *Cerro Azul,* the aircraft continued to climb in altitude until we came to the objective. Approaching from the south, my aircraft in trail, we came to a hover at least fifty feet above the trees, the slope dropping off drastically. The fast rope master signaled to the aircrew that we were too high, and the loadmaster gave the signal for standby. Without warning, the chopper barrel rolled to starboard, over the edge of the ridge, dropping altitude suddenly. Looking straight at the ground, the blades of the aircraft and the treetops were visible at the same time. The pilot then dropped the nose hard to the right, bringing the tail back around. The front of the aircraft was pointing straight toward the draw that dropped off parallel to our landing zone; and then with almost seamless effort, the pilot lifted the nose of the aircraft, diving just over the top of the trees and down the side of the mountain. We regained speed as we dove farther and farther down the face of the mountain. Then the pilot brought the aircraft back around to the right and flew back to the top of *Cerro Azul*. With an abrupt halt, the tail of the aircraft lifting, leveling the flight deck floor, the command, "Ropes," was given over the noise of the jet turbines and swept-back blades.

My Air Force buddy was sitting on top of the fast rope; and with a startled look on his face, he began trying to shove the rope out from under his buttocks. I helped; soon, the rope was clear. I watched it fall and land in the tops of the trees just a few feet under the wheel of the aircraft. I thought, *Hmm. Not too far down,* and then the fast rope master slapped my shoulder and shouted, "Go!"

Grabbing the rope and rotating ninety degrees, I came clear of the aircraft and started the downward descent into the trees, the weight of my rucksack pushing me through. My body leading, it dragged the rope through the trees. Looking up past my feet still on the rope, I could see my Air Force buddy getting ready to rope out as I continued falling backward through the trees, dragging the rope with me.

Branches snapped as I continued my descent into the forest when, suddenly, I gently hit the ground on my back, head facing down hill, unable to move as the rest of the team roped out and down, landing feet first on my chest and bouncing off and onto their feet. One by one, six or seven men came down the rope, each bouncing off my chest and stepping off into the woods.

The loadmaster, standing next to his mini gun, was leaning out the side window and looking down at me. Stars as bright as ever, they were shining vividly above us all through the heated vapors of the aircraft's exhaust. He reached over and released the rope from the aircraft. Before the rope could complete its fall, the pilot, with a rolling arch, took off out of sight, down the same gorge he had taken earlier.

Buried in the fast rope, somebody gave me a hand up as tracer rounds zipped by overhead. A considerable distance below the top of the ridge, the mountain was a lot steeper than we had anticipated. The troops on the first aircraft were engaged in a firefight, the sound of which was alarming, loud, as we began our movement toward it.

Soon, it was quiet as we continued to move up the trail toward the top of the hill, single file, in as close to a dead run as we could muster considering all the gear we had and the slope of the hill. The sound of an explosion came from up top as we halted just below the ridgeline. Soon the captain came over and said, "All clear! Mike, get on the horn and let battalion know we are at situation eighteen." Without a word, I moved off to find a place to set up my SATCOM radio.

From my vantage point on the south side of *Cerro Azul*, I could see all of Panama City. I set up my SATCOM radio and made contact with battalion.

"Tango Foxtrot Black, this is Romeo eight eight, situation eighteen. How copy? Over."

"Roger, good, copy Romeo eight eight, situation eighteen."

Having made contact with the task force, I continued to set up my radios. An FM radio, or Fox Mike, a frequency modulated radio that was used for line of sight communications between our team members and as a backup ground to air means of contact. Then I set up my ultra high frequency radio, or UHF, the primary ground-to-air radio for this operation. I settled in to monitor traffic and to provide support as needed.

To the south, the 82nd Airborne began rolling in over *Tocumen* International Airport. The entire Ready-Ready Brigade started jumping in. The aircraft seemed as though they were skirting along the top of the trees as the troops exited like clockwork, their parachutes barely perceptible from my high-altitude perch overlooking the entire scene.

The ground to air UHF started to crack with signals as the radio operator at the Pacora River Bridge, off to our east about ten miles, began calling in close air support. Our target was quiet, but they had no sooner completed their air mobile infill into a field next to the bridge when they came under fire from a large element that had halted on the other side. It was the entire Battalion *Dos Mil* (two thousand) that had halted on the other side of the bridge as our teams made their landing, and now the fight was on. The sound of gunfire could be heard over the radio as the operator called for support.

"Spectre nine zero, this is Romeo seven nine zero six. I've got military vehicles on the other side of the bridge with the headlights on. Over."

"Roger copy zero six. What would you like me to do?"

"Take 'em out! Take 'em out!"

"Roger copy zero six. We are coming in on gun run now. Keep your heads down."

With my night vision goggles I could see the infrared spotlight on the side of the AC-130 as it came around on gun run and opened up with its 20mm, multi-barreled cannon. A bright light, perceptible only through my night vision goggles lit up the sky around the aircraft, the sound (*boawhgggg-wooooup*) reported its familiar, comforting presence.

The aircraft continued firing with its Howitzer, Vulcan, and other weapons as vehicles exploded along a half-mile stretch of the *Carretera Interamericana* east of the Pacora River bridge. Then the pilot came over the radio.

"We've got some hot ones moving north into the woods. Do you want me to maintain contact?"

"Affirmative. Take 'em out! Take 'em out!"

"Roger."

The aircraft adjusted fire to chase the survivors that were fleeing into the woodline to the north. Then came the call everybody was waiting for.

"Romeo seven nine zero six, this is Spectre nine zero. All clear. Do you need anything else?"

With sporadic gunfire in the back ground, the response was, "Negative, nine zero. We've got it from here. I'll let you know if we need any more help. This is zero six. Out." The entire Battalion *Dos Mil* had been rendered combat ineffective in less than thirty minutes by a little over a dozen Green Berets and a Spectre gunship.

Out over Panama City, the Rangers and the 82nd Airborne continued their assault over the airport, gaining control of the eastern half of the city while the Seventh Infantry continued to mop up downtown. By morning, things had settled, pretty much, as the sun came up, evaporating the evening's dew from the grass, leaves, and our uniforms. Smoke was rising all over the city from the area down near the *comandancia,* downtown, and around the airport.

The captain came over to where I was at and said, "Turn your gear over to your buddy and get down to the main entrance with Russ and translate for the crew down there."

"Sure thing, boss! I'm on it!" Getting rid of my radio gear was a blessing, plus being able to participate in operations versus pulling radio watch was more in line with my liking. Sitting around listening for somebody to call was not my favorite thing to do.

As I moved down the hill to the main gate, there were two bodies lying on the side of the road. They had been the only resistance we encountered the night before. There isn't anything like a couple of dead guys laying there to make you think about life a little bit. A couple of the guys were wrapping them in ponchos, getting them ready for evacuation. That would be later this afternoon. 'Till then, we would cover them with ponchos and then place them into body bags before loading them onto a helicopter.

At the bottom of the hill, there were a few of our guys setting up a machine gun position to cover down the road, past the main entrance to the television tower site that we now occupied. I walked past them, down to the gate where Russ was standing, and talking to a couple

Panamanians who had Army duffle bags strewn over their shoulders. In his rudimentary Spanish, he was trying to discern what it was the two of them wanted. The site was laughable, as no real understanding was being met; so I asked in Spanish, "What do you have in the bags?"

The two men dropped the bags on the ground, setting them up, standing with the opening toward the sky. They opened up the bags, and inside were at least twelve RPG-17s in each duffle bag. These weapons are the East German equivalent to our shoulder-mounted, light anti-tank weapons, or LAW. The leader of the two also had another small, white bag that was apparently very heavy; so I asked him, "What's in the white bag?" He held it open. Looking in, I could see that he had about two dozen brand-new AK-47 bayonets, still soaked in grease.

He began to explain that an entire infantry company of Panamanian Defense Force members had moved across his farm the night before and that they had left all their weapons, gear, uniforms, everything underneath a large tree near his house. Russ was on the radio, calling the commander down to see what we had; and a Toyota Land Rover pickup with cattle railings around the back came around the corner and up the road. We stopped the truck and searched the men who were driving it. It turned out that they were with the two who had brought the weapons up. They had just held back so that they wouldn't all get shot, a really good idea since we were all a little jumpy, not having slept that night.

The commander came down the road, and we briefed him on what we had. In perfect Spanish, he asked the men if they would take us to the location where the weapons were hidden. They agreed, so the commander, Russ, and I, along with all four of the Panamanians, loaded into the truck; and we took off back down the road in the direction in which the men had arrived.

Underneath a large tree, the branches spreading out over the ground overhead, the men led us to a cache of weapons that was hastily buried under a tarp covered with leaves and brush. We discovered hundreds of rifles, rucksacks, uniforms, even medical equipment. Some of the uniforms had blood on them.

We gathered everything, loaded it up onto the Land Cruiser, and headed back up to *Cerro Azul*. Finding this many weapons and uniforms was a pretty good indicator that many of the PDF had evaded capture and perhaps death by moving into the mountainous area outside the city, exactly where we were at.

We drove past many houses, all of which were displaying a white flag of surrender as we went by. An older gentleman came running out to the road as we came around one corner. He was holding and waving a white flag in his right hand. Shirtless and in cutoff shorts, his body was glistening with sweat. His lanky muscles stretched his taught, black skin that shined in the morning sunlight. Without command, the driver pulled over and stopped in front of the old man's house.

With anger in his voice, he explained that several PDF soldiers had stolen his family's clothing that was hanging on the clothes-line. The clothing on the line wasn't enough for them, so they had drug the entire family out of the house and taken the clothing off their backs, leaving the family standing there, naked. This was a poor family to start with. They had no car, the house was made of wooden planks the old man had scrounged, and there were windows and no curtains. He had planted a garden with a few banana trees and was raising a couple pigs and some chickens.

With the same voice of anger, he explained that he was afraid to let his children, all twelve of them, out of the house because the soldiers left some small, black boxes all around his yard. We decided that we should check them out and immediately found that the PDF had left over two dozen Czechoslovakian plastic antipersonnel mines all around the old man's house. They were designed during the war in Afghanistan to prevent detection from mine detectors. Carefully, very carefully, we recovered as many of the mines as we could find. The commander gave the old man a voucher for each of the mines and explained to him that if he would take the voucher to Albrook Air Force Base, they would pay him for having turned them in under the weapons for money program that we were implementing.

A few days later, we drove by the old man's house to check on him; he came running out with a fist full of cash, screaming, "They paid me! They paid me!" We all had a great big laugh, a satisfied laugh, as he explained that they had paid him five thousand dollars for the antipersonnel mines. That was more than he would have or could have made in three years.

For several days, we continued to collect weapons for money; and then it was time to leave *Cerro Azul*. Satisfied that we had accomplished our mission, we commandeered a dump truck and returned to Panama City, victorious and ready for the next mission.

Immediately upon arriving back to the task force headquarters, we were scrambling to get ready for our next mission. There wasn't time to think things through as we busily stocked back up on ammunition, batteries, water, so forth and so on. Everybody was in hustle mode as we prepared for an impromptu rotary wing assault on the ninth military regional headquarters in La Palma, just a short distance from the border with Colombia—well, a short distance by air or boat. But as it turned out, to walk from the border to La Palma could take weeks—not so much because of the distance, but because of the dense jungle of the Darien province.

The company commander was in charge of this mission; and he was on fire, gathering as many bodies as he could in order to get it right. It was said that there were more than two hundred troops in the *cuartel* we were about to attack. These troops were supposed to be Noriega loyalists, hard core jungle fighters with a passion and a cause to fight for. They were, however, the last of the holdouts who hadn't as of yet surrendered to the American forces now occupying most of the country.

It was not even ten in the morning. We had returned as early as possible, hoping to get a decent meal; but now we were getting locked and cocked for another mission. None of us were sure why there hadn't been any better planning, but it was too late to ask. I went upstairs in the hangar, up to the command center, and found the battalion communications officer in order to get call signs and frequencies. He advised me that the current instructions were still in effect; and that made it a lot easier. All the frequencies, call signs, everything were already preset. I was ready to go. I went back downstairs and took my rucksack outside and set up my SATCOM and other radios and did radio checks with the command center. "All okay," I said as I completed the last radio check and signed off.

As I was closing up my rucksack, two Special Ops MH-53 Pave Low helicopters, with their protruding in-flight refueling rods sticking out from under the fuselage, flew in just over the top of the hangars. They landed quickly, tailgates opening up as the pilots brought the engine speed down to an idle.

Somebody stuck their head out of the hangar door and yelled at me to get it on as I was closing up my sack. The flight would only take about forty-five minutes. Down the coastline we flew, test firing our weapons off the tailgate as we cleared out over the ocean. Each air crew had three gunners on board. The flight crew of load masters and crew chiefs were manning two each 7.62 mini guns that were mounted on each door directly behind the flight deck, and then there was a .50-caliber heavy-barrel machine gun mounted on the tailgate. The aircraft were capable of putting out some fire power; but more importantly, each carried a precious cargo of a dozen or so assaulters.

Our plan was to air land on an LZ above the town of La Palma, an open field on a hilltop that overlooked the small fishing village and to communicate with the Panamanian Defense Force personnel inside the *cuartel*. We would use a telephone that was located underneath the communications cell tower that was also located on top of the hill. We were to pick up a security position around the LZ as the commander gave them an opportunity to surrender. If they refused, then we would take the *cuartel* by force.

Suddenly, the aircraft dropped altitude, diving nose first toward the water. Once the pilots were satisfied that they were low enough they continued on their heading until they had reached the gulf and turned to the left, skirting along the water, heading directly toward the target without hesitation or doubt. We continued on this heading until we reached the peninsula of La Palma. The pilots maintained their heading straight to the beach and then climbed, nap of the earth over the ridgeline, heading directly toward the old La Palma Airfield. Clearing the ridge, the pilots maintained their altitude, turning slightly to the right; then they dropped down nose first, pulled up hard to the left, and landed on top of the hill overlooking the town, the airfield, and the *cuartel*.

As the aircraft came to a landing, we were already standing up; and we barreled off the ramp, almost simultaneous to the wheels touching down. We all spread out and knelt, waiting for the aircraft to take off. In less than half a minute, they were gone, the high-pitched whine of the rotors and turbines still ringing in my ears. I followed the company commander over to the hut that had the telephone in it and busted the door off its hinges for him. Then I turned around and set up my radios and made contact with the air-to-ground control platform, an Air Force AC-130 gunship that was hovering overhead at about six thousand feet. In addition to the gunship, we had two of the A-37 Dragonfly fast movers on station. I called them 'those squatty body two-seaters that looked so funny.' They were not very big, only sitting a few feet off the ground; but they could carry two 500 pound bombs under each wing. I relayed the information to the commander, who was busy dialing the numbers we had been given for the *cuartel*.

Soon, he was on the phone, talking to somebody. I overheard him give them an ultimatum—"Surrender or die"—and the person on the other end of the phone was screaming a negative response. With that, he turned to me and said, "Mike, have those fast movers give me a fly-by directly over the *cuartel*. Just a fly-by as a warning!"

"Roger that," I said as I keyed the hand mike for my ground to air radio. "Phoenix three nine, this is Romeo eight eight. Give me a fly-by over the *cuartel*, just as a warning. How copy Phoenix? Over." Breaking squelch twice, the pilot acknowledged the request as they dropped from the clouds with the sun at their back, coming into view as the men on the hilltop cheered.

The two aircraft, heavy with their payload, dropped down in a swooshing motion on the opposite side of the *cuartel* from us out over the water, almost as if they were floating; they flew in a direct line, side by side, toward the *cuartel*. As they approached the beach, they turned skyward in a simulated bomb drop and climbed straight up, directly over the top of the *cuartel*. Reaching about two thousand feet, they turned left and right, splitting their formation. They maintained their heading for about three kilometers until they were almost out of sight; then they each turned nose down, dropping altitude until they were just above the ground, and they pulled up, facing each other with the *cuartel* pinned between them. I could tell that the pilots had given their engines full power as they approached each other at five hundred miles an hour, smoke pouring out from behind them. One skirting along the beach, the other out over the bay, they crossed simultaneously over the top of the *cuartel* and turned skyward again, up and then out.

The commander, still not having hung up, said to the person on the other end of the line, "You've got one minute to make up your mind."

Still screaming, the voice on the other end of the line indicated a negative response.

"Mike, get on the horn, and have that gunship come around on gun run."

Without hesitation, I called the AC-130 and requested that he come around on gun run and be prepared to fire on our command. Soon, the gunship was looming out over the bay, only five hundred feet off the water, so low I could see the Air Force insignia on its side and the guns sticking out from under its wings.

The low drone of the turbo prop fans hummed steadily as he banked it around to his left, bringing his guns around so that the village would not be in the line of fire.

The commander calmly said into the phone, "You have thirty seconds."

But this time, there was no response. Soon, a pair of dirty underwear on a stick protruded from the window of the *cuartel*, directly from the commandant's office; and with that, our commander said,

"Let's go, boys!" With a yell, we all stood and started running down the stairs, past the houses, people watching us from their front doors.

Over the radio, I gave the aircrew the command to stand by as we ran the two hundred meters down the stairs onto the main rumba, or street that ran the length of the village. Taking up positions along the outer walls of the *cuartel*, we held our place as the commander, using a bullhorn, ordered the men to come out with their hands up; but they didn't. I overheard him say, "Oh boy. Now they want to play." He yelled down the line, "On my command, men, open fire on the buildings!" Then he gave them another chance to surrender. Waiting for what seemed like an eternity, there was no response; so the commander said, "Ready, men! Fire!"

We all rose up over the wall; and in a scene reminiscent of a Bonny and Clyde movie, we opened up with our M-16s. I was amused at first, plaster falling off the walls, windows being shattered, curtains catching the breeze and bullets.

Somebody launched an M-203 round through an upstairs window and then another through the front door. With the second round exploding, the same dirty pair of underwear on a stick came out the window and a bullet cut the stick; the underwear fell to the ground. We all continued to fire for a few seconds until the sound of the commander screaming, "Cease fire! Cease fire!" was heard.

Once the dust settled, he told them to come out with their hands up; and they did. About thirty of them came out, most in their underwear for some reason. We all stood up from behind the wall. As the commander ushered them out onto the airfield, he gave the assault element permission to clear the entire *cuartel*. I went with him over to the airfield and helped provide security, then I got on the horn and waved off the close air support. They left, departing directly over our heads, the gunship waving its wings as the fast movers did victory rolls to our satisfaction.

Once they were out of sight, I set up my SATCOM and called the task force, giving them a situation report by simply stating, "All clear! Situation one eight!" Looking at my watch, it was still not even 2:00 p.m. "What a day. What a day," I overheard somebody say.

EL SALVADOR

The team was seated in small, wooden chairs; the entire chain of command occupied the seats behind us. We were at an isolation facility that the battalion had set up on an old Army camp somewhere in Florida. The heat permeated the tin building that had no windows, air-conditioning, or vents. With his briefing printed as a slideshow, using an overhead projector, the battalion intelligence sergeant, a slender, clean-cut, young, black NCO wearing Army-issue glasses, a set of starched fatigues, and spit-shined boots, nervously began his briefing. We sat there, intently listening, as he began to speak in a slight Southern drawl.

"A land dominated by volcanoes and earthquakes, the culture of El Salvador has been inherited from both the indigenous population of mainly Mayan Indians and the Spaniards who ruled the country until 1821.

"The history of El Salvador revolves around one central issue:

land. In this, the smallest and most densely populated country in Central America, land always has been a scarce commodity. Although private property rights are in the process of being established, the equal distribution of land is still controlled by the landed oligarchy, with the assistance of the military.

"The war in El Salvador is not a casual action. It is a bomb that has exploded in Central America, a bomb fed by inefficient government and social and economic crisis, conceived in secret by the Marxist-Leninist movements that cover themselves under the flags of popular reform groups with secret political and tactical objectives aimed at gaining power by the use of force.

"It is a product of the constant friction between east and west, and it has brought this tiny country to the frontlines of the cold war in a battle of ideologies that has had devastating effects for all involved.

"Between 1980 and the present, the Republic of El Salvador in Central America has been engulfed in a war between the El Salvadoran government and the Farabundo Marti Front for the National Liberation (FMLN), a communist revolutionary front that receives direct support from Cuba and Nicaragua and indirectly from the Soviet Union.

"This war has plunged Salvadorian society into a cycle of violence that ravages the countryside and has left thousands and thousands of people dead. The use of fear and coercion are tactics used throughout, denying Salvadoran citizens their civil liberties and exposing them to criminal acts of violence and violations of human rights by the forces on both sides of the conflict.

"As the war has intensified, its effects have rippled around the world. El Salvador has turned toward the United States in an effort to stave off a potential guerrilla victory that threatens to destroy the economic and political life of the nation. Washington has responded to the Salvadorans' appeals. And since the mid 1980's, El Salvadoran government forces have been gaining the upper hand in the field, having implemented our post-Vietnam counterinsurgency strategy.

"Following the election of Jose Napoleon Duarte in 1984 the U.S. increased its support for the El Salvadoran armed forces, and this became one of the most significant factors in turning the tide of the war. Since the American public will not support the introduction of ground troops into the conflict, Congress has limited military involvement and approved the deployment of only fifty-five advisors.

"These select few have faced the danger of intense combat actions targeted against them and the units they advise as they are tackling the massive task of reforming the El Salvadoran military and political landscape.

"Our strategy, until now, has been to stress pacification, human rights, civil defense, and population security rather than the destruction of guerrilla units. It has been our belief that the Salvadoran military should operate in small units with strict constraints on the use of firepower and that their activities should be subordinate to economic, political, and psychological operations designed to improve the image and augment the legitimacy of the government.

"Nonetheless, the conflict in El Salvador has raged on several fronts. In the field, a battle-hardened and politically indoctrinated corps of FMLN guerrillas has been frustrating the efforts of the armed forces to defeat them militarily. A low-intensity conflict, marked by indecisive armed clashes and a constant struggle for the hearts and minds of the rural population, has defined the efforts of both sides.

"In this dirty little war, all the participants have paid a heavy price. This conflict has brought this volcanic, intensely divided country to the forefront of the Cold War, and that is what brings us here today. Sir!"

The battalion operations officer stood up from his seat located in the back of the room. He moved forward, taking his position in front of the team, set his slides down, turned off the projector, and picked up his first slide then set it onto the projector. Without missing a beat, he turned the projector back on.

"Men, your mission is to deny the FMLN leadership sanctuary."

Pausing, he allowed his words to sink in as he read the faces and reactions of all the men on the team and those who were in attendance. Turning off the projector, he removed his first slide and replaced it and then turned the projector back on.

"Our intent is to capture the FMLN headquarters and drive them out of the redoubt they have held since the start of the war."

Again, he paused, allowing his words to sink in as he turned the projector off. Then he removed his second slide and replaced it with another and turned the projector back on.

"To accomplish this, you will conduct linkup with the Salvadoran First Infantry Brigade and provide support as required in order to achieve the commander's intent."

The operations officer wrapped up his portion of the briefing as the rest of the staff stood up and gave their section of it. Once they were finished, the battalion commander stood up and gave a speech that highlighted the importance of what we were about to embark upon. I listened; but in the back of my mind, I couldn't help but think that we were taking on more than we should. The entire team sat there, stoic, listening, as the impact of the mission statement and the battalion operations officer's words sank in.

Most of us had just recently returned from Panama after having spent the last six months rebuilding the national police force. Those days had been long and hard, and we hadn't had a break since before Operation Just Cause. In fact, doing a quick inventory of the men sitting with me, I realized that this team, although newly formed, was chock full of guys who had been involved in the most intricate details of mission planning and conduct of various operations throughout Panama and South America over the last few years. We were all somewhat hardened veterans ourselves; and with that thought, I felt comforted.

The briefing ended; and suddenly, the team was standing there, left to its own devices, to figure out what we needed to do next.

Somebody remarked, "Wow. Not a small task for a twelve-man team. Not at all. We should be able to do that."

With boisterous laughter, the entire team cracked up, slapping each other on the back and shaking each other's hands. This was one hell of a moment. We had been selected to do the mission that we had all been hoping for. We were going back into combat, back into the field as advisors to an infantry brigade. We had been chosen above all others. What an honor. This time, it was for real.

A few days passed, and the team gave its briefing back to the command. There had been only a few questions from the battalion commander. The group commander stood and gave us a few words of advice; and the group sergeant major was there, threatening everybody with a piss test if we didn't do well. It was his way of joking around, but we all resented the implication.

We loaded onto the back of a deuce-and-a-half and left for the airfield immediately. Once at the airfield, we boarded our flight, our gear packed, ready to go. The oxygen console was ready as the aircrew closed the clamshell on the C-130 as we taxied off the tarmac and onto the runway. With a screeching halt, the pilot stopped the plane and hesitated for a moment as each of us braced ourselves, reaching forward and grabbing hold of the paratroop seat straps. The familiar sound of the C-130's four turbo prop engines roared as the pilot let off the brake and, with a sudden jolt, we began to roll down the runway, all occupants leaning against the negative g-forces they we were experiencing, holding onto the red seat straps as the aircraft's nose lifted, and in a swooping motion it came off the ground and began its climb to cruising altitude.

All of our parachutes, rucksacks, and rifles were center-loaded along the midsection of the aircraft. This was only a five-hour flight, but we had time before we would don our HALO gear and other equipment. Our plan was to conduct a military freefall airborne operation from twenty-five thousand feet above actual ground level; freefall to pull altitude, around four thousand feet; form up on the lowest man; and land as a group on the drop zone that the El Salvadoran troops had secured for us. The drop zone itself was not much larger than a football field, but it was large enough to accommodate our small team.

It was already dark outside as the load master began to open the rear of the aircraft, lowering the tailgate. We had been pre-breathing oxygen for an hour or so, having rigged our parachutes and equipment during the flight. The jumpmaster was standing at the end of the oxygen console with his back to the rear of the plane. Stars and moonlight filled the cabin with ambient light as the jumpmaster, using his index and middle finger on his right hand, pointed to the top of his left wrist. Then he stood back a step or two and pumped his arms forward with all ten of his fingers extended, not joined. He pumped his arms twice, letting us know, "Twenty minutes."

Twenty minutes until we would jump. I checked the oxygen flow indicator. It blinked each time I took a breath. Each breath, the sound of which was magnified by the fact that we were wearing earplugs, represented another moment closer to the jump. The man next to me seemed to be having a problem. His eyes were open wide, the whites showing on all sides as he indicated that he couldn't breathe. With a quick glance, I could see that he had accidentally disconnected his air hose. I reached down, connected it, and gave him two thumbs up. He relaxed instantly, slouching under the weight of his gear.

It was impossible to get comfortable. Even though we were seated, the weight of all the gear pulled down heavily against our shoulders as we sat there, watching the jumpmaster, who was now kneeling on the starboard side of the ramp, holding on with one hand while he leaned out over the edge, under the side of the open fuselage. I could feel the aircraft turn as the pilot adjusted his heading according to the jumpmaster's commands. He would indicate with his right hand, "Five degrees left," making small adjustments in five-degree increments. He did so by pointing the direction he wanted to adjust the flight, and the crew chief would relay the commands to the pilots. Standing up, the jumpmaster extended his hands with all ten fingers open, indicating, "Ten minutes." With that, he leaned forward and, in a motion that made it look like he was blowing into his hand, gave the signal for winds. Then he stood erect and extended his right hand with his index finger and middle finger opened, indicating two knots. And then he drew a slash across his chest with the same hand, his left hand still holding onto the aircraft. And he made another gesture. This time, all five fingers of his right hand were extended. "Winds at two knots, gusting to five," was the signal. Not bad. Not really any wind to speak of. This jump was going to be a go. There was no reason it wouldn't—not at this point.

The jumpmaster stood there, looking down, as the curvature of the earth floated out and away, far below the tailgate. The engines roared, requiring full power to maintain this altitude as the black exhaust swirled behind the aircraft and then crystallized, forming four inwardly-swirling moonlit white contrails that quickly merged into one solid trail. The moonlight shined through the round windows on the right side of the plane as we were now on track for jump run. The jumpmaster kneeled down and protruded his body outward, using the frame of the aircraft as a handhold; and we sat there attentively. He was looking for major terrain features that would indicate our location in relation to the DZ. Still looking out, he placed his hand on the floor of the aircraft, raised it over his head, and gave us a thumbs-up, indicating that we were on track and that it was time to stand up.

We all stood up, disconnected from the oxygen console, and flipped on our bailout bottles. The bailout bottles gave us all up to fifteen minutes of oxygen to breathe, more than enough to jump out and reach pull altitude before disconnecting our masks.

We moved forward to the hinge for the ramp and started checking each other's equipment. Over the edge and far below the ramp, I could see the beach line and the ocean. There were small towns, dimly lit, drenched in yellow light smothered in smoke and dust. The jumpmaster singled nonchalantly, "One minute." We moved to the edge of the ramp in a tight group, each with a chemical light taped to the top of his helmet. The jumpmaster stood up; motioned for us to follow him; and, in a diving motion, leapt into the darkness. On his cue, we followed immediately, diving over the edge of the ramp, our feet and rucksacks pointing upward, still in the view of the flight crew for just a second as we caught the air dam coming off the bottom of the aircraft.

The aircraft roared away, the outline of it in view as my body was still facing head down; and in a moment of silence, it seemed as though we were all hanging there in slow motion as our bodies transitioned after exit and slowed to terminal velocity.

In unison, the group formed up in a V formation around the jumpmaster, trailing behind and above him at uneven intervals as we began to freefall toward the earth at one hundred and twenty miles an hour. Freefalling at altitude gives you the sensation of flying more so than falling. The air whipped past our faces and around our helmets, making a roaring noise that went unnoticed as the freefall continued. The formation ebbed and flowed as each man positioned himself within it, trying to reach the same altitude as the jumpmaster, who was still the low man. The outline of the other men was highlighted by the chemical light on the top of their helmets.

Falling in an almost perfect V formation, the team was demonstrating its ability to concentrate as each man held his arched position, rucksack between his legs. A quick glance at my altimeter, and I noticed that we had not gone through twelve thousand feet actual ground level as of yet, and the mountainous terrain was still very far below. The moonlight was perfect as the team flew its way toward the drop zone, which was lit by a strobe light that from this altitude seemed to only be a small flicker directly below us.

Looking around, I could see at least five other teammates and the jumpmaster, who was still slightly below me and to my right. Pulling my hands in tight and arching my back as hard as I could, I brought my feet in over my rucksack, bending at the knees a bit more than normal, in order to bleed off air and drop altitude. This worked as I brought myself down even with the jumpmaster's altitude and positioned myself flat, dumb, and happy about twenty-five yards behind him. I kept my eyes on him, making adjustments as needed.

Checking my altimeter, I realized that we were coming through seven thousand feet. I looked back at him and noticed that he was waving everybody off, crossing his hands in front of his head, waving them three times; then he tucked his arms back, stretched out his legs, and went into a dive away from the formation. We all followed suit, waving off; turning sixty degrees, away from the formation; and diving out and away. I let it ride like this for a few seconds, watching the ground, observing how much distance I had moved away from the now even larger strobe light on the drop zone.

A quick check left and then right; all was clear. I checked my altimeter as I cleared past forty-five hundred feet. I waved off quickly three times; reached in; found my ripcord; and thought to myself, *Don't you dare drop it.* With that thought, I pulled the ripcord, pushing both hands out straight in front of me. This would tend to raise my head above my feet and dump the air off my back, allowing the pilot chute to deploy, thus pulling my canopy out of the pack tray and permitting it to open.

Looking back over my left shoulder, I could see my pilot chute laying there on my back; so with the motion of looking over my shoulder, I pulled my right arm inward, smacking my elbow against the pack tray simultaneous to doing a slight roll to the right. This dumped the dead air off my back, and the pilot chute shot into the air, upward; and the main canopy dumped out, catching some air as I continued falling.

I reached up and grabbed the risers, shaking them once, twice, three times. Still no good canopy was over my head. I reached as high as I could, gaining hold of as much of the risers as I could, and pulled down hard. With that, the canopy opened in a sudden, jarring snap. The force of the opening translated into my thighs, as the parachute harness took on the chore of supporting all the weight of my body and combat gear.

Breathing heavily, I reached around to the left side of my face; and with my right hand, I disconnected the facemask. I turned off the bailout bottle, which was connected to my side, under my left arm. I could smell the smoke from the various camp and other fires that were burning below. Looking around, I noticed that the strobe light on the ground was still blinking. There was a red light and a green light on the DZ, indicating the direction of the wind. *Red to green, you're clean. Green to red, you're dead,* I thought to myself as I began to work my way toward the light.

I picked up on the formation that was now snaking or S rolling back and forth. This helped to dump air or drop altitude as we approached the DZ. I fell in behind and above the man in front of me and followed suit. One by one, we landed as we approached, dropping our rucksacks that were tethered to our gear with a lowering line made of one-inch tubular nylon. We all came swooping in, one by one, rucksacks hitting the ground first—each man flaring his chute, landing feet first, standing up, turning and dumping air out of his parachute. We all landed in an area only twenty-five meters in diameter.

The two American military advisors that had been working with the brigade for the last year had done an excellent job of setting up the Drop Zone. We gathered our gear and loaded into an awaiting truck as the security element of Salvadoran infantry moved back in and loaded with us. This was our first meeting; and silently, they patted us on the back and asked for smokes using the international hand signal.

The adrenaline rush from the jump began to subside as the trucks pulled into the brigade's bivouac site. Even though it was still dark, there was all kinds of activity, as the entire brigade was busily setting up for the long haul. They had already set up a series of green, general purpose, medium-sized tents. Each of them could house about thirty troops, and all of them were set up in neat rows.

The bivouac site was set up about ten miles from the volcano that the FMLN occupied. The unit was already in the field, ready to commence operations. They were only waiting for us to arrive, waiting for the support we could provide. A Salvadoran NCO led us to a tent that was to be our home for the next several days. The Salvadorans had already set up two rows of cots, six each, lining each side of the tent. The ground had been swept clean; and the sides of the tent were rolled up, mosquito nets hanging around the sides.

As the sun came up, I was at the water buffalo brushing my teeth, cleaning up, getting ready for the day. I could hear the distinct sound of artillery rounds being fired from the nearby battery and then reporting their mark as they exploded a ways off in the distance from the direction of the enemy redoubt. The brigade had already started prepping their target in anticipation of coming operations. Helicopter gunships, six of the old UH-1H Huey's left over since the Vietnam War, flew overhead. The Salvadorans had painted them black with snarling fangs on the front. They had also noticeably outfitted them with large rocket pods that loomed larger than life as they passed directly overhead, heading toward the enemy positions on the volcano.

My particular portion of this mission would be to take an infantry company around to the back side of the volcano and set up a series of ambushes, using small units of two or more squads in order to block the escape routes the enemy might use to avoid capture as the brigade swept up the mountainside, captured the enemy trenches, and drove them from their hideouts. I didn't mind not being part of the primary push. It didn't suit me. I liked working on my own, in the jungle, with my guys. I wouldn't have much time, only a few days, to prepare them for this mission; but my instinct told me that these guys were probably already more than capable, with or without me.

Walking with the rest of the team, we made our way through the camp toward the brigade's headquarters area. Led by an American lieutenant colonel who had been assigned as one of the unit's advisors for over a year now, we walked with a purpose—each carrying his rifle, slung at the low ready, our load-bearing equipment hung low on our waists and our jungle hats shaded us from the sun.

Although there was still grass between the rows of tents, it had been dry for some time; and the dust hovered over the entire area. There wasn't enough of a breeze to keep the air clear, as the heat wilted everything and the Central American humidity wrenched the sweat out of our bodies. Our green fatigues were soaked under the arms and down the center of our backs as I looked at my watch and realized it was still early morning, not yet eight o'clock. We pushed past the chow hall that the Salvadoran troops were using, all lined up, waiting for their ration of beans and rice. If they were lucky, they might get a hardboiled egg. Probably not today.

We had eaten our meals ready to eat, or MREs. I never really enjoyed MREs as much as I had the old long-range reconnaissance patrol packets, or LRRPs, a dehydrated meal that required only water in order to reconstitute a meal of spaghetti or corned beef hash. They filled you up, and you didn't have to combine a lot of different ingredients to get your meal ready. There was also a lot less trash; and that was a big deal, tactically. But today, we ate MREs and wore our old jungle fatigues as we walked together through the camp, all eyes upon us.

Entering the brigade commander's tent, I noticed that the walls were covered in maps and there was a single folding table with a few chairs in the middle. The brigade operations officer greeted the captain as we occupied spaces around him, trying to listen to what was being said. The usual pleasantries and introductions continued for about ten minutes, until the brigade commander entered the tent.

At that moment, a Salvadoran NCO shouted the command, "*Attencion!*"

We all came to the position of attention as the commander greeted the captain and the rest of the team. It wasn't until after the Salvadoran colonel had satisfied himself with the introductory process that he asked us to relax. He summoned the intelligence officer to give us a situation briefing as young troops brought in more chairs for us to sit on.

Taking our seats, the battalion operations officer started his briefing. He was professional, very experienced, as the scars on his face and hands indicated. On his face there were scars from lacerations across his cheeks on both sides of his face, and his hands were burnt to the point that they were pink in color versus his natural dark complexion. He spoke with an air of authority, knowing that he was the expert in his field. I couldn't help but admire this man.

How hard it must have been for them to fight a civil war, a war that pitted brother against brother, mothers against sons, and so on. How difficult must it have been for these men to attack villages that they had grown up in, where their families were from. A civil war is tough. Finding the motivation to fight must have been the most

THE NIGHT EAGLES SOARED

difficult thing to do. But somehow, these men carried on, working toward a better future, toward the day that they would know peace in their land.

The briefing continued as the brigade operations officer stood up and gave his portion. We already knew most of what was being said. The only thing that was different was the assignment of units to the advisory team. I picked up A Company, 1st Battalion, infantry, which was one of the youngest units in the brigade. The majority of my men had just completed basic training, and their average age was almost seventeen. After the briefing, I linked up with the company commander of the unit I would be working with. A lieutenant who had worked his way up through the ranks, he had been selected for officer candidate school and to attend the US Army Ranger school. He was not only competent; he was well-versed in the art of war as it pertained to this particular situation. He was solidly supported by his first sergeant, who had been leading troops in combat for over five years. The first sergeant had also worked his way up through the ranks and had the battle scars and a slight limp to show for it.

We all walked over to the company area, where the troops were waiting in formation. They had their faces all painted; and around their right shoulders, they wore an armband made from a white and black scarf, each folded perfectly to show the letters that indicated their unit designation as being part of the First Brigade. With their oversized steel pots, they looked a lot like a lamp with a lightshade on it; but deep down, these young men were strong. They were ready for their mission as they held their Vietnam era M-16's with pride, over their right shoulders. As we approached, an NCO called the unit to attention. The group stomped their feet in unison and then snapped into position with the distinct sound of their heels clicking together. A small cloud of dust hung over them as the commander introduced me and directed the platoon leaders to move the company down to a site near the river, where they were to receive training that I would be presenting. On command, the unit turned to its right and began to march off. I fell in behind them, with the lieutenant and the first sergeant; and we walked, comfortably making small talk as they asked me questions about from where and who I was. I would answer in my best Spanish.

My Spanish language skills by this time had been honed, allowing me to converse openly; but still I had a distinct accent that made it hard for others to understand what I was saying. There were times that I wouldn't know a word for what I wanted to say, but the troops were always willing to work with me. I think they respected the fact that I was trying to speak their language. They always complimented me on my ability to do so.

Near the river, there was a huge tree standing tall and apparently unmolested by the war with its high canopy spreading out as if it was an umbrella over a hundred feet tall. We gathered in the shade; and the troops cleared out an area by stomping down the grass with their boots, and then they took their seats. I stood there in front of them for a few moments, looking them over after the company commander had turned them over to me. Looking into their eyes, I could see their youthfulness underneath all that paint. Some smiled at me. Others looked down or away. All sweating a bit, they had a smell about them; the kind of smell only an infantry man could appreciate or perhaps understand. It was the smell of dirty clothes; body odor; and smoke from a plethora of cigarettes and, of course, cooking fires. There were enough of them all together, so many that you could hear them breathe, over a hundred of them in the group.

With me I had an easel board that some of the troops had carried for me, along with a class on how to conduct an area ambush written on large paper sheets that hung from the easel board. With my rifle slung around my upper body so that it would hang at the low ready, I retrieved a few magic markers with my right hand from my cargo pocket. I had black, blue, red, and green—all the essential colors for describing military operations. Usually, I am not at a loss for words in this situation; but for some reason, I couldn't quite get over the fact that I was going to teach these guys how to conduct an ambush the right way. I couldn't put my finger on a reasonable justification as to why they would want to. *This is a war,* I thought to myself. I knew that the situation was difficult. These men were fighting against their own countrymen, their own families in some respect. Their motivation must come from someplace I had yet to recognize or even allude toward understanding myself.

Looking over their heads, into the tree branches overhead, I asked the question, "Who here has ever been ambushed by the enemy?" Only a few hands were raised, most notably the company's first sergeant. So I asked him to tell us what happened, and he began to explain how his patrol several years ago had been ambushed by an FMLN element. He described how they had set off explosions that knocked him unconscious. The shooting that ensued brought him back to his senses, and he realized that not only had he lost his weapon but he had also lost his left foot in addition to having been shot in the buttocks. He raised his pant leg to show the prosthetic device that was attached to the eight-inch stump below his knee.

I asked him, "Did the enemy assault through the kill zone after the ambush?"

He said, "No. They just set off their charges, fired at us, and then they ran."

"Well then," I said. "So you survived the ambush, and now today you are leading an entire infantry company back into combat against them, right?"

He answered, "Yes."

So I asked the group, "Can anybody in the crowd tell me what the enemy did wrong when they ambushed the first sergeant's patrol?"

One person raised his hand, and so I pointed at him to answer the question; and he said, "They didn't kill the first sergeant!"

With a smile, I answered, "Yes, you're right, but not quite.

"You see, men, the only way to win a war is to make contact with your enemy and to maintain that contact until you've either destroyed him or destroyed his will to fight. As you can see, they did neither to the first sergeant, and now they are going to pay dearly for that mistake.

"My purpose here with you today is to teach you how to destroy your enemy so that he will not come back to haunt you a year from now. I am going to teach you how to survive and fight again. I am going to show you how to conduct an ambush and how to assault through the kill zone so that you won't have to worry about people like the first sergeant coming back to kill you someday." I paused for a moment then.

"The bottom line is what this war at our level is all about: killing your enemy before he is able to kill you. Do you understand what I am saying?"

With a loud yell that lasted for at least ten seconds, they let me know that not only did they understand but they wanted to learn. So, with that, our training began.

We ran mock ambushes all day, walking through each step. We did it out in an open field where everybody could see how it was done. Then we did it at half speed, and then at full speed. Once everybody was ready, we did a company live fire ambush. It was incredible. I watched as these young men, assaulted across the kill zone, mock killing everything that moved. They were ready. That night, we would move out and head in the direction of the volcano, a ten-mile hump, a river crossing, and then we would set up our ambushes and wait for the main push from the brigade to begin. This was a big deal. If we could get the G's to come down off that mountain, the war would probably be over.

The movement toward the volcano was uneventful as we kept off the roads, using cattle trails and crossing fences as we went. The lieutenant kept the company out of sight, using the terrain and the darkness as his allies. The only part of the movement that made me worry was the river crossing. It would be the only time we were exposed. Most of his men could swim, but some couldn't. Our plan was to swim across with ropes in order to set up several rope bridges that the men could use to hang onto as they pulled themselves and their equipment across. It all hinged on how fast the current was and if the intelligence survey of the crossing points had been correct. We expected the water to be no more than six feet deep at its deepest point, and that would not be too much of an obstacle. The riverbed, however, was almost one hundred meters wide, and that could prove to be a formidable obstacle.

We continued, moving in single file, covered in darkness, up then down, around we snaked over the terrain in a single file, stopping only to cross an obstacle. The lieutenant and the first sergeant were in control of the unit as we approached the river crossing sight. The patrol came to a stop, each man stepping in unison to the left and right side of the trail, picking up security. I moved forward until I linked up with the headquarters element. The lieutenant was giving orders to the platoon leader who would be in charge of setting up the rope bridges. There would be four ropes set up, one for each platoon. They would set the ropes up along a two-hundred-meter stretch of river located between two bends. The lieutenant picked one platoon to send security teams to the left and right in order to set up near side security before the men began to swim with the ropes. Once the security teams were in place, he sent the swimmers across. I watched as they disappeared into the water and the darkness; and we waited with anticipation, watching the ropes unwind on the bank as they continued to be pulled downstream and across. After about fifteen minutes, the ropes appeared to be completely unwound; and then, one by one, the men on the other side began to pull them taught. Using the glow in the dark light from his compass, the swimmer's team leader signaled that all was clear by swinging the compass in a half circle or pendulum motion. We both observed the light signal, the lieutenant and I; and that was that. He sent the far side security team across. One by one, the two squads of men lowered themselves into the current, quietly hooking their rucksacks to the rope using a snap link. Then they each pulled themselves along with their rucksacks across the river.

We waited for quite some time for the far side security element to get across. As they crossed, the lieutenant asked me for a smoke; but I didn't have one. I hadn't smoked for years because it made me feel as though I couldn't breathe. In this business, staying in good physical condition was imperative; and smoking just wasn't something that was conducive to being able to do the types of physical activities we were required to do. We sat there in silence until we received word that all was clear. Slowly, the rest of the company crossed the river.

I crossed with the lieutenant. The first sergeant had already crossed and was waiting for us as we got to the other side. He reached down and helped me out of the water as I reached the far side. As soon as the company had completed the crossing, we moved back into the jungle and stopped to listen and watch, making sure we hadn't been compromised. We decided to make this our objective rally point. From here, we would send out our ambush elements. We were close to the volcano, and there wasn't much sense in getting compromised by moving as such a large element. The lieutenant sent word for his platoon leaders to gather up in the center of the makeshift patrol base he had established. Looking at my watch, I could see that we had used almost five hours to make the movement from our base camp and to cross the river. That wasn't too bad for an element this size. We still had time to get the ambush location set up before the sun would start to rise. I pulled out my small radio and did a radio check with my team leader, giving him the code number we had designated to indicate that we had crossed the river safely. Our team radios were not secure, so we used pre-designated codes to communicate operational information in order to prevent the enemy from determining what we were actually talking about. We decided to move together, the lieutenant and I, with second platoon to the primary trail that came down off of the volcano on our side of it. This trail was well marked and could be seen from the aerial photography that we had obtained. I'm not sure where the photos had come from, but they were excellent. They were good enough for us to know that we could set up an L-shaped ambush there without a problem. The first sergeant went with first platoon since the lieutenant had more trust in the experience of third and fourth platoon leaders. They would be setting up various squad-sized ambushes along smaller trails to our left and right flanks.

The soil at the base of the volcano was rich. It had a granular texture that seemed strange to me; but it smelled like earthworms, a sign that it was very rich. The trees grew tall, and the jungle was layered. *Triple canopy,* I thought to myself. I liked the fact that we had a decent jungle to cover our movement now. Crossing the open farmland that we had been on made everybody feel a bit nervous; but now that we were in the jungle, we could breathe a bit.

The lieutenant was doing everything right. He asked me what I thought, and so I told him he was doing an excellent job. He had established his objective rally point, set up all his security elements, briefed all the platoon leaders, and had given them the criteria for initiating their ambushes along with a five-point contingency plan, should there be a compromise while moving into their ambush site. Everything was going smoothly, and we were getting ready to move into our position. He and I had looked it over, and it was perfect. There were large boulders on one side of the trail that we would be watching. They were rectangular in shape, laying sideways at about a forty-five-degree angle along the side of the trail that wound back and forth down the side of the mountain in a line that originated from the mouth of a large cave about two thirds of the way to the top.

From our position, we could see a few small cooking fires on the side of the volcano as the G's began to wake. The fires made it easy to see their positions. Using my night vision device, I could clearly see them; so I made a note as to their locations just in case I needed to call in an air strike. The smell of coffee brewing permeated the air, arousing my hunger as we all finally settled in along a curve in the trail that turned almost ninety degrees from left to right.

We set up on the outside of the curve, with a couple machine guns in the center and one on each end of the ambush line. On the far side of the trail, there was a rock wall, handmade, approximately four feet high, that would tend to trap the enemy between it and us. It, however, could provide cover for them should they escape over the top of it. I mentioned that to the lieutenant, and so we decided to put some Claymore mines over there just in case. His plan would be to set them off before we assaulted across the kill zone, making it easier for us to clear the other side of the wall if and when we did have to cross over it in pursuit. He had set up a half dozen Claymores on that side and another dozen or so on our side, all pointed to create the greatest effect.

He worked the line, talking to each soldier—especially to those who had drawn the responsibility to set off a Claymore. He let the men know not to set them off until he set off the first one. That would be the signal to initiate the ambush. The first explosion was the signal for everybody to open fire—the men on semi automatic, the machineguns on full auto—the rest of the Claymores. He also designated an entire squad to fire on full auto—a different technique than I had learned, but I felt it would be effective nonetheless. The lieutenant had reserved the extra Claymores for me to fire off, the ones on the far side of the wall. I had no problem with that. In fact, I appreciated the opportunity.

We waited as the sun came up. We waited as it got hotter. Mosquitoes buzzed around my ears as I lay there on my side behind a large rock, Claymore clackers set up to my front. I had a perfect view of the entire line. But so far, nothing had happened. I laid there, waiting, along with the rest of the men—most of them out of sight but not out of mind. It was quiet except for the locusts. Their buzzing was almost deafening, and it was loud enough to cover any noise we might be making. The fact that they were making their noise was a good thing for us. If somebody was about to approach, they would get quiet and alert us. I looked at my watch and wondered why the rest of the brigade hadn't initiated any action on the other side of the volcano as of yet, so I pulled out my small radio and contacted the team and let them know that all was quiet on my end.

The humidity was so high that my uniform was already soaked through. As I looked at my watch, sweat dripped off my hat onto the lens. It was only 0745. The main assault was supposed to kick off at 0800. No telling how long it would take for fifteen hundred men to take this mountain. Like clockwork, the artillery pieces from their positions near the base camp began to fire. The rounds raced by, high to our front, and exploded in muffled thuds on the opposite side, away from us.

I looked through my binoculars and quickly located several squads of men moving across the mountain along a trench that was parallel to the base of the mountain. They were moving to reinforce the opposite side. The enemy had probably spotted the brigade moving forward under the cover of the artillery fire. I handed my binoculars to the lieutenant, and he got on the radio to request an air strike. Soon, two American-made A-37 Dragonfly fast mover jets with two five-hundred-pound bombs mounted under each wing, appeared over the target. The men in the trench moving across the volcano looked up as the aircraft swooped over them, first one and then the other gracefully letting go of their pay loads. I watched as the bombs dropped in what seemed like slow motion as the aircraft lifted and turned tightly into the air, straight up, away from the imminent violence they had unleashed. The bombs struck their mark, napalm spreading across the charred rocks as the men in the trench disappeared in a cloud of fire and black smoke.

At the peak of their ascent, the two aircraft turned away from each other, bellies toward the sky, as the pilot and navigator sat there, side by side, watching their handiwork do its thing. Simultaneously, they turned downward and raced back toward the earth— one to my left, the other to my right—making an almost perfect circle. They pulled up, facing each other, and raced back over the target area and dropped the remainder of their payloads as they passed by each other.

Twisting and turning, they pulled up and climbed out, watching as their bombs found their mark and exploded. Their napalm covered the ground with fire on a five-hundred-meter front directly over the trench the enemy had been using. The flames shot into the air in another cloud of dark smoke and red flame. It was all I could do to keep from applauding as the two jets turned down and flew along the sides of the mountain and turned toward our position, crossing again directly over our heads with the aircraft upside down, bellies toward the air. I imagined that they were giving us a salute as they passed. As soon as they passed overhead, they climbed out in a victory roll directly over our position. Their exhaust contrails twisted each other like baked pretzel sticks all the way up as they reached egress altitude. Then as suddenly as they had appeared, they were gone. They would probably be heading back to their base, back to reload and return.

Clearing, the smoke climbed into the air, leaving behind the burnt mountainside, exposing the black volcanic soil beneath what little vegetation had been able to survive all the attacks that had been launched against the redoubt since the beginning of the war. The scarred volcanic flows of black lava were now joined with the scorched earth man had created with his armaments.

We waited from our jungle hiding position most of the afternoon, the heat building, patience wearing thin as the battle on the other side of the volcano raged on. Smoke filled the sky above the mountain as the brigade continued its assault. The occasional sound of a ricochet echoed overhead. Some of our elements had picked off a few small patrols. Perhaps they were reconnaissance patrols looking for a weakness in the noose we had placed around the enemy positions. There were gaps in the line, but we had so many ambush positions set up around the base of the mountain that it was difficult if not impossible for them to find a way out. Most of their movements could be detected. At least the larger elements stood out like a sore thumb on the now-denuded mountainside.

There was a cave opening about two hundred yards from our position, and it seemed as though the trail we were on came out of that cave—although there were trenches and trails leading to the left and right of the trail, so it was difficult to say with any certainty how big or deep the cave might be. Then, just before it started getting dark, hundreds of men came pouring out of the cave, heading straight for our position down the trail. Our ambush site wouldn't be large enough; but we waited patiently as the lieutenant called in an artillery strike on the cave opening. In the distance, the battery began to make itself heard again as it fired on that position. It seemed like an eternity waiting for the rounds to impact as men continued to pour out of the cave. With amazing accuracy, the rounds started exploding on both sides of the trail just below the opening. The men who were caught in the barrage began to spread out, but they continued down the hill.

I contacted the team and found out that the assault had been successful. The brigade had penetrated the trench system that protected the openings of the cave system the FMLN had been using as their headquarters for so many years. *Well,* I thought, *that explains why so many people are coming out of that cave opening on our side of the hill.*

The battle on our side of the mountain continued as darkness fell. The battery kept firing illumination rounds, providing us with the light we needed to maintain our positions. Tracer rounds seemed to bounce off everything as the machine guns and the men continued firing at anything that moved. I kept working the line, checking on men, putting bandages on, sharing my ammunition, and giving encouragement. I bumped into the lieutenant, who had a huge smile on his face.

He said, "We're getting them good this time!"

Our plan to ambush patrols had turned into a blocking position. It seemed as though the G's just couldn't help themselves. They just kept running into our trap.

All the Claymores had been used, so the men were now using hand grenades and their rifles. From time to time, there would be small hand-to-hand skirmishes as the G's kept coming down off the mountain. By the time the sun came up, our little patch of jungle was torn and burnt, smoke rising from the ashes, as the battle subsided and we counted our men.

Altogether, the company had lost eight men; and almost everybody had some sort of wound. I didn't have a scratch on me, although I had a headache from dehydration. Looking for my canteens, I realized that they had both been cut open by shrapnel. But still, I had not one scratch on my body. *It is miraculous,* I thought to myself as the lieutenant sat there, smiling at me. The medic was putting a bandage around the lieutenant's right thigh. He had taken a piece of shrapnel and hadn't even noticed until this morning when the medic grabbed him and made him relax for a while.

I looked around and found the company radio operator and told him to request some rotary wing support to get the wounded off the mountain; and that is when I saw him laying there in a pool of his own blood, the top of his head crushed. The first sergeant was dead. He had been killed outright, not having suffered much; but his men were devastated as they carried his body over to the company position. He would be sorely missed. His troops told me that he had been jumped by several G's and that they had crushed his skull with a rock before anybody could get to him. The first sergeant was dead.

After sending the worst of the wounded off on the medevacs, we turned the dead over to an El Salvadoran element similar to that of our own graves registration; and the company picked up and moved off the mountain returning by foot to the brigade's bivouac site. This time, we walked down a dirt road, over to the highway, and across the bridge not worrying about the FMLN. They were on the run. The war was close to being over. We all knew it.

As we marched into the camp, troops from some of the other units lined the trail and chanted the brigade's combat chant, making us all feel great. Forgetting about our aches and pains, we all joined in.

"*Somos antiterrorista, anticomunista, hasta el fin, hasta el fin, hah, hah, hah!*

The company picked up the pace and jogged the rest of the way into the camp, sounding off as we shuffled into our own company area.

That afternoon, the team boarded a set of deuce-and-a-half trucks, then we were driven to the airfield at Ilopango and we departed ahead of the Friday afternoon head count on American advisors. In its effort to minimize U.S. involvement in the conflict, Congress had passed a law requiring the Ambassador to confirm that there were only fifty five advisors on the ground at any given time. The count would be sent to Washington every two weeks on a Friday afternoon by 1700 hours. This afternoon, there were still only fifty-five advisors on the ground at that time. Officially, we hadn't been there. What we had accomplished never happened, we did not actually exist. We departed without symbolism or celebration on a National Guard C-130 heading out over the Pacific Ocean, climbing to altitude as we turned north and flew back over the Gulf of Fonseca and over Honduran airspace out over the Caribbean. We had only been in El Salvador for a few days, and it was over. We had done what we had come for. We had succeeded.

The pilot came across the loudspeaker and announced that we had run out of flight hours for the day and that he would be forced to land in order to get crew rest. The loadmaster came over and said, "We are going to the Cayman Islands, and you can bet your bottom dollar I am going to break this plane so we can stay for a few days."

He was true to his word. We landed on the island and spent three days on the beach, drinking beer. The only drawback was that we didn't have any civilian clothing with us, so I bought a pair of flip-flops and a bathing suit, and that is what I wore the entire time.

Watching the news, we were all surprised that our battle for the volcano, to drive the FMLN leadership from the redoubt that they had held since the start of the war, had not made the headlines. It was as if the war in El Salvador didn't exist in the United States. We commented on that with each other and all decided that it didn't matter. We knew what we had done.

Finally, the plane was fixed; so we boarded and flew back to Fort Bragg to find it still there—nothing changed. We dropped our gear in the team room and went home without fanfare, unable to explain to anybody what had happened. Nobody knew but the few of us, and that was the way it was.

"Nothing more needs to be said about that dirty little war," the captain had said as we left the team room, got into our cars, and drove home.

I went to the NCO club and had a few beers and then went back to the barracks and racked out. Formation the next day took place as if nothing happened. We did our physical training, and the team sergeant cut us loose for the day. I went to the gym and sat in the steam room for several hours and tried to put the memory out of my mind.

PRESS RELEASE:

On 16 January 1992, President Alfredo Cristiani and the leaders of the FMLN signed a peace accord that brought an end to the twelve-year conflict that had engulfed the entire country in a rage of violence, destroyed the economy, and caused so much suffering.

The constitution was amended to prohibit the military from playing an internal security role except under extraordinary circumstances. Demobilization of Salvadoran military forces generally proceeded on schedule throughout the process. The Treasury Police, National Guard, and National Police were abolished; and military intelligence functions were transferred to civilian control. A purge of military officers accused of human rights abuses and corruption was completed in 1993 in compliance with the Truth Commission's recommendations and the military's new doctrine, professionalism, and complete withdrawal from political and economic affairs has left it the most respected institution in El Salvador.

Simultaneously to the signing of the peace accord, a national celebration erupted as the Salvadoran people could finally look forward to the possibility of peace and prosperity. The wounds inflicted throughout the conflict would forever live in the national conscience, but there was a willingness to forgive as both sides came together and formed a new nation under the banner of reconciliation and reconstruction.

In the counter-insurgency laboratory of El Salvador, the post Vietnam War strategy of the United States proved to be successful. One of the most interesting parts of this strategy was the impact a relatively small number of American Special Forces advisors were able to have. Their accomplishments were great despite the obstacles and dangers that they faced.

THE CHURCH LADIES

The phone in the team room rang; one of the guys answered it, stating the last four digits of the phone number.

"Four four two three. This is a non-secure line. Sergeant Miller speaking."

Our team rooms at the time were located on Smoke Bomb Hill at Fort Bragg, North Carolina. Having remodeled several World War II vintage barracks down by area G, we occupied one quarter of the upper floor of an A-frame building that had been built during the war.

The windows were open, and the sound of helicopters flying past overhead could be heard as Sergeant Miller said, "Hey, Mike. The sergeant major wants to talk to you down in his office, ASAP," as he hung the phone up, shouting over his shoulder.

I was in the back of the team room, cleaning my rifle—a bolt action, 7.62mm long gun with a fixed 10-power scope. It was brand-new, so new that we had only trained on these rifles a few times during sniper school. Throughout training, we had used an M-21, which was a modified M-14 with a heavy-duty National Match barrel. The M-21 had been glassed in using fiberglass to fill in the gaps between the metal components and the wooden stocks. I liked the M-21. It had a ten-round magazine, but the scope was nowhere near as good as the new one with its mil-dot reticules. Getting accustomed to the bolt action rifle was something I needed to do. Training was a priority at this point. I didn't think I would be ready to do a mission with this rifle for some time, but I was soon to find out that time was not a luxury at the moment.

Knocking three times authoritatively on the sergeant major's door, I sounded off and he invited me in. Entering his small office, my team leader and the company commander were seated to the left; to my surprise, the battalion commander was seated at the desk while the company and battalion sergeant majors were seated to the right. I stood at the position of attention approximately two feet from the desk, and reported with a salute as somebody closed the door behind me. I wasn't sure what was going on, but I knew I hadn't done anything negative enough to warrant attention at this level.

Standing at the position of attention, I listened as the battalion commander said, "At ease, Sergeant."

I relaxed slightly, putting my hands behind my back.

Then he said, "Sergeant, I understand you're the best tracker in the entire group."

"Affirmative, sir!"

In a doubting tone, he asked, "How did you learn to track so well?"

Hesitating for a second, I responded, "Well, sir, back home, hunting and tracking deer and bobcats, among other things, sir."

He asked, "Do you think you could track down a human being?"

"Affirmative, sir. I've been trained to do so. I'm ready to do what needs to be done anytime, anywhere, anyplace, sir."

With that, he said, "Well, have a seat, Sergeant."

There was a small wooden chair against the wall. I picked it up and set it down with my back against the door so that I could see all of their faces without turning. The five of them began to brief me on a mission downrange that would require me to track down and find three women. Three missionaries that had been taken hostage a few years earlier by the G's in Colombia. Apparently, the women had been working with some of the most recently discovered Indian tribes along the Panamanian-Colombian border when the communist guerillas (Narco terrorists) caught up with them. There had been various opportunities to gain proof of life, the most recent of which had been earlier that morning. The G's had allowed the women to speak over a high-frequency radio, and Intel felt as though they had pinpointed the location down to an area of twenty-five square kilometers or so near the small Columbian village of *Puerto Libre* along the *Rió Atrato* near the Panamanian border.

"The area west of *Puerto Libre* is densely forested with triple-canopy jungle and swamp. There are rivers on two sides of the area of operation." He said, "So you'll have to brief me in a few days on how you plan to get in there without being detected. You'll probably have to use the river as an avenue of approach. Let me know what options you come up with. Then we'll decide on how to continue. Do you have a sniper buddy?"

"Yes, sir, I do."

"Well then, the two of you will go into isolation immediately and start your planning process. Have your commander let me know when you're ready to give me a brief back."

"Yes, sir!"

I stood at the position of attention as the entire party stood, and then the company commander motioned for me to leave. I saluted, turned, moved the chair out of the way, and exited the room without hesitation.

Returning to the team room, everybody wanted to know what was going on. I couldn't say anything. I just secured my equipment and called Jimmy, my sniper buddy, who was over at battalion drawing weapons, and told him to meet me at the isolation facility as soon as he was done.

We spent about four days looking at the operation in great detail. There was no real way to get into the region using rotary wing aircraft, and a rough-terrain jump was too risky, considering that there were only the two of us and the trees were over ninety feet tall. We decided to fly in using commercial aircraft after having shipped our weapons and other gear downrange via military airlift. Then our guys in Bogotá could pick up the gear and we would link up with them to retrieve it.

We requested a ten-thousand-dollar operational fund—money to be used for transportation, bribes, medical care, anything we might need it for—and then we packed our gear and got it ready for the flight.

After having briefed the group and battalion commanders on our mission plan, they approved it; and off we went. The two of us took a taxi to the local airport and boarded a flight bound for Bogotá via Miami. Upon arrival, Jimmy and I rented a pickup truck, a Toyota Hilux 4x4, and drove to the linkup site with our guys. There, we picked up our weapons and other gear, checking them all and loading the pistols and an M4-Carbine. We started our journey northwest toward Medellín. We drove all afternoon but didn't get all the way there, so we decided to rest overnight in a small village called La Union. We checked into an inn, and downloaded all of our gear. There was a night watchman, so I asked him to keep an eye on our vehicle and paid him about three dollars. With a huge smile, he agreed. That night, we took turns pulling security. One of us would stay awake for a few hours and keep an eye on things. Then we would switch out. It was quiet, nothing to worry about really, although this entire part of the country was well-known for its Narco traffickers and their dislike for anything or anybody that might resemble the DEA.

As the sun came up, I could smell coffee being brewed and decided to check on the truck. I walked outside and there the night watchman was, proudly pointing at the truck and saying, "Es okay! Es okay!" Smiling, I nodded and tipped him a few dimes and asked him where I could get some coffee and breakfast. He pointed out a small kiosk across the street, so I crossed and picked up several small, deep-fried bread pies with meat in the center called *empanadas* and a couple cups of coffee.

Jimmy and I sat on the porch of the inn, which was really a house; but the little old lady running it had converted it in order to make ends meet I suppose. It wasn't so bad. There were flowerbeds and a young mango tree in the yard, along with a couple of lime trees and some plantains. She had a large, multicolored Macaw sitting on a perch near the front door; and it was contentedly eating some fresh bananas. Every now and then, it would let out a screech that could burst your eardrums; and then it would go back to eating its fruit.

We loaded up and departed without drawing much attention to ourselves. We looked liked we could be regular civilians, perhaps tourists from Europe or from farther south. Both Jimmy and I spoke impeccable Spanish, and we could emulate the Castilian accents of the folks from perhaps Uruguay. We kept our weapons concealed. I was carrying my nine-millimeter pistol along with a shorty, an M-4 Carbine with a ten-inch barrel and a paratrooper stock. I kept it in a shoulder bag, and the pistol I had tucked under my shirt. I had on a pair of dark beige Dockers with cargo pockets and a brown pair of Gortex boots, the pant leg pulled down over the top. All this, along with my ball cap and sunglasses, made me look like just any other tourist I hoped. I had my long gun hidden behind the backseat of the rear cab of the truck. On top of the seat, we placed the rest of our gear and luggage. Our three-day assault packs were neatly tucked away inside.

We drove all day, passing checkpoint after checkpoint, each time bribing our way through without question. Passing through *Medellín* was a bit tricky. The streets were confusing, and it was a lot larger than we had anticipated. Neither of us had ever been there. Using his GPS and a road map we had purchased, Jimmy navigated as I drove carefully through the city, trying not to attract any attention. Finally, we cleared the city and decided to stop at a large, Colombian version of a truck stop to rest our legs a bit. While there, Jimmy asked for directions; and soon, we were back on the road, traveling down Route 11, heading through the mountainous jungle toward the Gulf of *Uraba*. We drove all day, stopping to rest as we passed through places like *Sevilla*, *Obregón*, and *Dabeiba*. We entered into the coastal valley of the gulf, arriving at the town of *Chigoradó*, and decided to rest overnight. We needed time to decide what our next step would be.

Our plan had been to continue from here via the highway into the town of *Turbo* and then charter a boat from there and have it take us across the gulf and up the River *Atrató*; but as we entered *Chigoradó*, we noticed that there was a small airfield with a sea plane. We decided to approach the owners in the morning to see if it would be possible to contract a flight.

In the morning, we had our breakfast at the hotel where we were staying. It was a nice hotel, somewhat modern, no hot water; but it was clean and the food was pretty good. I had a fruit salad along with some bread and local cheese. It was filling, and the coffee was very strong—small espressos with lots of sugar. I didn't dare drink any cream or milk. Many times I had tried, and many times I ended up very sick. This time, I didn't have the luxury of going down with a stomach virus; so I abstained.

After breakfast, we loaded our equipment, making sure to keep the weapons out of sight, and then drove over to the airfield. The folks there were more than happy to see us as we explained that we were on a fishing trip and we wanted to do some fishing along the lakes near the *Rió Atrató* and the small town of *Puerto Libre*. They agreed to the idea, and we coordinated with them to pick us up in three days, should we not contact them via the telephone first. We were carrying satellite cell phones that we could use to make a call from any place at any time. The only problem with these phones was that they didn't work well in the jungle. We needed a large, open area in order to have a direct line of sight for the satellite.

Before we departed, we contacted the command and let them know that we planned on doing our exfill in seventy-two hours and asked that they have fixed and rotary wing assets available to pick us up as planned or, as an alternate, we wanted to be picked up at the *Chigoradó* airfield on request. With that, we were done.

We parked the Toyota under a small grass hut at the insistence of our pilot, and we loaded our gear onto the plane and prepared for takeoff. We discussed our pickup time with the pilot, and it was all agreed; he would pick us up in seventy-two hours from the time he dropped us off. It wasn't that we actually wanted him to pick us up. It was just part of our cover, and perhaps knowing he would be some-place at a specific time could support an alternate plan if needed.

Jimmy sat up front in the co-pilot seat in order to continue his chores as navigator; and I sat in back, concentrating on our next moves. We had planned on coming into the operational area from the opposite direction, from the main river. Now we would be entering the area where the ladies might be located from the east. That made a big difference. The night before, I had plotted our route, determined the azimuth's and distances, and then commit-ted it to memory. Jimmy and I had discussed the concept, and we both agreed that this was the best way to proceed. The only stickler was coming in on the airplane. It could spell disaster, should we be compromised, should we be spotted by the G's; but we felt that the aircraft had been seen in this area before and shouldn't raise any more suspicion than a boat on the river, a boat that didn't usually travel that far upstream. We had picked out a landing zone with the pilot, and we didn't plan on being on the lakeshore for long. We would land, disembark, and move out; and the pilot was to take off immediately, without waiting around.

He flew over the jungle, about five hundred feet off the ground, climbing or turning from time to time as the terrain changed below. He was very familiar with the area, and I'm sure he was probably accustomed to doing business with most everybody in this region, to include the G's. Below, the ground looked like a blanket of green as we cleared over the highest ridge to our front, the tops protruding from the clouds. To our front, there was an opening in the clouds; and we could see the lakes.

Pointing down at them, the pilot said, "It will only be a few minutes now," as he dropped the nose downward, passing through the clouds.

I wondered how he knew there wasn't a mountain in the clouds as my heart beat a little fast. I felt nervous about the landing, but I wasn't sure why. Perhaps it was because I had never landed on water before. Perhaps it was because I was accustomed to jumping out versus landing anywhere.

The pilot brought the aircraft in for a picture-perfect landing and coasted up to the beach we had decided upon before takeoff. This guy knew what he was doing. We quickly down loaded our gear and waved good-bye as he turned the aircraft around and took off. Less than two minutes on the ground and we were golden. We both took a look around, trying to see if we could see any boats or people. There were a few plumes of smoke from what looked like cooking fires about five kilometers to the south, but who knows from what or from whom they could have been. For the moment, we hadn't been compromised as far as we could tell; and that was all we needed to know. We recovered the gear and moved off into the jungle, following a small creek bed for almost three hundred meters before stopping for a listening halt. We sat there for an hour, listening quietly, and prepared our equipment. I unpacked my rifle, loaded it, and put on my retention holster.

Loading my pistol, I looked at Jimmy, who was doing the same, and said, "Let's cache the rest of the gear over there by that big rock. We should be able to find that no problem."

We carried the extra equipment and luggage over to the cache site and piled it up next to the rock. Then we gathered branches and leaves and covered the stuff up. It was unlikely that we would even bother with this stuff; but if we needed it, we would have it. There were some extra medical items, bandages, painkillers, intravenous injection sets, and other basics, along with our luggage and extra clothing.

With my long gun slung over my shoulder and my M-4 hanging at the low ready, I picked up my assault pack and followed as Jimmy picked up a heading on his compass and started taking us toward the last location we had for the ladies, according to the Intel folks back at Bragg.

Our first leg would take us straight toward the small fishing village of *Puerto Libre*, about twenty kilometers through the lowland surrounding the *Rio Atrató* lakes. This ground was covered with triple canopy, and there was lots of water. Most of the time, it was at least ankle deep, sometimes deeper. It wasn't as bad as we moved farther away from the lakes; and after about five kilometers, we discovered some very nice triple-canopy jungle so dense that it blocked out the sun and prevented the undergrowth from growing. This made our movement much easier; but first, we stopped and took off our socks. Wet socks in the jungle just don't cut it.

"Better off going without socks," muttered Jimmy.

"I couldn't agree more," I said.

We sat there for a moment, drinking water, listening. So far so good.

As we began to approach the village, we could smell the difference a human population made on a place—mostly the smell of smoke. But soon, there was the distinct odor of raw sewage and rotting trash. We were still over a kilometer from the town, but the smell was very distinct. We stopped for a moment. Jimmy placed his finger under his nose and made a face. Nodding, I pointed toward both of my eyes with my right hand index finger and middle finger and then made the motion of walking with them pointing in the direction to the left of the village. Using the knife edge of my hand, I indicated that we should go around. Jimmy nodded and picked up the pace. Quickly, we moved around the village, skirting the edge, catching a glimpse of it from time to time. It was almost dark, and we wanted to put some distance between ourselves and these people before it was too late.

After about an hour, we slowed down. Sweat was pouring off the brow of my ball cap.

We took a knee, and Jimmy said, "This should be good right here!"

I agreed, and we decided to rest overnight right there. As the sun went down, we kept quiet, not starting a fire, sleeping one at a time, killing time, and waiting for the sun to come up again. One thing that worried me was that the locals would be out hunting monkeys at night. If they were, they might pick up on our trail. We needed it to rain; but this was the dry season, and it wasn't likely. Besides, we needed to find the trail of the missionaries. If it was the rainy season, we never would. All night long, we swapped off sleeping and keeping watch. I used my night vision goggles to keep an eye out. Everything was quiet. It seemed as though we might have been able to get in here without being compromised. That was a good thing. I took a deep breath and chewed on a piece of jerky and thought about what might take place the next day. If we were lucky, we would find the trail and perhaps the women. We waited, fitfully resting in the cool night air, listening to the birds and insects and the occasional howler monkey. There was a three-toed sloth somewhere near. I could smell him but couldn't see him, so I listened for his movements until the sun came up; and there he was, two feet over Jimmy's head, hanging upside down, looking directly at him. I laughed to myself as I reached over with a stick and woke Jimmy up. He opened one eye to see the sloth looking right back at him. Slowly, Jimmy rolled over and came to his knees and said, "Man that thing stinks!"

Smiling, I said, "Let's go."

We packed up our gear and secured our weapons. Doing a press check on my pistol, I slid it back into my holster; and we moved out. The terrain seemed to steadily climb as we moved toward the river and our target. We continued for several clicks when Jimmy stopped, holding his right fist tight next to his ear. He pointed with his index finger, indicating an enemy to our front. I dropped down onto my stomach as did he, and I crawled forward to his position. Lying there side by side, we could not believe our luck. We had walked up onto the G's who were taking a bath in a stream about fifty meters to our front. I counted eight of them—four in the water and four keeping watch. With my left hand, I indicated that number to Jimmy; and he shook his head no. He pointed to the left;

and there were two more guys, sitting on a platform up in a tree about thirty meters to the far side of the crew at the water hole. We sat there for what seemed like an eternity, studying them, making mental notes about their weapons and appearance.

They were tattered, that's for sure; skinny but muscular. There was one man—a tall black man—who seemed out of place.

I whispered to Jimmy, "Cuban?"

He shrugged his shoulders, not knowing the answer. We watched until they moved out. They headed back toward the river, back toward the location we were looking for. We decided to track them for a while and see what they were up to.

Their trail was easy to follow. Obviously, they didn't expect to be tracked. They felt absolutely safe out here. And why not? This was completely isolated. With my shorty at the ready, I continued tracking the group for about an hour until they led us to their base camp.

Jimmy and I moved off the trail, trying to make as little sign as possible. The ground was completely flat, and the jungle was thick and dark. We found an outcropping of rocks and some trees that had fallen and decided to set up there. We climbed inside the maze of branches and hollowed out two portholes to look through and watched the group as they gathered around a small cooking fire. Jimmy pointed to the left side of the camp; and there, under the branches of a mango tree, sat a cage with three white faces pressed against the chicken wire window in the door. The cage was made of wood, and the only opening we could see was on the door. All three ladies had their faces pressed against it. The surprise of seeing them there made my adrenalin crank as my heart almost jumped out of my chest. Jimmy and I looked at each other, and he made a signal with his hand saying wait. So we did. We waited, watched, and listened. They didn't know that we were right there; close enough to hear what they were saying. I counted fifteen guys altogether. Then Jimmy pointed out a lookout, again in the trees on a platform. Luckily for us, he was asleep.

After sitting there for about an hour, six of the G's collected the women from their cage and drug them off in the direction of the watering hole. Jimmy and I followed, being extraordinarily careful not to make a noise or be seen. We followed down the same trail they had used earlier, keeping the group just out of sight. When we got close, I stopped and set up a Claymore mine along the trail between the two groups. I set it up using a ten-minute time fuse, setting my stopwatch. We moved down the trail another twenty yards or so and set up another using a twelve-minute time fuse. We ignited the time fuse and then moved forward. Jimmy and I agreed to assault the group. At seven minutes, according to my stopwatch, I would take out the external security and he would take out the internal security. Then we would get the women and move out. The time fuse on the Claymore should provide us some cover as the other groups still back at the base camp responded. Even if the Claymores didn't kill anybody, perhaps they would make them think twice before they followed us.

The women were standing on the edge of the water hole, unwilling to undress in front of their guards. The six guards were standing there with their backs to us, unaware of our presence. They had forgotten about their own security, only wanting to see the church ladies naked, and perhaps they would rape them. Nevertheless, they were all standing there with their backs to us, so Jimmy and I walked up behind them and stood there two meters away, watching as the scene unfolded to our front.

I said, "Hey," and the men turned around.

As they did, Jimmy and I both opened up with our shorties, cutting them down in a quick burst of automatic fire; and then it was quiet, so quiet you could hear a pin drop.

One of the women began to scream, so Jimmy started saying, "We're American soldiers here to get you out!"

The first Claymore went off, and screams of pain came from that direction. Suddenly, bullets started cracking all around us; so we quickly grabbed the women and pulled them along with us as fast as we could.

Jimmy kept saying, "We're Americans here to get you out!"

With that, they seemed to calm down a bit and cooperate with our effort to get them away from their captors.

We had moved about a hundred meters when the second Claymore exploded; and again, we could hear screams of pain. I stopped, telling Jimmy to keep moving. Then I set up another Claymore and then another. I said to myself, *If these jackasses keep chasing us now, then we are in trouble.* I set them both up with five-minute time fuses, setting one up and pulling the fuse igniter; and then I set up the other one. Once I was done, I picked up my gear and took off at a dead run, following the obvious trail Jimmy and the ladies had left. Catching them, we continued moving as fast as we could until both Claymores had exploded. We stopped for a second to catch our breath and listen. We waited for some time, watching and listening; but it seemed as though we had not shaken our pursuers.

We knew that there was more than one guerilla element out here. This was their terrain, so now we had to be careful. We had two choices. We could move back toward the lake and wait for the Colombian pilot to pick us up, or we could make the call and have the rotary wing extraction we had planned for. The only question was would the Navy be in place this quick in order to come get us? We were several days ahead of schedule, not having expected to find the ladies so soon. We had planned on calling in their location and having the Navy conduct the rescue, but now we didn't know if the Navy would be ready to launch. There would be in-flight refueling requirements, among other things, that had to be coordinated. Regardless, we needed to find out; so we kept moving until we found a nice opening in the jungle canopy. Then I made the call using our sat phone. I made the call back to Fort Bragg.

As I talked to them back at Bragg, the excuses began to pile up. The Navy was still not in place, and there were no other rotary wing assets available for the following two days. I advised them that we would move back to the lake and hope for linkup with our asset, the pilot. If that didn't work, we would improvise, perhaps commandeer a boat along the river and work our way down toward the gulf. Either way, perhaps the Navy could pick us up at the lake.

"Well," I said to Jimmy, "we've got to move to the lake and hope that that pilot picks us up. If not, we are in for a long wait. It could be two days before the rotary wing extraction is able to take place."

Smiling, he said, "Well, lucky for us these ladies are in okay shape. If they can make it to the lake, we should be okay."

With that, we picked up and began to move—Jimmy at point, the three ladies in the middle, and I brought up the rear. We kept moving for about an hour and came to the top of a ridgeline.

This is a nice vantage point, I thought to myself.

From there, we could see the lake and *Puerto Libre.* I pulled out my long gun and looked through the scope, down at the village. There was a road that led from the village to the lake, almost directly to the point where the plane had dropped us off. It wasn't visible from our satellite imagery; but from this point, it was clearly obvious.

Something in the village caught my eye, and I noticed that there were several armed men wearing civilian clothing walking down the main street. I showed them to Jimmy, and we agreed they were guerillas. From that location, I couldn't take them out with my long gun. Even if I could, who knows how many there might be in town. That ruled out trying to commandeer a boat in the village. We decided to rest in place overnight. We would move out in the morning. It was about twenty or so kilometers to the lake; but from up here, we could pick and chose our path, perhaps depart early in the morning and make it on time to meet our contact.

It hadn't been our plan to attempt a rescue. We were just supposed to pick up the trail and see where it led us. Nobody could have predicted the events as they had turned out. Neither of us had discussed it. It wasn't something we had planned. The situation was as it was, and now we would have to deal with it. We had no emergency exfill plan for this situation, and that was an oversight. We were ahead of schedule on the mission profile, and that was that. We would have to wait it out until morning and then take it from there. Perhaps by then those fools at Bragg could figure something out.

In the meantime, we were on our own; and that was okay as far as I was concerned. No sense in getting too many folks involved in this.

I watched the G's in the village through my scope, and they seemed to become more and more agitated as the word of what we had done reached them. The large, black Cuban was stomping up and down the street, pointing and waving his arms. Soon, they gathered a group together; but it was too late. It was almost dark, and they wouldn't be able to pursue us through the dense jungle at night.

The poor church ladies were starved, their eyes sunken into their heads, their elbows protruding larger than their biceps. They were healthy but emaciated; weak; and very, very tired. Jimmy and I gathered the rations we had in our assault packs and opened them up for the women. They were shy at first; but then they dug in, satisfying their hunger and thirst as they drank from our canteens. I couldn't help but feel sorry. Jimmy explained the situation to them, their eyes reflecting anguish and fear. They were dirty, their clothing tattered. I smiled to myself as the thought occurred to me that their clothing was tattered and holy. They were quiet, not speaking to each other or to us. They ate in silence, enjoying the meal as if it was their very first or perhaps their last. I retrieved a poncho liner from my pack and handed it to them, saying, "There will be no fire tonight, ladies. Take this, and try to keep each other warm."

I set my long gun up so that it was overlooking the village and checked my shorty as I pulled the magazine and noticed that I had almost used all thirty rounds. *Should have changed it out after the fire fight,* I thought to myself. *Oh well. No need to beat myself up now.* I put the empty magazine into my pack and retrieved a small bottle of lubricant, and then I pulled the rear pin, separated the upper receiver from the lower, and pulled out the bolt. Taking a rag from my pack, I cleaned the bolt, placing the pieces on some paper I had placed on the ground. Satisfied, I used the rag to clean out the upper receiver and then put the bolt back together and installed it. Closing the rifle up, I pulled the charging handle to the rear and lubricated the bolt some more. I continued to pull the charging handle to the rear three or four times, observing that it was smoother and smoother each time as the lubricant worked its magic. From under my brow, I noticed one of the church ladies watching me. I loaded the weapon, placing a fresh magazine into it; and then I gently allowed the bolt to slide forward, loading a round into the chamber. I did a quick press check, making sure it was loaded, and then checked once again to make sure the weapon was on safe. Satisfied, I raised it over my head, removing the sling from around my shoulders; and I placed it on top of my pack. Again, I noticed the church lady looking at me. I made a shrugging motion, insinuating the question, "What?" She looked away and stared at the ground. Her brown hair hanging across her cheeks, she began to sob uncontrollably; and the other two tried to console her. Jimmy smacked me on the shoulder with the back of his hand, as if to say dumbass, and I looked at him with another shrug. "What?" I hadn't done anything to her, so I wasn't sure what was going on. But Jimmy stood up and went to her. Kneeling, he placed his hand on her shoulder; and the four of them began to pray. *I don't have time for this,* I thought to myself, so I stood up, retrieved my shorty, and moved down the trail back in the direction we had come from and stood watch until the sun went down.

Later that night, Jimmy relieved me; and I returned to the camp, noticing that the church ladies were asleep, using our assault packs as pillows. They were covered up with the poncho liners we had given them. *Perhaps now they were finally able to rest,* I thought to myself as I sat with my back to a tree, facing out into the darkness toward the village. I fell asleep thinking of my kids. Long since divorced, they lived with their mother and new stepfather, a dentist in Wilmington, a court order preventing me from being anywhere near him or his new bride. Not really a problem; I preferred to be right here where I was—in the jungle—doing what I do. This is what I am, a soldier; and that should have been good enough. But I guess being gone most of the time didn't help much. I vowed to go see them as soon as I got back to Bragg. I would go visit my kids and perhaps go to the beach. I fell asleep with that as my dream.

Putting his hand on my left shoulder, Jimmy woke me up.

Looking at my watch, I could see that it was already before morning nautical twilight or BMNT.

"Time to stand to," he said.

Wiping the sleep out of my eyes, I stood up and checked to make sure I still had my pistol and my rifle. I retrieved my long gun and slung it around my back. We decided to let the church ladies sleep; I retrieved a coffee packet from my pack, opened it, and poured the dehydrated coffee crystals into my mouth. I held the coffee on my tongue as I opened a sugar packet along with a creamer and poured the powders onto my tongue. Filling my mouth with water, I swished it around, stirring up the concoction with my tongue, enjoying the pungent flavor of the coffee as it combined with the cream and sugar. Swallowing, I noticed Jimmy looking at me. He just shook his head, and I said, "Hey, I love a good cup of coffee in the morning when I wake up." Smiling, we stood there, our backs to each other as we prepared mentally for the day, watching, listening for anything that might indicate a threat. It was quiet as the sun came up. I watched the village through my scope as Jimmy woke the ladies and told them to get ready to move. They packed up the gear as Jimmy busied himself sterilizing our campsite.

There was activity in town as the large black Cuban exited one of the houses, the only house that had a tin roof, in fact. He walked out into the street. A slight breeze was blowing perhaps three knots from left to right. I split the center of his face with my crosshairs as I watched him gather his men. I wanted to take him out. I could feel myself slipping toward the trigger, but I couldn't do it, not yet anyway. Perhaps I would get my chance before we were exfilled.

"Let's move," Jimmy said to me quietly.

Looking down and exhaling in disappointment, I lifted myself up onto my feet and picked up the rear as Jimmy led the way down toward the lake. We had less than twenty four hours before the pilot would get there. That didn't leave us much time to move the twenty clicks or so to the landing zone. The church ladies kept moving. Quiet, they didn't speak at all. I thought that was a bit strange, but perhaps the G's had beaten them to keep them quiet and they weren't quite yet sure how we would react if they did speak. Regardless, we had to move; and their cooperation was imperative. Staying quiet was also important since we were still so deep into this region, an area owned by the G's. We walked fast, but only as fast as the ladies could handle.

They are in great shape, I thought to myself. I suppose they had been walking a lot with their captors moving them from camp to camp, staying one step ahead of the Americans who were feverously searching for them. We weren't out of it yet, and we all knew it; so we kept moving.

It started to rain slightly as we reached a stopping point along the trail. Winded, we were almost halfway to the lake; and we still had almost 24 hours before the aircraft would arrive. I sat down; facing the direction we had come from, and took a drink of water off the leaves of a banana tree next to me. As I allowed the water to drip onto my face, the distinct crack of a bullet flying past overhead sounded off; and then the *thump, thump, thump* of an AK-47 being fired caught our attention. Somebody had fired at us, fired at us from the direction we had just come. Their aim was off, having fired too high in the air. Perhaps they were tracking us and had fired some rounds off to see if we would respond. I looked at Jimmy, who had moved over to my position.

As he knelt, he said, "Sounds like they are about two hundred meters to our six."

I said, "Are you thinking what I'm thinking?"

He said, "Yes. Let's move."

With that, we stood and moved, making a hard right-hand turn to three o'clock, continuing on this track for about fifty meters. We stopped as I set up a position using my shorty as a primary. He moved the ladies in behind a large tree and told them to stay put until one of us came and got them.

Returning, he asked me, "See anything yet?"

"No, but I can hear them stomping through the brush on our original trail." I had a perfect view of the spot where we had stopped as the group of guerillas moved in, stopping to read our sign.

There were four of them, well armed with AK-47's and hand grenades.

Probably a recon element scouting for our trail, I thought to myself.

One of them had a small, two-meter band handheld radio; he started trying to contact someone on it when Jimmy opened up on full auto with his shorty, standing with his rifle up to his face, his left leg forward as he leaned into the weapon, dropping the entire magazine in their direction. I followed suit, taking sharp aim, firing controlled pairs at targets I could see when he said, "Magazine," and stopped firing. I switched my selector switch to full auto and let go a good burst of twenty rounds or so before my weapon clicked, empty. "Magazine," I yelled as Jimmy bolted forward down the trail toward the G's. Reloading on the run, I followed. As we crossed through our hasty kill zone on a quickstep march, we found the G's laying there on the ground, bleeding. We double-tapped each one, making sure they couldn't follow. I found their handheld radio, held it up for Jimmy to see. He smiled and started picking up their rifles and gathering their ammunition. Soon, I heard a voice on the radio calling for the group we had just ambushed, asking for a status.

I keyed the push to talk button; and in my best Spanish, I said, "They are all dead, and so are you."

We both got a quick laugh out of that one as we picked up what we could and moved back to the location the ladies were at.

Jimmy handed them the rifles, loading each one, and explained to them how to use the safety and how to shoot on full auto. "Use these to defend yourselves should anything happen to Mike or myself," he said.

The elder church lady said, "Thank you! Thank you!" as the three of them hugged our necks and kissed our cheeks.

With that, we moved out, listening to the radio, heading for the lake.

It wouldn't take long for the main group of guerillas to find the bodies of their friends, so I told Jimmy to go ahead while I set up some booby traps. I had two bouncing Betty mines, perfect for this situation. Left over from the Vietnam days, they used a trip wire so thin it was almost impossible to see. Once tripped, the mine would bounce into the air and explode, thus maximizing their effectiveness. I set up the first one at the site from where we had initiated the ambush. Then I moved back down the trail Jimmy had made with the ladies, and I set up another. Not having any more mines, I decided to move back down the trail toward the dead guerillas and wait. I wanted to see how long it would take for their buddies to find them.

Suddenly, the large black man, the one I had seen in the village, the one I assumed was probably a Cuban advisor, stepped into the scene, directly to my front. I drew a bead on him with my long gun, aiming at his chest as he started barking orders. Not paying attention to how many people he had with him, I fired one very well placed round, striking him in the chest, penetrating his sternum, and fracturing his spine. He dropped to one knee, stunned. His arms hung motionless as his jaw dropped open. He collapsed, face down, and died right then and there.

Like a hailstorm, bullets came pouring at me. His men opened up with all they had. They couldn't see me, but they knew from which direction I had fired. Branches and leaves rained down as the bullets zipped by just overhead, all around me, as I tried to make myself as small as I could. I crawled like a cat; face down, for about twenty meters as they started assaulting through the area where I had been.

With the jungle hopefully shielding me, I came to my feet, still crouching as low as I could, and bolted down the hill down into a low area. They didn't see me. Instead, they kept moving up the hill toward our original ambush site. I realized that they had tripped the wire on my trap as I heard the distinct springing noise made by the mine as it bounced into the air. It exploded head high, and the screaming and shouting that followed let me know that it had been successful. I picked up my pace and tried to lead the crowd that was now licking its wounds away from Jimmy and the church ladies to no avail. They stood down and started looking for the trail. Deciding to circle back around, I moved up to a position that allowed me to have the high ground overlooking the trail and the last bouncing Betty I had left behind.

Over their radio, they reported in the status of the patrol. I imagine it was to a headquarters element back in the village. They reported that the large Cuban, named Simon (pronounced, *cee moan*) had been killed along with two others who had been hit by the mine. There were two others with minor wounds; and then, to my surprise they announced that they only had thirty men left to continue the patrol.

Thirty men, I thought to myself. *This is going to be a great day. If only we can make it out of here.*

I waited there for some time before the patrol came back up the hill. Three or four men passed over the trip wire, and I worried for a moment that I hadn't placed the wire high enough off the ground; and then that distinct springing noise announced itself and I felt a bit of satisfaction for my success as the mine exploded, killing several men outright and leaving a few others on the ground, wounded.

The entire patrol sank down onto the ground as the mine exploded. Not knowing how to react, they were frozen in place as I bolted down the trail, down the hill, through the middle of them firing, double-tapping, aiming, taking out as many as I could before they were able to return fire. I suppose I got five or six of them before I decided to change my direction. Deciding it was time, I quickly ran off to the left side of the trail, leaping down the hill and out of sight.

Happening upon a large tree, I jumped over the roots and then looked back, checking to see if anybody was following. I stood my ground as three men came down the hill. Waiting, I watched as they got closer and closer. Several others took up positions behind them, waiting to see if anything happened. The three of them continued down the hill, quickly overtaking the ground between me and them. As they approached, I rose up over the root on my knees and used a six-round rhythm drill to drop all three of them in their tracks. The group farther back opened up as I ducked back down behind the tree, rolling out and then jumping up, the terrain covering me, I ran down the hill and found a stream. Climbing into it, I floated down and away from the mayhem. Quietly, I escaped as the disoriented patrol tried to collect itself.

Plenty of time had passed since Jimmy and I had split. He was still with the ladies and likely pretty close to the pickup point. I floated downstream for a bit, and the rain stopped. It had only been a light rain, and now the sun was coming back out. It didn't make much difference though, not in a triple-canopy jungle like this. I climbed up out of the stream and retrieved my compass. Shooting an azimuth toward the lake, I took off at a modified run, similar to the airborne shuffle; but I had to pick my feet up a little higher as I continued moving. The scrub brush along the ground, the vines, and other things mandated that. I kept running for about thirty minutes when I heard two helicopters fly directly over my head. *The Navy must have come through*, I thought as I picked up my pace, frantically trying to make it to the lake. It was then that I heard the squelch break on my own handheld radio. It was Jimmy calling for a jungle penetrator. I knew that you could only seat three people on one of those things, so Jimmy wasn't planning on getting out, so I called on the radio, "Rock Head. Rock Head, this is Gunny. How copy over?"

"Gunny, are you okay?"

"Yes. I'm moving toward the linkup point. Are you going to be able to get out with the ladies?"

"No. There isn't time. I'll see you at the linkup."

Without hesitation, I keyed my radio and said, "Roger that. Good luck!" and that was that.

We both knew what we had to do: make it to the linkup and hope that ol' boy with the sea plane made it back. I kept running, listening as the helicopters hovered, their mini guns reporting contact as they would burst a few seconds and then wait and then burst again. One of the aircraft kept flying a track back and forth between Jimmy and the enemy patrol that apparently was working its way down the trail toward the jungle pickup site Jimmy had selected. It seemed like an eternity. The choppers were only a few clicks away from where I was, but I could hear them, especially when they fired their mini guns. Without announcement, the choppers lifted and they were gone, their rotors thumping off into the distance.

I called on my radio, "Rock Head are you still with me?"

He answered, and we both continued moving toward the linkup point, down to the lake, to the landing zone where we had infiled.

As I cleared through the jungle and out into the sunlight on the landing zone, I saw Jimmy there, taking his last dip from his can of Copenhagen. He placed it into his mouth, between his lip and gums, and worked it with his tongue a bit. He was a strange one. He never spit, just swallowed the juices. It seemed as though he never ever spit out a dip. I guess one would go out as one was going in. He seemed to just eat the stuff. I couldn't figure it out, but I knew how he was without it. He must have known I was there. He had probably been listening to me huff and puff as I made my way out of the jungle because he didn't even look up or anything.

He just said, "That you, Mike?"

I replied, "Yup. Look what I brought ya!" Reaching into my pack, I pulled a fresh can of Copenhagen out of it and tossed it to him.

He smiled and said, "You've had this the whole time?"

"Yup. The whole time."

"You sorry no good. I've been chewing redip since last night."

Smiling, I said, "I know."

With that, he picked up; and we moved off, back into the tree line, back into the jungle to wait.

We rested there overnight until the next morning, and as promised the sea plane appeared over the hilltop on the other side of the lake. Using a signal mirror, I flashed the pilot; and he dipped his wings from side to side in acknowledgment. Dropping altitude, he swooped down over the lake, lining up directly upon our position. He roared in, touching down onto the water only a few hundred yards from shore, and coasted up to our position. We knew the guerillas would be on our trail pretty quick. They couldn't have helped hearing the plane coming in for a landing. Jimmy and I both started waving our hands for him to hurry. The pilot pulled up short of the beach, flung the passenger side door open, and waved for us to get in. We waded out into the water, not worrying about snakes or anything, and climbed into the aircraft. As I buckled in, I could see the release of tension go out of Jimmy's body as the plane taxied out and took off back in the direction from which it had arrived. We both released a big sigh of relief as we climbed up and out, back toward *Chigoradó*.

Landing at the airfield without incident, we found the pickup we had left behind, underneath the grass-roofed hut, and loaded our gear into it.

The pilot slowly walked up to us and asked, "Did you catch anything?"

Jimmy and I both looked at each other and smiled, and I said, "Yes. Yes we did." And with that, we climbed into the truck and left.

When we arrived into Bogotá, Jimmy broke out a cell phone and called our guys there in order to coordinate a linkup. Without much conversation, we turned over our gear to them.

We were just about to leave when the young captain that was with them said. "Hey, guys. I'm supposed to tell you that the colonel wants to see you as soon as you get back to Bragg."

We looked at each other, Jimmy and I, knowing that we were going to have our hats handed to us for not sticking to the plan, for doing what we had done. We got back into the pickup and drove toward the airport.

I looked over at Jimmy with a smile on my face and said, "What are they going to do, stamp our meal cards 'no dessert?'"

DESERT STORM

Having deployed to Saudi Arabia on a routine training mission with the Saudi National Guard, the news of Saddam Hussein's invasion of Kuwait struck us with almost complete surprise. It wasn't something that we had expected; now the Saudi military was on full alert, worried that he might come across and attack the kingdom. King Fahd, our unofficial code name for Saudi Arabia, was now on high alert as American troops and their equipment began to pour into the country.

My time in the desert had been limited, having spent most of my career in Central and South America. I had been reassigned to Fort Campbell, Kentucky; and subsequently, I had spent almost the first six months of my assignment in the deserts of Saudi Arabia, staying constantly deployed. My time in Kentucky had not been pleasant. I longed to be reassigned back to where I had been; in

Central America at least we had a mission, at least we weren't sitting back stateside, waiting for something, anything to happen.

When we found out about the invasion, we moved from our training base near Medina to the coalition headquarters near Riyadh. It was there that we would receive our mission to find the Scud missile launchers that were wreaking such havoc on our forces and on the Israeli public.

As always, it was hot and dry. There was no real shade or trees to speak of. Heated dust covered everything we owned. Keeping our rifles clean was a priority, but still not possible. The heat boiled up out of the ground, breaking through your clothing, feeling as though it was melting your skin. We were used to it, but we didn't like it. We had occupied a tent city that had been set up as an isolation facility to support our mission planning. The mission brief was typical, straight by the book. The intelligence officer, followed by the operations officer, communications, and then supply and logistics. The commander stood up and gave us the usual speech, the one that explained the importance of what we were about to do. It didn't matter. We just wanted to get out of this dump and back into action. There wasn't a real need for this formality, but we went through it regardless. All we needed to know was what they wanted us to do, and we would take it from there.

To this point, the coalition forces had been staging for an assault into Kuwait; but they hadn't received word as to when they could go. The entire Navy, it seemed, was in the Persian Gulf with Marines waiting onboard with great anticipation of what was to come. My younger brother was on one of those ships. I worried about him, but there wasn't anything I could do. I knew he was going to be okay. He was a tough little dude, too hardheaded to listen to me or anybody else for that matter. He went ahead and joined the Marine Corps, despite my best effort to talk him out of it. Some guys are just meant to be Marines, so I guess he was one of those types. That didn't mean I wasn't proud of him. To the contrary, but I was Army through and through and wished he was too.

Once the briefing was over, we got down to the nitty gritty

of mission planning; it wasn't a lot of fun, but it was interesting, to say the least. Our team leader liked to use a system he called "brainstorming" to come up with the basics of a plan; and then we would sit down and write out all the specifics, prepare our briefings, and then commit everything to memory. We accomplished our brainstorming sessions by writing out the obvious elements to the operation, infiltration, movement, observation, reporting, and exfiltration, so forth and so on. He would write the word on an easel board, and then we would sound off with ideas on how we could execute that portion of the mission.

For this one, we decided to go the tried and true method, a rotary wing insertion to an offset location; conduct a foot movement into our area of operation; set up hide sites; and observe the area from various vantage points in order to identify the Scuds. It was cut and dry really, and then we would report our locations and call in air strikes as needed. Once the air strikes were completed, we would exfill via rotary wing back to our headquarters at King Fahd—a simple recon. We had all trained for this for decades. Barring any unforeseen obstacles, we didn't expect any real problems. Nonetheless, we brainstormed scenarios and discussed decision points and reactions until we were satisfied we could answer any questions the staff might hit us with. With that, we went to bed after three days with very little sleep while the captain notified the command that we would be ready to brief by 0900 hours the next day.

The brief back went off without a hitch, the captain and the team sergeant giving it as we all stood by, watching and listening. I gave the communications brief and turned the stage over to one of my teammates and waited for it to end. There wasn't much ceremony, although we realized that finally, the conventional Army was recognizing our ability and perhaps gaining an understanding of our capabilities and their lack thereof.

The Army as a whole had fallen behind in its ability to conduct unconventional warfare. They were still trying to fight the battles of WWII second-generation warfare; and those days were rapidly coming to an end, having already experienced the prospect of defeat at the hands of the North Vietnamese, who had used fourth-generation warfare or guerilla tactics against the United States forces. The lessons hadn't been learned.

It didn't matter much though. Saddam had organized his forces based upon the Russian principle of mass versus the combined arms concepts the United States had developed using airmobile, ground, and other forces to conduct blitzkrieg-type tactics that would work well in the desert, perhaps in flat, dry terrain, but not so well in other places, like Vietnam or, say, the Middle East, outside of the current situation we were now faced with. No. This would be the last hurrah as far as I was concerned for the conventional-minded heavy armored divisions and commanders like Stormin' Norman.

He had handed this mission to the Joint Special Operations Task Force (JSOTF) commander as if he was throwing a dog a bone, tossing it out there to see who would pick it up. The Scuds were, I guess, of strategic importance but hardly a threat to the overall outcome of the war. We had already rolled out our latest technology—the Patriot missile batteries—and with some success, they had started bringing down a few of Saddam's Russian rockets. That scared the hell out of not only the eastern Europeans but the entire world. The product of Reagan's Star Wars research, the Patriot missile batteries gave us an edge that nobody could counter. They possibly would give us a first-strike capability; and that didn't set well with many of our enemies, not to mention many of our supposed allies. Nevertheless, the press and many in our own military establishment relished in that success as did the American people, most of whom probably had never realized how far we had advanced in our antiballistic missile technology over the last decade or so.

We gave our briefing and accepted our mission wholeheartedly as we departed the isolation facility for the range to test fire our weapons. I brought my long gun and enjoyed spending a few hours confirming my zero and taking down a few targets, sort of showing off as we moved back to eight hundred meters and plinked a few rounds. Everybody wanted to try it out; so I let them all have a shot at it, making promises to help them get into Sniper school when we got back to Kentucky. It was a good day at the range, although it was very hot, hot and dry. We had been issued some decent sunglasses; and to us, this was something special. We all commented on how much we liked them. They were very expensive Oakleys, and they worked. Not only did they work, but we thought that they looked cool. Thus, so did we.

That night, we boarded two (JSOTF) helicopters, two Black Hawks; and we took off leaving Riyadh behind as we flew low over the sand dunes heading toward the border, toward our operational area, away from the major fight that would take place in Kuwait. We felt as though we had been relegated to a lesser role, out of sight and out of mind so to speak, away from where we felt we needed to be—in Kuwait, dealing with the real fight. It didn't matter though. At least we had a mission, and it was important.

The aircraft continued on their heading, flying just over the tops of the dunes that in the moonlight were clearly visible. The dunes were shaded in the low areas, the tops of the hills were lit up; the sand reflected the bright moonlight and my imagination ran wild as if we were flying over the surface of the moon, on our way to attack an alien invader.

The Black Hawk's shadow dropped down and moved up across the dunes as we flew level with intent, with the determination of getting to where we were going without hesitation or doubt. There would be several false insertions to confuse the enemy as to our actual LZ; it was part of our deception plan. The pilots would come to a hover as if they had dropped something off and then pick up and continue the flight. Eventually, the team started exiting the aircraft in groups of three, each team capable of calling in air strikes, each team capable of operating on its own. We spread out over an area of over one hundred kilometers. Our ability to observe the entire area would overlap as each team had a designated area to set up its observation site.

My feet dangling over the edge of the aircraft floor, I could see the right side front wheel just under my feet. The door gunner was seated comfortably to my left, holding onto the handles of his mini gun, fingers on the triggers. The gun protruded with its multiple barrels out the side of the aircraft, and the ammunition linkage wrapped upward from the ammunition can on the floor, into the receiver of the weapon. It looked like a rectangular-shaped snake, filled with venom. The rotor blades swirled overhead, more like a disk than a set of four blades independently beating the air. The swept-back blades gave the Black Hawk a distinct sound, unlike that of the Huey's loud chopping. The Black Hawk was smooth, although it did have a very slight high-frequency vibration that gave it a whining pitch that, without ear plugs, could make you deaf in a heartbeat.

We had crossed the border; and after two or three false insertions, it was time for us to get ready. We would be the first three-man team of four to be inserted by this flight. The pilot seemed to pick up speed, and his flight pattern changed slightly. He seemed to be trying to hug the ground a little tighter than he had before. In the desert night, these aircraft stood out like a sore thumb. Perhaps he was getting a bit nervous now that we were out over Iraqi airspace.

Only a few moments passed before the pilot pulled the nose of the aircraft up into the air, basically hitting the brakes; and then he plopped the entire ship onto the desert floor, the wheels beneath my feet absorbing the impact along with the large shock absorbers that connected them to the plane. Leaning forward, pulling on the weight of my rucksack, my feet hit the ground; and I bolted out past the edge of the rotor blades and took a knee. My two buddies did the same, and we formed a quick little perimeter right there as the aircraft lifted straight into the air about fifty feet and then tilted forward and zoomed off into the night. It got quiet real fast, our ears still humming from the extreme noise created by the Black Hawk's twin turbo jet engines.

I reached up and pulled my earplugs out, holding my long gun under my left armpit, the barrel across my lap. We knelt there for a second, scanning for any threats. There didn't seem to be any. My first thought was that dropping into a standoff location out here was crazy. It was wide open for as far as the eye could see.

Making this movement wouldn't be so difficult, although I soon learned differently. The terrain was flat, but we had to cross wadi after wadi, many of which formed incredible obstacles with thirty to forty-foot-high sheer rock walls on each side. At times, we could find trails that would lead down into the dry gullies; and there were other times we couldn't. We soon realized that it was best to skirt around them. Taking heed of the terrain, we figured out that we could skirt around the head of each wadi or move downstream and find the shallower end where we could cross without much trouble. None of them had any moisture in them whatsoever. I thought for sure we would find at least one with a spring in it, an oasis I suppose; but that was a romantic notion. *How can people survive out here in this desert? There is absolutely no water,* I thought to myself.

We moved almost all night, following Bob, the senior man on our little three-man team. He was using the plugger, a new GPS device we had been issued to navigate our way across this desert floor.

He stopped suddenly and said, "This is it. We are within three meters of our designated observation site."

"Hallelujah," I pronounced, losing my composure for a moment.

It had been a long night, and I guess I had just about had enough of this marching out in the open. It was nice to be able to relax for a moment; and then we went to work, digging a hide site. At first, the ground was so hard we couldn't break through. I worried about the noise. Sound travels great distances at night; but eventually, we broke through a layer of rock and dirt and hit finely packed sand that was easy to extract from its ancient resting place. We dug down into the ground five feet or so, filling up tan-colored sandbags that we hoped would match the color of the terrain. We took turns finding rocks and stacking them over the sand pile we had created, trying to make it all blend in naturally. Using the sandbags to build a small wall around our little hide site, we stretched an old, thick, green, winter poncho over the hole and then stacked another layer of sandbags over that and stretched another, thinner, summer poncho that had a desert camouflage pattern on it over the top of the entire project. Then we stretched desert-colored infrared netting over the top of the entire thing and stood back to check our handiwork. *Not too bad*, I thought to myself. *It only sticks up a few inches above the normal terrain.* We had spread the sand out around the entire area, making the impression we had created on this place seem more like part of what had always been there. We were satisfied that it would suffice, and so we moved our gear in and set up shop.

For me, this hide site was perfect. I could use my long gun on all sides with clear fields of fire for three hundred and sixty degrees. *Excellent*, I thought to myself. I set my weapon up, however, pointed toward the east, imagining that it was pointed straight at Baghdad and the obvious direction of any enemy threat. Bob and our other teammate, Rick, set up their observation scopes while I set up my SATCOM radio and made a radio check. "Tomahawk zero niner, this is Road Runner one six. Radio check. Over."

A second or two passed, and then I heard the radio operator on the other end quickly respond, "Road Runner one six, this is Tomahawk zero niner. Roger out."

We had communications, and that was a good thing. Next, I put the antenna on my ground-to-air ultra high-frequency radio and did another radio check.

"AWACS, this is Road Runner one six. Radio check over."

Almost immediately, the air-to-ground air traffic control platform responded, "Roger copy, Road Runner one six. This is Barnyard, confirm your location. Over."

With a quick check on the plugger, I called in our position to the air controllers and received their acknowledgement. Quickly, I got back on the SATCOM and called headquarters and let them know that we were in position. After that, there wasn't much more to do. I listened as each of the other elements came up on the SATCOM net and reported their status. Everybody had made it to their hide sites. We were all in position, and now the only thing to do was sit it out and wait; and so we did.

Time drug slowly on out there as the wind swept across our position. The dual layers of ponchos we had created a roof, which kept our little hole nice and cool throughout the day, although it was very, very dry. We immediately started trying to conserve our water. The march that night had really taken its toll on all of us, and we had consumed more water than we had anticipated. Water was just one of those things that we had to have out here to survive. We had drunk our fill after having exerted so much energy; but now we conserved both in an effort to succeed, to fulfill the requirements of our mission, and to survive. We really had no idea how long we would be there. We had planned for five days but could stretch our supplies for at least eight if required.

We rested, two at a time, while one kept his eyes open, watching and listening for anything that moved. From time to time, a group of buzzards would fly past, circling high into the atmosphere—so many that they created a shadow across the way, circling upward and outward to the top of their imaginary cone, a cone of live creatures looking for something dead to eat, a living cone of death, evil birds hunting and salivating at the thought of eating rotted flesh. The wind currents keeping them aloft as the heat rose up from the desert, creating a draft that supported their large, cumbersome bodies. They came and went throughout the day, their shadows a chilling reminder of just how uncertain and interdependent life is for everyone and everything in a place like this.

From time to time, we would see a herder with his flock of goats and sheep off in the distance. Using our poised point of observation and high-powered telescopic sites on my rifle and observation scopes, we could see them clearly two to three kilometers out. Larger items we could see at a greater distance, and we noticed that there was a village just out of view. The smoke from their cooking fires rose up over the horizon, and we counted at least a dozen. It wasn't much of a village; but it was, nonetheless, a village, and perhaps a hiding place for a Scud missile launching crew. We did know for sure that if there was a crew in this area, they would need to go to that village in order to get supplies; so we watched attentively, never taking our attention away from that direction for very long.

We lived in that hole for days, never leaving except under the cover of darkness. During the day, if we had to do anything, we did it in that hole. We brought plastic bags to urinate or defecate into just in case we couldn't hold it. Of course, trying to do either in front of these guys was an open invitation for a good ribbing, like "Look at the size of that," or "Who you gonna satisfy with that little thing?" Our mood was lighthearted, although we hadn't seen anything of importance and time was passing slowly.

We knew that soon, we would exfill back to the world; but first we would have to do a resupply. That meant that we would have to wait for darkness and abandon our hide site and move a few kilometers off to receive it. It would be coming in as an airdrop bundle, and we had to have the target set up for the air crew. Mostly water and food, we needed that resupply in order to survive the extreme climate out here in the desert. It did get cold at night, which we could handle. It was the one-hundred-and-twenty-five-degree temperatures in the day that could kill us. We needed that water, and who wanted to die of thirst? What would that prove, our own stupidity? Not us, brother. No way, we had made up our minds. We would get that resupply, and we would continue our mission.

My lips were dry and cracked as I packed my radios and other gear back into my rucksack in preparation for the resupply op that night. It would take most of the night; and then we would be back here, back in our hole. We would leave it set up and just reoccupy it when we got back; but first, I packed my gear, saving and savoring the last bit of water I had in my canteen.

If we didn't get water tonight, we would have to request extraction, unless we could find another source. So far, each night, we hadn't been able to find any water; and that was troublesome. From the reports we had received from the other teams, they hadn't found any water either. We weren't in trouble yet, but we could be if things didn't go our way. The situation brought a song by the rock and roll group Dire Straits to mind, a song called, "Water of Love." So I started humming it as I packed my gear.

Rick shouted, "Shut up, for crying out loud, shut up!" startling me, leaving me a feeling of embarrassment in my heart and nausea in my gut. I couldn't help it. It just came out. The song was on my mind, and I couldn't shake it. So I kept it to myself and continued to play it back through my consciousness. There was one line from that song though, one line in particular that was stuck in my mind. It kept going, replaying in my mind, just one line from that song that I couldn't shake. *Water of love, deep in the ground but there ain't no water here to be found. Someday baby when that river runs free, it's gonna carry that water of love to me.*

Time slowly passed, the three of us sitting there in our little hole, looking out at the world, wondering what might happen next. Thinking about how much water we had, it dominated our thought process. At least it did mine. But I didn't say anything. It didn't matter how much we tried to forget about it. We couldn't.

Soon, Rick apologized. "Sorry, man. I guess we are all a little jumpy," he said.

So that started the conversation about water. We talked about the ocean, the beach, the lake back home, and the swimming pool on post. The day got hotter and we thought about it more. Soon, as the sun was high overhead, the mirage across the desert floor resembled a large lake or ocean; and even if we tried to stop thinking about it, just one look outward reminded us of it.

Suddenly, a young boy walking along with a stick came to within a few hundred feet of our position. He was carrying a small, handmade birdcage. In it he had a few swallows. He must have trapped them, I guessed. We sat there looking out through our binoculars at the young fellow as he walked along, a few goats following him. There were a half dozen or so goats, light brown with some white spots on their backs. There was one billy goat, his beard long, his horns twisted upward and then spiraled down and around, pointing toward his face. The billy stopped for a second and looked in our direction, raising his nose into the air, sniffing, trying to determine what it was he smelled. We had just finished our meals ready to eat; and the trash had a smell to it, as did we at this point. The billy must have thought we were food, or perhaps a female goat by the smell of things; so he started putting his head down and snorting, sticking his tongue out and looking in our direction, causing all kinds of commotion. The boy took notice and started to investigate. I drew a bead on him with my long gun. The fixed ten-power scope made his face clearly appear, the dust around his nostrils, the sweat on his brow. He couldn't have been more than twelve years old, but he had a black turban wrapped around his head. I watched the expression on his face as he realized what he had seen. The sheer look of terror in his eyes caught me off guard. Hesitating, I didn't fire as the boy darted off behind a dune and disappeared out of sight.

Before anybody could say anything, I exclaimed, "He was unarmed, damn it. He wasn't a combatant!"

Bob replied, "Sure as hell not a combatant, but you know that he is going to beat feet back and let his folks know what he saw out here. It's only a matter of time before the Iraqi military gets wind of it. We've been compromised, perhaps. If he tells anybody, perhaps he won't. We'll wait it out until dark, and then we'll move to the resupply point tonight and take it from there. Does everybody agree?"

All three of us agreed to wait and see if the boy had mentioned it. We all agreed to wait and see if there was any sort of reaction from the local militia or military.

Bob got on the radio and called the situation in to battalion, informing them of our plan to continue the mission for resupply that night. It didn't take long though, only an hour or so after the boy had spotted us, for two military vehicles, a pair of tan Toyota Land Cruisers to pull into view. They were on the hard ball road that ran across our right flank, about two kilometers from our hide site. It curved in a bend that brought the traffic to within a kilometer of our front; and then it turned away from us, heading for the high dunes off to that side of our position. They stopped on the apex of the curve almost directly to our front. I watched them through my scope as they disembarked their vehicles and stood next to them and scanned the desert in our direction with binoculars. After a few minutes, three large trucks, Russian troop carriers like our deuce-and-a-half truck pulled up and stopped behind the land cruisers. They were still out of range for my long gun but close enough for us to see them.

I looked over at Rick and Bob and said, "Let's not wait, let's call in an air strike now, before they get too close."

They nodded in agreement, so I picked up the hand mike for the ground-to-air radio and called. "Barnyard, Barnyard, this is Road Runner one six. Fire mission. Over." I waited for what seemed like an eternity as the trucks and Land Cruisers pulled off the road and started heading in our direction. Rick and Bob were both watching through their observation scopes, calling off the distance between us and them. Soon, the squelch broke on the radio.

"Road Runner one six, this is Barnyard. Go ahead. Over."

"Roger, Barnyard. I've got enemy troops in the open, fifteen hundred meters to the east of my position, two-thousand meters to the west of a village on the curve of the hard ball road at grid coordinate mike papa two zero six niner niner three two four seven five. Two jeeps and three trucks. How copy? Over."

A moment passed, and the AWACS came back up on the air. "Roger copy, Road Runner one six. Switch to frequency alpha two, and contact Mako one one. A flight of F-16's inbound your target now. Go."

Without hesitation, I reached into my cargo pocket and retrieved the signals instruction booklet that I had and looked up the frequency. I found it as Bob sounded off, "They are only twelve-hundred meters to our front." Changing the frequency as fast as I could, I heard the pilots on the air calling for us. "Road Runner one six, this is Mako one one inbound your target area now. How copy?"

I responded, "Roger copy, Mako. We have enemy troops and vehicles in the open, approximately twelve-hundred meters to the west of my position along the curve in the hard ball road two clicks east of the village, marking my position now."

I reached for my signal mirror that was in my left breast pocket and flashed at the flight of four F-16's inbound from the west. The pilot came back on the air.

"Roger copy one signal mirror. I have a visual on the target."

Just as the flight passed overhead, the pilot said, "You boys keep your heads down," and they shot skyward, dropping their payload as they did, each aircraft lobbing two MK-82 five-hundred-pound bombs in the direction of the Iraqi vehicles. The bombs hit their mark, destroying two of the three large trucks and killing most everybody in the entire patrol. The flight of four leveled off, turning nose down, and returned again, firing their load of 20mm High Explosive Incendiary bullets. They fired over and over, all the way down as the target area erupted in a series of explosions. A huge cloud of dust climbed over the Iraqi position. I watched through the scope on my long gun as survivors ran for their lives, smoke billowing off of them. We didn't fire upon them, hoping that they hadn't seen our position, figuring they were out of it by now, hoping they wouldn't continue to seek us out.

The flight leader split his formation at five hundred feet. Two of the aircraft trailed off to the left, two to the right. The first two made a large circle around the target area while the other ones disappeared out over the horizon. The two remaining aircraft circled once and then climbed to altitude and dropped two more CBU-87 Cluster bombs. This time the bombs exploded over the target area about three hundred feet off the ground, spreading smaller anti-personnel bomblets out over an area the size of five football fields. Then, suddenly, the entire area erupted into explosions destroying everything, smoke, and dust filling the sky.

Bob shouted out, "Woohoo, Mike! Did you see that?"

"I sure did. What do you think? Should I call the Makos off?"

"Yeah. I think they are all dead now," he said.

I got back on the radio and called, "Mako one one, this is Road Runner one six. Excellent work, my friend. That should just about take care of things. Over."

He replied and offered to stick around and scout the area for any more activity.

"Roger. That is a good idea, Mako one one. I'll continue to monitor this frequency until you depart the area."

His affirmative response was signaled as he broke squelch twice and continued his patrol around our operational area for the next thirty minutes or so, and then he came back on the air. "Well, Road Runner, you boys are free and clear down there. Thanks for the work. See you for a tall one when you get back. This is Mako one one. We are outta here."

And with that, the remainder of the flight was gone, leaving us there alone in the deafening silence of the desert and under the ominous shadow of the buzzards that were now gathering over our kill.

We sat there all afternoon, wondering if there would be any further response from the Iraqi military, but there wasn't. Perhaps we had rendered the military in this area incapable of responding, or perhaps they were busy elsewhere and couldn't or just did not want to respond. Regardless, it was quiet; so we called battalion and gave them a situation report. It only took about thirty minutes for the battalion commander to respond. We would be extracted that night from an LZ less than two miles from where we were located. We were all smiles with that news. So we waited for dark; retrieved our gear; and got the hell out of there, moving as quickly and in the most direct line as we could to the extraction point.

Keeping our eyes and ears open for anything that might pose a threat as we moved with a purpose, there were never any three guys in the world more anxious to get the hell out of Dodge than we three that night. Unfortunately for the rest of our guys, they wouldn't get extracted for a few more days. They had to make their resupply mission that night and stick it out. Most all followed the same fate as we had, never seeing a Scud—not one. Many had been compromised by small children playing, old women washing clothes, one old man walking along all alone ... None of our guys took the shot. All called in air strikes against the Iraqi response; and except for a few blisters on our feet, none of us got hurt.

Back in the rear, we looked up the Mako squadron, and we all had a few tall ones, spending an evening together, enjoying a few moments of camaraderie as only those of us who had shared that experience could have. We must have said thank you a thousand times.

SEARCH AND RECOVERY

It seemed as though the war in the gulf had ended so long ago. My time in Kentucky ended; and I was sent back down South, back to Panama. I had spent so much of my time in the military living in the Canal Zone. I still had a lot of connections and old friends there. Soon after I arrived, I picked up on my old habit of getting up early on Saturday mornings to go to the open air market in Colon to buy seafood and other items. Seafood was readily available down on the wharf, in a 1930s vintage warehouse next to the docks where the fishing boats would moor and unload their catch. Getting there early was a necessity. Arriving late would negate the purpose of getting the freshest items. Usually by ten o'clock, most everything would already have been sold. This was a busy place pretty much every day, but Saturday was the best day to go.

The fish market was set up in two aisles that joined back to back in the center, and two aisles lined up along the outer walls, which created two long passageways on each side of the structure running the entire length of the dock, all of it neatly protected under the roof of the open-air facility. I had a friend—I guess I should say an acquaintance—there who sold boiled iguana eggs and other edibles from the jungle. Small in size, the eggs were a very tasty treat, easy to peel and eat. There was always some sort of fresh fruit and other foods there that had been gathered directly from the jungle. One of my favorites was the fish from Gatun Lake, Peacock bass, commonly referred to by the locals as Los Sargentos due to the stripes on their sides. These bass were plentiful; and for a few dollars, I purchased two dozen or so and had them dressed into filets.

On Monday, it was a normal dry season day in the Canal Zone, hot before eight, humid even for that time of year, but not a cloud in the sky. I entered the team room to find the captain and my team sergeant waiting there for me. Both of them looked up as I came in. At first, I figured I had drawn their attention solely because I was the first person to return after physical training (PT) that morning.

After PT that day, I had gone over to the gym for a shower; and I spent about thirty minutes in the sauna, trying to loosen the tightness I felt in both of my heels. Every day after our exercises, I had been going to the sauna. It helped me deal with the heat; but also, my ankles were in such bad shape from all the years of carrying a rucksack. It was primarily my heels though. They were in constant pain. And if I sat down for just a few minutes, they would start to ache; and then it would take another thirty minutes of walking around to kill the pain.

I tried ibuprofen, aspirin, and a few other drugs the medics had given me; but none of them worked. I decided to just work through the pain, according to doctor's orders. The doctor at our base clinic said that it was only planters' fasciitis, bone spurs on both heels; and the arches of my feet had hairline fractures that just wouldn't heal due to all the marching and running we did.

When I say marching, I mean doing physical training with a prescribed weight on our backs—at least sixty-five pounds—two or three times a week. This was in addition to our five-to ten-mile runs that we did every other day. Fridays were the best. We would hump our rucksacks up over tank top hill and down to dock forty-five, along Gatun Lake, and then turn around and come back up the hill and down to the battalion to drop our rucks, which was just less than five miles. Then we ran two miles throughout the base, around colonel's row, over to the swimming pool. Then we would climb the fence, strip down to our shorts, and swim at least two clicks. Afterward, it usually took a good thirty minutes of stretching before I could walk without limping. Then if I was to sit for any time, my feet would start to ache; but that didn't stop things from happening, and now I was standing there in front of them and I knew that they had another mission for me.

They explained that I had been selected by another team to accompany them on a mission to Ecuador. A Panamanian twin engine Cessna had crashed somewhere along the Ecuadorian and Peruvian boarder with two US citizens on board. The company had been directed to provide a split team that included each requiring a medic and a radio operator along to deploy down there and try to find it. Since that other team only had one radio operator, I was chosen by them to go. The captain and team sergeant didn't seem too happy about it. I guess they didn't want to lose me for any period of time, or perhaps they thought that I had finagled my way onto the mission behind their backs or something; but I hadn't. Nevertheless, I didn't or couldn't have cared less what those two thought at that particular moment. I had other things to worry about. I recovered my personal gear from my wall locker and reported in over at the other team room as quickly as I could.

The guys on the other team welcomed me as I came through the door and started explaining that so far, the Ecuadorians hadn't been able to locate the plane in the dense jungle. There was a contingent of US rotary wing assets in country already working with the Ecuadorian military, and they would be diverted to work with us. The team would deploy onboard an Air Force C-27, a twin-engine cargo plane that looked like a C-130 but was only about half the size. We would fly to a small airstrip near the Andean town of Macas and pick up a few rental vehicles; and from there, we were to drive for several hours through the mountains to an Army post near another small village called Patuca. This was as close to the border as we could actually get by road. The rotary wing assets would meet us there. Apparently, they had been working in southern Ecuador; and now they were being diverted to support us. The place where we were headed was a place that hadn't seen an American man since probably World War II. We only had a few hours to be at the air base; so we hustled up, packing our gear as fast as we could, and loaded out into three Hummers. There was also a blue Ford twelve-passenger van waiting to carry the rest of the team over to Howard Air Force Base to catch the flight that was waiting for us to arrive.

The drive across the isthmus took over an hour. Traffic was heavy as we passed the old checkpoints that had been such a pain in the neck back before we had taken down Noriega and his crew of thugs who ran the country back before Operation Just Cause. Memories of those days passed through my mind as I drove one of the Hummers, trying to keep up with the van. We turned off of the trans-isthmian highway onto what we called Jungle Trot Road, a narrow concrete, two-lane road through a patch of jungle that had been preserved by the Panama Canal Authority, although it wasn't as pristine as the jungles on Fort Sherman. The drive through it, however, was sometimes a hair-raising experience, especially in the rainy season. There were no shoulders, and the road itself was very narrow. Busses leaving out of Panama City headed for Colon would often take this route as a shortcut with less traffic. They would fly around the corners, often crossing over the imaginary center line that at one time had existed. There were various wrecks, the bones of busses and autos, stripped, burnt-out husks of vehicles that hadn't made it through, littering the entrance to the forest, welcoming its visitors with a reminder of the dangers that waited along the way.

We crossed over the Bridge of the Americas in tight formation, quickly clearing over the arch, downward to the main gate at Howard. We turned into the entrance and proceeded through the gate without being stopped, the security police waving us through as we zipped past his post. Upon arrival to the airfield, we went directly toward hangar three, passing through the gates and driving straight into it. There were a few of the guys from the company there, the supply sergeant, air operations NCO, and the ammunition specialist, the three of them waiting for us. They had pallets waiting with ammunition, rations, and other items already stacked up. All that was needed was our gear and we would be ready to go. There was an Air Force hazardous cargo specialist busily inspecting the ammunition and other cargo already on the pallet, barking orders to our guys, making sure everything was labeled correctly.

We pulled the Hummers in close to the pallets and started unloading our gear without waiting for instruction. The doors to the hangar were wide open on both ends; and a swift breeze passed through, keeping it nice and cool inside. We threw a large plastic bag, a pallet bag, over the load and rolled it up, turning our hands inward so the roll would be to the inside of the bag. An airman drove a large forklift around the corner and into the hangar; another followed with a K-loader, a large vehicle able to carry up to four pallets.

A K-loader is a fairly high-tech apparatus. It has a large platform that is outfitted with rollers, the same type system you find inside the cargo planes it was used to load. The driver sat in an offset driving compartment and was able to manipulate the angle and height of the platform using hydraulics. Its maneuverability would make Los Vatos in Southern California with their low riders very jealous. The vehicle itself could carry forty to fifty thousand pounds of cargo at any given time. However, we were limited to less than eight thousand pounds, including our own body weight since we were flying the C-27. It was a very small aircraft, barley wide enough to carry an old Army jeep. It didn't have much of a payload capacity when required to fly for any real distance. It was a puddle jumper really, but it was nice to have; and in this case, it could land on the short runway that we expected and needed it to. The pilots of these aircraft often referred to themselves as bush pilots, able to land in places most would never dare to consider.

The company commander and his entourage showed up as we drew the cargo netting over the top of the pallet and attached the side straps onto it. We pulled the straps downward as hard as we could as somebody shouted, "Put some weight into it, man!" The downward motion cinched the top netting tightly over our rucksacks. The team's leadership stood in conference with the commander and the others as we ground guided the forklift and had him place the pallet onto the K-loader. The driver of the K-loader quickly started his engines; raised the platform slightly, rolling the pallet down to the center of the platform; and locked it into place, securing it as he reversed out and left the hangar.

The entire process hadn't taken more than thirty minutes, and the pallet would soon be loaded onto the waiting aircraft; and then we would be ready for takeoff.

The command group summoned us all over to where they were standing, and the sergeant major said, "Gather 'round here, men. The commander wants to have a word with you before you go." Then the commander said:

"Men, this is a recovery operation, not a rescue, so take your time and be thorough. Don't let the pressure of the moment overcome your ability to make rational decisions. There is plenty of time, so don't worry about trying to get in and out as quick as you can. Take the time you need to get the job done right and come home safe. Does everybody understand my intent?"

He hesitated for a few seconds as we all looked down at our feet, shuffling them slightly, rocking from left to right.

There were no takers to the question, and he responded, "All right then. Get the hell out of here, and we'll see you when you get back. Good luck!"

We all moved past the two of them, the commander and sergeant major, and shook their hands. One by one, we proceeded through the line and onto the bus that was waiting there to take us out to the plane.

Once we were loaded up, the two of them stood there and watched as the bus pulled away, out onto the access road, following the red line out to the tarmac and to the C-27 and its flight crew, both of which were ready to go.

We took off from Howard Air Force Base, flying north, and then turned right and crossed back out over the canal and over the mountains, over *Cerro Azul*, one of the targets we had hit during Operation Just Cause; and then we crossed over the beach, continuing our flight out over the Pacific Ocean and its calm pristine waters, which by now were over twenty thousand feet below us. The drone of the two turbo prop engines hummed steadily, the sound of which made us all a bit sleepy. I dozed off without noticing the time and without care, snoring so loud that at times one of the guys would wake me and say, "Knock it off." But I'd just fall back to sleep; and in a few minutes, I would be snoring away once again, waking only when the aircraft touched down in *Macas*.

The aircraft came in hard, wings tilting from side to side, the engines roaring at full power as the wheels touched down, brakes screeching as the pilots reversed the thrust on the propellers, slowing us down pretty quick. I looked out the window to see the side of a mountain towering over the runway. Ecuador is one of several countries that are located along the Andean Ridge, as we called it, or mountain range for the rest of the world. They are tall, jungle-covered mountains. Densely forested, they are very rugged and unforgiving. This was a place only the Ecuadorian Indians dared to enter. The upper reaches of the Amazon, the beginnings of the streams and creeks that fed into the dense jungles of the Amazon River basin all started here, and the jungle was alive.

The pilots parked the aircraft in front of what looked like a fairly modern airport terminal, killed the engines, and opened the doors. The sound of the jungle and the smell of the village instantly overtook my senses as I wiped the sleep from my eyes, recovered my rifle, and stepped out of the aircraft down the few steps and onto the two square blocks of new asphalt that made up the parking area for our bird and a few other host nation military aircraft to include a couple of small helicopters.

We all walked together over to the terminal, and an Ecuadorian

Air Force officer greeted and ushered us inside to enjoy the air-conditioning. It was not as hot here, at this altitude, as it had been in Panama when we left; but it was humid, and the equatorial sun seemed to sting. My fair complexion did me no favors in a place like this. I sunburn easily and being on the equator compounded the issue. The equatorial sun beat down on my skin like a flame thrower. I had always ignored my mother warning me to stay out of the sun as a child but now the strength of the sun in this place was stronger than I had ever seen before and I could hear her warning in the back of my mind. It didn't take much time for me to start noticing, and I was glad that I had brought a large supply of sun screen with me.

The captain and team sergeant spoke with the Ecuadorian officer for quite some time as we waited there, listening to music being played over a small boom box that sat in the far corner from where we had taken seats. The sound was soothing, some type of flute, one of those bamboo things the Indians made by hand I imagined. It sounded like the forest, like the jungle was singing to us; and the rhythm was such that it didn't readily escape my memory.

Outside, a group of men, each of whom was driving what looked like a brand-new dual cab Chevrolet Luv pickup pulled in and parked outside the terminal. There were four trucks, and they were ours to use for the rest of the trip. I had never seen a dual-cab Chevy Luv pickup before and found it curious as to why they didn't sell these in the States. One of the guys said, "Brazilian made," motioning toward the trucks with his chin. We sat there looking at them for a few moments; and then, without saying a word, we all stood almost in unison and walked out the door to check them out.

We stood around the trucks like a bunch of good ole boys back home and carried on mindless conversation, killing time until finally a forklift driver pulled up with our pallet of equipment and set it down onto the ground directly behind the trucks. Quickly, we undid the cargo netting and straps and pulled the pallet bag off. One of the guys said, "Save that bag. We'll need it for later," so a few of us folded it neatly and placed it into the back of one of the trucks. It didn't take long for us to unload the gear and then load it into the trucks. There was plenty of room in the four of them as everybody started divvying up seating and driving arrangements. I called the passenger side rear window seat in one of the vehicles and occupied it as the team leader and team sergeant came out of the building and walked over to the trucks, saying, "Let's go boys," and we hit the road, driving through town, people staring at us as if we were in some sort of parade scene that would play itself out several times over that day as we passed through one small mountain village after the other.

The road from *Macas* to *Patuca* was treacherous to say the least. High in the mountains, its gravel trail twisted back and forth around and across one ridgeline after another. Often, the road was barely wide enough for one vehicle to proceed over its single lane at any given time. Happening upon oncoming traffic was a harrowing experience, especially when passing large trucks. They would pull over next to the side of the mountain and allow us to pass on the outside, which gave us the vantage point of looking down at our impending death over the edge of an uncertain labyrinth and dense jungle hundreds if not thousands of feet below.

The jungle hung heavily over both sides of the road, blocking the sun for the most part, as we kept the windows rolled down, allowing the cool breeze to flow over us. We tried the radio; and to our amazement, there was actually a station. Although we didn't understand the Indian dialect that was being spoken, we did enjoy the Andean music that was piped out over the airwaves as we settled in for the three-hour drive that took us all day.

We stopped in one village. A Pepsi sign hung in front of one thatched roof hut, so we stopped and went inside and had lunch. It was incredible to see how fantastic the meal had been prepared—delicacies from the jungle. There was a type of stewed meat—we assumed it was wild pork—with an onion-based gravy and long-grain brown rice along with a type of hard bread that tasted like a saltless cracker. The nice lady brought us freshly cut papaya for dessert; we ate it all, savoring the aromas and flavors as we drank our bottled Pepsi that she had set out for us. It was amazingly cold. She had a refrigerator and electricity—perhaps the only person in town to have electricity. The team medic was curious, so he asked and she showed him the kitchen and the solar-powered setup she had to keep the soda pop cold. He returned with a smile on his face, commenting that the kitchen was clean. And then he laughed out loud. "You know what kind of meat that was?" he asked us all at once, and we all shrugged our shoulders unknowingly. He laughed even louder now and exclaimed, "Capi Bara! It was Capi Bara."

We all laughed out loud, and I thought, *That was the best-tasting rat I've ever eaten.* We all laughed and asked for more as the old lady smiled, all three of her teeth shining black and silver. You see, Capi Bara is a type of rodent that lives in the jungles and swamps of South America; and in many places, it is considered a delicacy fit for the highest of kings. We were none the worse for wear as we walked out and back to the trucks, our bellies full and our hearts content.

Outside waiting for us was practically every child who lived in that small village. They were all standing in a tight group, some sucking their thumbs—a little girl held her doll tight to her chest—their little, dusty, brown faces looking up at us quizzically, perhaps wondering if we were giants. I looked around; and almost every guy on the team had a huge smile on his face as some dug into their pockets and retrieved chewing gum, candy, or chocolate—whatever they had—and gave it to the kids. Satisfied, they marched off singing a song, the words of which none of us understood, as they sang in their traditional dialect.

The word spread of our presence in the area, evidenced by the greetings we started receiving in each of the small villages as we passed. We were in eastern Ecuador, as deep into the jungle as any American or foreigner for that matter had gone in decades perhaps; and the people greeted us with open arms and kindness. Children would line the street as we came through town and run alongside the trucks and chant, "Cho-co-la-te, cho-co-la-te, cho-co-la-te!" as they sprinted, the larger ones keeping up with us until we finally relented and relinquished whatever we could. I for one really enjoyed our newfound celebrity. Many of the guys tried to play it off, act tough as if it hadn't affected them; but deep down, we all felt a sense of joy and happiness inside.

Most of the day had passed since we had left Panama. We had flown for several hours; driven just as many; and then, finally, we got to our destination: a small military camp near the village of *Patuca*. The village actually turned out to be just one large house just outside the military camp. The camp was situated next to an abandoned and badly overgrown airfield that had been carved out of the mountain years and years ago. Grown over with elephant grass and small trees, the outline over the airfield was clearly visible; so we had the unit commander spread the word. That afternoon, men started arriving, loaded onto the back of anything that could transport them. They arrived for work, and we hired as many men as we could. We hired them all and immediately started having them clear the airfield by using their bare hands, machetes, shovels—whatever they had brought with them. It didn't take long. Before sundown, we had a large enough area cleared out to receive the two Black Hawks that would arrive the next morning. The area was cleared and ready for them.

The host nation unit commander sent a runner to escort us to what he had described as officers' quarters near the soccer field. The quarters actually turned out to be one-room mud huts with thatched roofs and a dirt floor; but they were better than sleeping outside in the jungle without a roof over our heads, so we gladly accepted and set up shop then and there. Finally, we were settled in as the sun had already set on the other side of the mountains, leaving us drenched in the evening twilight for some time before it actually got dark.

The temperature dropped fast, and a heavy fog moved in over the side of the mountain and our small post next to the airstrip. The fog was heavy with moisture; and although it didn't rain, it did soak everything that wasn't covered or protected from its penetrating moisture that clung to everything. As darkness fell, I climbed into my sleeping bag. Lying on the floor, I used the back strap of my ruck as a pillow and fell soundly asleep, only awaking for my shift of guard duty and then finishing off the night by going back to sleep, resting peacefully. I couldn't remember a time that I had felt so relaxed. The air up here was thin, but the smell of the jungle hung heavy in the night air. I slept soundly 'till morning.

There was a small stream running near the huts where we had slept the night away; so as we roused in the morning, I meandered over to it and noticed that the water trickled out of some rocks on the side of the hill, clear, fresh, and clean. I used it to brush my teeth, wash my face, and wet my hair. I took a small cloth from my shaving kit and soaked it with ice-cold water that poured out of the rocks and washed under my arms and then my crotch. Comfortable, I put deodorant on, combed what little hair I did have, and put my t-shirt back on. I had awakened first; so I started a small cook fire and made some coffee using my canteen cup as the rest of team started moving around, getting ready for the day.

A runner came over and invited us to have breakfast at the officers' mess hall, saying that the commander had requested our presence. So, with that, we all made ourselves ready; and we walked together, as a unit, over to the dining facility, which was nice considering the isolation of this place so far out in the jungle. We had a breakfast of two eggs fried hard; white goats' milk cheese; fried, ripened plantains; a type of sausage—we didn't ask—and some salty black beans that had been puréed and mixed with chopped garlic and onions. There was espresso coffee as black and thick as I had ever seen. One shot was like a jolt of lighting, strong, very potent. I had two and felt as though the top of my head was tingling by the time I had finished my breakfast. The food was good, the facility was clean, and we all enjoyed the hospitality of the local officers and the staff.

Throughout breakfast, the discussion centered on the downed aircraft; and the commander felt as though he knew where it might be located. Some locals had described to him the area, but he would have them come to our huts later that morning to explain to us exactly what they had seen and where they had seen it. Meanwhile, we waited on the rotary wing folks to arrive. Without them, we were grounded and couldn't do much. After breakfast, we all returned to the huts and rested while the leaders made their plans. *I haven't had this much rest in months,* I thought to myself. *I could get used to this.* Then I said it out loud as some of the other guys came in and started making themselves comfortable.

We relaxed for several hours until we heard the chopper pilots come up over the radio, declaring that they were inbound to our location with sling-loaded equipment and needed support on the ground to identify release points and to park their aircraft. We had already marked the landing zone for them, so all we had to do was ground guide the sling-load operation and have the pilots land, a simple task that we were already prepared for as the choppers made their presence known, climbing over the ridgeline from the west. The sound of their rotor blades unmistakably announced their arrival as we ran out to the landing zone to great them.

Loaded heavy with the equipment slung underneath, the rotors beat the air into submission, keeping the aircraft and its cargo in the air, lifting it high enough to clear the mountaintops, chopping away uncharacteristically to the normal flight of a Black Hawk. We watched as they expertly surveyed the landing zone we had prepared, circling twice before they gently placed their loads onto the exact locations we had marked for them. They landed without incident, and the crew went to work while the pilots shut the engines down and ran through their post-flight checklists.

The workers had been at it for several hours already, but they stopped and watched as the aircraft arrived. I imagined that they hadn't seen aircraft like these before, carrying sling-loads underneath. They seemed to be enjoying themselves, as their conversation in their local dialect grew louder and more excited. They worked hard, chopping and hauling away the small trees, root balls, sticks, and rocks. The captain had arranged for some truckloads of gravel to be delivered; and as they arrived, the workers gathered quickly to spread the load as the trucks would start to dump it and then start rolling down the runway.

We needed this runway to finish the job we had started. We needed supplies and fuel, and we needed to get an exfill platform in here to take the bodies out when the time came. The choppers wouldn't do. The bodies had to be taken back to Quito, and that was just out of their range. Besides, their job was to get us in and out of the jungle, not to exfill the bodies back to the states. Our plan called for replenishing the airfield and then having the C-27 return, pick us and the bodies up, and fly us all the way back to Quito and then on to Panama.

It only took three days, and we were able to have the runway up and running. The first C-27 landed; gravel flying everywhere as its wheels touched down onto the newly resurfaced runway. It came to a stop at the far end, just short of diving over the edge of the mountain, turned around, and taxied back to the where the Black Hawk crews waited. The plane had brought in two more fuel blivits—two round, collapsible containers made of rubber that were filled with JP-5 jet fuel. They also brought in some spare parts for the choppers and rations for the aircrews. The aircrews couldn't eat the local food. The pilots couldn't risk getting any sort of stomach infection.

I asked why, and one said, "Imagine trying to fly that thing and having diarrhea or needing to vomit. It just doesn't work out very well."

I tried not to imagine it but couldn't. The idea imprinted an indelible mark upon my mind that just wouldn't go away. I decided that it was better that they didn't eat the local food.

That afternoon, the commandant summoned the team to the headquarters building; and waiting for us there, we found three Indian males wearing cloths over their groin area, their buttocks showing. They had markings like brandings the shape of raindrops in a line, making a permanent necklace around their necks. They had bamboo shafts running through their pierced ears; and their hair was cut tight over their ears, and a short braid hung from the backside of their heads. The braid was wound tightly with beads and feathers tied into it; and on their backs, they had another set of brandings running the length of their spine, on each side of the bone. The commander sent a runner, and soon he returned with a young man who was in uniform but his hair was similar to the three men. The young man translated for us in the men's native tongue as we asked questions of him in Spanish, learning that the men had seen an aircraft in the jungle several days ago and that they could show us where it was at. When they learned that we would go by helicopter, they refused, deathly afraid of the machine. They offered to take us to the site on foot, to guide us into the exact point of the crash. We had them look at a map of the area; and they seemed to understand the concept of it, pointing to a location that we were able to judge as the probable location they wanted us to go to.

We all agreed that three of us from the team would go with them. A driver from the host nation unit would take us by vehicle and drop us off along the road, as close as he could.

The team sergeant selected two of his men and then pointed at me and said, "Take Mike with you. He will be your commo man."

Almost dismayed, I tried to hide my disbelief that he hadn't selected his own radio operator to go instead of me; and without saying a word, I left with the other two to retrieve my gear.

Shaking hands, smiles all around, we climbed into the back of the Ecuadorian Army truck, an old Mercedes Benz six-wheel drive, probably made in Brazil. I handed our guides a handful of meals ready to eat and a few bottles of water; and off we went, trailing dust down the road past the camp, deeper into the jungle, away from our little outpost that was now starting to take shape.

The two guys from the team kept to themselves somewhat as I tried to communicate without success with our guides. They only spoke an Indian dialect that I had never heard before, so we made do with hand signals. God only knows what they may have meant to those men.

After about an hour, the truck came to a stop and the driver came around, back to where we were seated, and dropped the tailgate. We climbed down and stood in the middle of the road for a few minutes while our guides got their bearings and we determined our location on our GPS. The two other men from the team released the driver, satisfied that they had a good geo coordinate of our position; and so he left, reversing out and then turning around. We stood there and watched him as he made the maneuver with considerable effort. The power steering on that old truck didn't appear to be working.

The team sergeant had selected his assistant operations sergeant, Frank, and the team's junior medic, who we called Doc, to lead our group. I never learned his real name. That was beside the point. It was Frank, Doc, and I following three Amazonian Indians into the jungle to find a downed aircraft that was somewhere nearby apparently. We started walking down the road for about a half mile before the guides found a trail they were looking for, and we stepped off the road and into a completely different world. The atmosphere on the road had been dry and hot; but once we stepped into the jungle, we were in the shade. The temperature dropped noticeably, and the air hung heavy and wet. The pungent odor of rotted fruit and vegetation saturated the environment, inundating my nostrils with the deluge of the jungle's aroma. There was a clan of Howler monkeys in a large tree to our left, their lion's roar warning us to not come near as we continued to move in a line following the guides as we skirted around channels of erosion that created ravines sometimes sixty to one hundred feet deep. The soil was dark red, muddy clay that stuck to our jungle boots weighing our feet down. From time to time, we would stop to scrape the mud off; and then we would continue. We quickly learned to use the water at the bottom of the shallower ravines as we crossed to clean the mud off. Our feet were wet anyway, and we had enough experience in the jungle back in Panama to know that they would be wet until we got back out of this place.

We walked downhill for a while, until the sun started going down behind the mountains, making it almost too dark to see down on the jungle floor. The triple canopy overhead kept out most of the light anyway, but now it got a little darker with each step. We came upon a small waterfall, perhaps thirty feet high; and beneath it was a pool of crystal clear water.

The guides stopped and started to drink their fill, and Frank said, "This looks like a good place to rest overnight."

We set up camp, put up our hammocks and strung our ponchos over them, using bungee cord to stretch the sides tight and then another to pull the hood of the poncho tight and up by connecting the bungee cord to a spring like branch overhead. Satisfied with my effort, I set up my radio and called in our location to the team back at the airfield while Doc built a fire.

He said, "Take off your boots. Let's see if we can dry out our feet."

The fire was nice, and my feet felt warm. My boots sitting on the ground next to the fire steamed as the heat dried the green canvas and black leather.

Two of our guides had departed but returned after a half hour or so with a young monkey they had killed. They cooked it for their meal and shared with us. It wasn't very tasty, but it was juicy; and at least we knew we could kill monkeys ourselves and cook them, having observed their method with inquisitive wonder.

It rained hard that night. It rained hard and then drizzled until the sun came up bright and clear, reflecting off of the wet leaves. Heavy banks of fog lifted over the ridgelines as we broke camp and started moving again, this time at almost breakneck speed. We pushed hard as the parrots and Howler monkeys alerted to our presence. The jungle was alive, and it responded to us as we moved through it.

With the airfield up and running, the choppers were ready to go. They had plenty of fuel, and the pilots were chomping at the bit to get back into the air. They came up over the radio and alerted us to their flight as we continued heading toward the location the three guides had pointed out on the map. Over the radio, the pilots said that they were going to conduct an aerial reconnaissance of the area near the location the guides had indicated; although it wasn't necessarily the location we had originally been directed to search.

The aircrews flew the target but couldn't see anything to indicate an aircraft had crashed in that area, so they lifted their search to include a larger area and the original general location we had been directed to search.

The six of us continued to move. It seemed to me that the concept of time and distance for our guides was perhaps a bit different than our own. I thought that they had said that it would only be a few hours from the road to the objective; but we had now been moving well over eight hours, counting the day before, and we still had not reached the crash site. Impatiently, I continued to follow along, hoping that we would find the site soon.

We stopped for lunch under the shade of a cliff that rose high into the sky along the mountain. It reminded me of so many other places, particularly the ridgelines up in the Appalachian Mountains there in North Carolina, the mountains we had used to finish our training, to conduct the final field training exercise of the Q-course, Robin Sage. I allowed my thoughts to wander back in time and realized that it had been almost twelve years since I had graduated Special Forces training. *What a life,* I thought to myself. *This is the kind of stuff they write books about.* Closing my eyes, the memories flooded over me like a waterfall, bringing a chill down my spine as I sat there, drenched with sweat from the heat of this tropical cloud nine.

Frank said, "Let's go!"

Opening my eyes, I could see that they all were on their feet, looking down at me. Perhaps they wondered what could be going through my mind at a time like this. We picked up and started moving. We moved until it was almost dark; and Frank found a nice, flat spot and decided that it was the place for us to rest overnight. We repeated the same process as the night before, pitching our hammocks and ponchos and setting up a fire and trying to dry our boots. I got on the radio and called in our position to the team back in the rear. Apparently, the aerial recon didn't turn up anything, so we were to continue our mission the following day and hopefully then we would find our target.

I slept well, not waking for the rain, not waking until it was time for my watch. I sat there in the dark, holding my eyelids open with my fingers, trying to keep from falling asleep as I listened to the jungle breathe in the night air. Frank and Doc were snoring loudly, and I was glad that I didn't have to wake them and make them stop. There was no real threat out here, no physical threat against us from any other human beings anyway; but there were a lot of snakes, very poisonous snakes. But I couldn't think of what they were called at that moment, so I put the thought out of my mind and waited for three hours until it was time to wake Doc.

Morning came quickly. Groggy, I couldn't open my right eye, which had dried shut while I slept. Rubbing my eyes, I could see that the sun had yet to come up; but Doc was sitting there stoking the flames, drying his socks. I asked, "Why don't you just forget about socks and go barefoot in your boots? I do and my feet dry fast."

He looked up at me, not saying anything; picked up his socks; and tossed them off into the darkness. Then he said, "Damn things never dry out, just keep your feet wet all the time."

I smiled in agreement and lay there, staring at the fire, slipping in and out, my mind in a haze. I laid there until the sun did finally come up and it was time to move once again.

We picked up and moved for several hours. The sun was high in the sky when we finally did stop for a break. I looked at my watch to see that it was only 1100 hours. *Still a lot of daylight left,* I thought to myself. One of the guides was beckoning us to continue, leaning over toward our small group. He pushed his left arm outward, his hand holding a walking cane; and he mumbled words that we couldn't understand. Then he made the sound of an airplane while at the same time raising his arms to mimic the wings. Excitedly, we got back on our feet and following the group of three, stomping through the jungle toward the location they were leading us to.

Suddenly, we stopped. Out of breath, I leaned forward and tried to get some air but couldn't.

Then I heard Frank say, "Oh my God. Would you look at that?"

I dropped my rucksack. The weight of it crashed through some small fern saplings and went *thud* onto the ground. Looking up, I could see it but didn't believe my eyes. It wasn't the Cessna we were looking for. It was a WWII-vintage C-47 goony bird, hanging just off the ground, inverted. It was suspended tail high from thick vines that hung from the huge trees. The jungle canopy here was thick, as thick as it had been; and in the shadow of the trees, we could see through the broken windshield into the cockpit. It looked like somebody was sitting there, looking out. Frank told me to get on the radio and call this in while he and Doc checked it out. I watched them as they dropped their rucksacks and climbed the embankment up toward the aircraft that hung there helplessly, as it had for what looked like a long time.

I got on the radio and called in our location and reported our findings. The captain instructed us to see if there were any bodies in the aircraft and to remove them. We were to look for evidence of identification and then call for the choppers to come in and take them out as soon as we were ready. I walked over and stood underneath the aircraft and relayed the message to Frank. This wasn't what we had set out to find, but we did find an aircraft. Apparently, there had been a slight misunderstanding. Perhaps our intent had gotten lost somehow in translation. Frank asked for a couple of body bags, so I retrieved them from their rucksacks and carried them up the hill and tossed them through an opening, a tear in the underbelly of the aircraft, up to them and then walked back down. It was at that moment that one of the other guides got my attention. He was shaking his head no and pointing as if to say go around. I made a motion using my right arm to indicate go around, and then he nodded and motioned for me to follow him. I followed him; and we walked, following the streambed for about two hundred yards. He pointed back to the right; and as I looked, there it was. Only a hundred yards on the other side of the goony bird lay our Cessna, the wings gone; windshield busted; the tail section broken off; and the front end, to include the engine, shoved back into the fuselage. There was luggage strewn about the area, and it was silent. I called out and received no response, so I picked up my handheld radio and called Frank and told him what I had found. He couldn't believe me, he thought I was messing with him at first; but when he recognized my resolute tone, he and Doc came running.

We all three stood there for a moment, scanning the scene. It was terrible, not likely that anybody could have survived the impact. What a coincidence that it happened in almost the same exact spot as the earlier crash. We couldn't believe it. It was just almost too incredible.

Doc commented first. "I can't believe it! I just can't believe it," he said.

Quickly, we gathered our senses and went to work. I retrieved my rucksack and got back on the radio and called in our discovery. The captain on the other end questioned me in disbelief as I explained what we had found. Doc and Frank went to work, yelling out requests for me to bring more body bags over to them. There were six people on the Cessna, two on the goony bird. We had just enough body bags, as we tried not to mix the parts; but that was difficult, especially on the Cessna, which hadn't fared as well as the old goony bird, which was much larger. When we had done all that we could, I called for the choppers to come in with a hoist to extract the bodies. While we waited, we made a small clearing using detonation cord to fell a few small trees; but we didn't have enough explosive to make a complete landing zone for the choppers. We cleared the landing zone as much as we could, our guides lent a hand with their machetes, and then brought all the body bags over and we waited for the helicopters to arrive.

It didn't take long—perhaps an hour—and the Black Hawks were hovering over our position that we had marked with yellow smoke. The first one came in while the other did race tracks around our position. The first one came in and hovered over the small LZ we had created and lowered a metal basket using its hoist. Once it was on the ground, we put two body bags in; and they raised it up and into the platform. We repeated the operation a few times until they had retrieved the cargo we had provided them.

Quickly, we tied Swiss-style rappelling seats around our waists using one-inch tubular nylon and attached a snap link to the front along our belt lines. Then we attached a three-foot section of tubular nylon to our rucksacks and attached another snap link to it as the second aircraft came in and hovered about sixty feet up. The crew chief was looking out the side window and the face of one of our teammates could be seen looking down out the side door. He was a fast rope master, and we were going to extract using our fast ropes. He and a buddy kicked the ropes out both sides of the aircraft; and we watched as the ropes fell, almost as if they were in slow motion, onto the ground directly to our front. Without hesitation, the three of us snapped onto the Kevlar rope inserts that extended out of the bottom of the fast rope, a white rope handle for us to use. I snapped my snap link onto it and then attached my rucksack. Frank and Doc did the same and when we were all three ready, we raised our right hands, giving the crew above a thumbs-up.

As the slack was taken out of the fast rope, Frank yelled out, "Hold on tight. Don't let go!"

The tension removed, the pilot lifted us gently off the ground, straight into the air, our bodies hanging about ninety feet below the chopper as he lifted us skyward and away. I looked down to see the three guides waving up at us and realized that we hadn't taken the opportunity to tell them thanks for their help. The look of amazement on their faces, however, told me that there would be no need as we floated away.

Dangling far below the Black Hawk we wrapped our arms around each other in mutually supporting effort. The camaraderie we felt at that moment was without question branded upon our conscious minds; but when all was said and done, there was no need to speak of it. We had accomplished our mission, and that was what really mattered.

HOME ON LEAVE

Many years had passed since returning to Panama. I had been down here for a long time. Two years earlier, I had been promoted and earned a slot as team sergeant assigned to a special mission unit, an advanced urban combat team, similar to a SWAT team; and we trained hard for an eventuality that had not yet happened. At least it hadn't happened on my watch.

There had been no rescues, but there had been the occasional alert and unit blow out to reinforce security at an embassy here and there. We did deploy a few times on a no-notice status. We deployed to reinforce security for American firms drilling for oil or other US government agencies that required our support. They would send us out in the middle of the jungle to rescue Peace Corps volunteers, missionaries, or tourists. Each time, we arrived to find that the situation was clear.

We hadn't had one single mission, although we almost did several times. We had done more than our share of training exercises with other military units of similar background and charter from different countries throughout Central and South America, even the Caribbean. We trained them while we trained ourselves, we developed new tactics, we honed our skills to a razor's edge; but it was over now. We were closing out, closing down the Panama Canal, turning over all the bases, turning that Canal over to the Panamanian's, leaving it all behind.

There had been a treaty signed in 1979 between the United States supervised by President Carter and the Panamanian dictator Torrijos. Now, late in the spring of '99, twenty years had passed; and it was time for all American military forces to leave Panama for good. There were hundreds of families that had already packed up and left, flying out of Tocumen International Airport or Howard Air Force Base as fast as they could. It was a classic military draw down, a reduction in force, the elimination of the US presence in Panama. We had drawn down to just a skeleton crew. School was out, and most of the families had left. The units would follow before the end of the year.

I on the other hand, had come to the end of my last tour in Panama and had been reassigned, back to Fort Campbell, back to Kentucky. I was glad. At least I had broken that cycle of being assigned back and forth between Panama and Fort Bragg. It also meant that I had avoided being assigned to the schoolhouse. I had avoided becoming an instructor as part of the Special Forces qualification course or any of the advanced skills courses they ran at the special warfare center for that matter. That in itself was an accomplishment, something most of my contemporaries had not been able to do. I suppose it would hurt me in the long run, hurt my chances for promotion; but that was okay. I didn't expect or want to get promoted any higher. I just wanted to make it to twenty; cross over that threshold; and retire, retire from the Army with my body and honor intact; retire from the Army and go back home, back home to Oklahoma and the family farm just south of Norman, down along the South Canadian River, to live a normal life, to regain that which I had given up so many years ago.

I only had two years left in the Army, and that was just enough time to start getting things ready for the transition back into the world as a civilian; not an easy task, my friends and I would joke, when you've been institutionalized like we had been for so long. I felt as though I had been institutionalized; I had been created; I had allowed myself to become part of the machine, part of the big picture. I was tried and true, part of the institution; and I had no idea if I could ever leave it for good, leave the life behind, become a normal citizen again. I wanted to.

I hadn't taken leave for the last three years, so I had applied for and was granted ninety days leave—incredible—ninety days off to go home, just in time for the wheat harvest, just in time for the summer, just in time to see my pop before he passed, just in time because I needed a break. I was exhausted from all the training, the late nights, the physical training without stop, the deployments, site surveys, ADVONS (advance team), loading out the main body, building pallets, three-o'clock show times, Friday afternoon maintenance, support cycle, training cycle, deployment cycle, military schooling, airborne operations—you name it. It wasn't all that so much that wore me down. What took a greater toll was being on a beeper, being required to always be within thirty minutes of the unit without exception, without fail. It wore us all down.

I needed this break, and I deserved it. And for a change, I actually wanted to go home for a while. It was time. It had been over seven years since my last visit; and this time, I planned on sticking around to try to reunite with my younger brother, Clay. After he had gotten out of the Marines, Clay had stayed home and taken care of things. I wasn't there when our mother died, he bore the burden. Although he never mentioned it, I think that perhaps he resented the fact that I wasn't there to help.

Time had taken its toll on our relationships, primarily my relationship with the entire family. They were all still a tight-knit group of folks. I was "the one who had gone off to the Army," they would say; and that made me an outsider, pretty much somebody not to be trusted. I felt that the Army had changed me in their eyes, somehow, after all these years.

I can't believe that it's been seven years since the last time. Seven years. I don't know why it's been so long. I guess it was just the way things had to be and were. But now my time in the Army was getting close to being over; and I felt—or should I say wanted—to reconnect with my family, to explore the possibility of coming back to live and work on our farm. My worry was that too much water had passed under the bridge and that I might no longer be welcome. The only thing left to do was go home and find out, explore the possibility, and make a decision about my future, about what I would be doing after I retired from the military in December 2001.

The familiar drive to *Tocumen* International Airport was uneventful. The window washers at each stoplight still bum rushed our vehicle at each intersection. My driver, one of the junior sergeants from my unit, turned on his windshield wipers to protest and waved his fist at the crowd, who returned the gesture with a few slaps against the side of our vehicle, jeering anti-American rhetoric the whole time.

"Gringo, go home!" they shouted, among other things.

"A bunch of ungrateful freeloaders if you ask me," I commented to the young sergeant, who just nodded his head in agreement, his face contorted with frustration as he drove aggressively toward our destination.

Pulling around the turnabout in front of the airport, we veered into the lane that was marked for departures and pulled to a stop directly in front of the American Airlines sign.

"Here you go, Mike. Have a good trip."

"Thanks. See you at Bragg someday!" I retrieved my suitcases and headed inside, avoiding the bellhops and beggars, as the young sergeant drove away. I watched from inside the terminal, peering out through the window as he avoided the taxis and busses and made his way through the congestion at the airport and found the exit back out onto the highway.

Deep down, I felt a sense of loss, as if something wasn't right. I knew that it would be the last time I saw this place, a beautiful country. My time here had been exciting and vigorous. There were memories of places like *El Valle* up in the mountains outside Panama City and the Hotel Bambito out near the Costa Rican border. This was a beautiful country; and deep down, I didn't want to leave. This had been my home for such a long time, but I had to leave now.

Working my way through the ticketing counter to get a boarding pass, I moved through customs and immigration. The common dislike for Americans demonstrated itself through the face of the agent at the counter, who was a classic bureaucrat with a stamp. She was obese and barely fit into her chair or her uniform. Her arms shook as she pounded her rubber stamp down hard onto my passport; and then, extending her hand palm up, she gruffly demanded twelve dollars for an exit visa. Without saying a word, I paid, observing the crowd around me as she took her time making change, which she tossed down onto the counter. I said thank you as I gathered the money and placed it into my pocket.

I took my time, holding the line for a moment as I gathered my suitcase and looked around, pondering my next step, until she ushered me onward with an upturned wrist. I smiled and slowly walked away into the passenger side of the airport, into the famous duty-free zone, where you could buy a fake Rolex, bootleg jeans, a bottle of perfume, or bathtub gin for a cut-rate price without paying taxes. What a deal!

I meandered past all the stores and the stuck-up girls in their knee-length black skirts, their cleavage showing through the opened top buttons of their white blouses as they made themselves busy behind the counters, their stiletto heels making the task even more difficult. It was a small terminal, and it didn't take long to find my gate and a seat. I waited there, observing until it was time to leave.

A sleek American Airlines DC-10 aircraft pulled off the runway and onto the ramp in front of the terminal where I was seated. It stopped at the gate, and an operator drove the flexible walkway out a few feet to meet the plane. I could see through the windshield and watched as the pilots went through their checklist, one of them reading it off and the other checking each item as the turbines slowly wound their way down, the intensity of sound diminishing in proportion to the velocity of the fan.

Folks began coming out of the tunnel that came up through the flexible ramp, some wide-eyed tourists from Europe; a few Panamanian soccer players worn out from their travel, trying to avoid the press; some short-haired Americans, wearing blue jeans, t-shirts, and tennis shoes, stood out from the crowd as military personnel; and, of course, the businessmen from all over came out. Perhaps there was a convention in town.

The people came pouring out like salmon swimming upstream. They leaned forward, pulling the weight of their carry-on luggage with them. Some had backpacks. Others had suitcases. A few had those little bags on rollers with the handle sticking up. They came out, so many I lost count. *There must have been three hundred people on that plane,* I thought to myself as I watched the crowd trickle down. And finally, there were no more passengers exiting.

On the ground, a fuel truck had pulled alongside the plane; and catering trucks were lifting their cargo to the galleys that awaited them, one on each end of the plane. A crew of cleaning ladies chatted their way past my seating area and disappeared down the ramp. Their laughter brightened my mood as the minutes seemed to fly by.

It wasn't long before we were allowed to board. As we entered, the aircrew met us, the pilots and stewardesses; and the one and only steward whose name was Ramon greeted us. Ramon introduced himself to me, saying his name with a Spanish accent; but it was obvious that he was from someplace like Nebraska. I just smiled and said hello. The crew was very efficient as they worked the crowd, helping out where needed, stowing luggage, and checking to make sure everybody had their seatbelts on. They put in a safety video as the pilots brought the engines up and the ground crew pushed the aircraft back away from the terminal. The familiar sound of the engines made me feel sleepy; and within a few minutes, I was out, sound asleep, totally unaware that we had taken off, heading out over the Pacific Ocean, and then we turned north across the isthmus and out over the Caribbean.

It was only at the moment we started dropping altitude for an approach into Miami International that I awoke. There would be two more connecting flights on my way back home, one in Atlanta and one in Dallas. But first, I had to navigate my way through immigration here in Miami, find my luggage, and recheck it for the domestic flight. *Thank goodness I'm well rested,* I thought to myself as the aircraft parked and we stood to deplane.

The doors opened, and the crowd shuffled out onto the international concourse; and we walked through doorways and down long hallways made of glass, uphill and downhill and then up again, until we reached the immigration and customs enforcement station. We entered on the left side of a row of thirty or forty kiosks manned by immigration officers. On the far right-hand side, there was a sign that read, "U.S. Citizens Only"; so I continued on my way through this familiar section of the airport, past the immigration official, who welcomed me back to the United States as he stamped my passport.

I went down the escalator and into the baggage claim area and retrieved my luggage. It took awhile; so I stood there, observing the hustling crowd of people from all over the world as they nervously searched for their luggage and gathered their bearings.

An old Jamaican lady asked me, "How you get outta dis place, young fella?"

Smiling, I pointed toward the customs checkpoint.

Satisfied, she just walked away, head held high, as she headed straight to the spot I had indicated.

Soon, my luggage came; I retrieved it, making a note of the new scrapes and scratches on it. *There isn't much you can do about it,* I resigned to myself as I continued onward toward my next destination, the domestic passenger terminal, and my connecting flight to Atlanta.

Again, I slept as my flight continued. The pressure of the world having been lifted off my shoulders was releasing itself from my body as the weight of the stress that had built up over the last few years dissipated from my soul with every moment that passed. I felt so relaxed. I couldn't imagine feeling this way just a few short hours ago.

Through Atlanta I went, catching my connecting flight to Dallas; and again, I slept, drowsily nodding off, my head bouncing off my chest, waking me from time to time until I could sleep no more. We arrived in Dallas, touching down, bouncing twice before the pilot was able to settle the aircraft firmly onto the paved runway. The reverse thrust of the engines slowed us quickly as he braked hard in order to make the turnoff in time for our terminal. I thought to myself, *Must be an Air Force Reserve fighter pilot on his off time.*

I looked at my watch and realized that I only had thirty minutes to make my connection to Oklahoma City. Pulling the chart of the DFW airport out of the seat back folder in front of me, I noticed that I had to cross several terminals to make it to my next destination; from experience, I knew it was a pretty good distance, so I would have to make it fast.

The time flew by as we pulled into the gate. Checking my watch, I knew I only had about ten minutes to get to the next gate in time to board my flight. The crew opened the doors, and the people slowly began to work their way out. Some Texan with a tall hat blocked my view as we moved forward. Anxiously, I hoped we would be out of this plane quick. The moment we cleared the doorway, I started walking fast. Turning toward the main hall of the terminal, I found the moving walkway; and I jogged on it, making great time. I felt as though I was running like the wind as I passed pedestrians walking on the normal floor next to the tramway. I stumbled as I exited the first one, not realizing how fast I was moving; but I caught myself in time to catch the next conveyor, and I was off and running again. Three sections had passed before I came to my connecting terminal, and I doubted my luggage would make it as I hurried to make my flight. A bit of sweat poured down the side of my face and the back of my neck as I showed my boarding pass to the lady there and walked down the tunnel to board the awaiting twin-engine puddle jumper.

The folks onboard, mostly from Oklahoma, were a bit nervous as the pilot fired up the twin turbo prop engines, one on each side.

A lady in the back asked out loud, "Do you think this plane will make it?"

It must have been her husband who responded when he said, "Sure it will, all the way to the point of impact."

The entire planeload of passengers burst into nervous laughter at the thought; the one stewardess, standing by the cockpit door, was not amused. Her hair was touching the ceiling as she leaned slightly to keep her balance as she ran through the preflight safety briefing and the pilot whipped us around and out onto the runway. This plane was agile; I felt comfortable, although I might have been alone in that feeling as we took off and leveled out at ten thousand feet or so.

The pilot brought the plane around the city as he picked up a northern heading following Interstate 35 that was easily recognizable from out my window at this altitude. He followed along this route, crossing over the Red River, almost dry at this time of year, the sand clearly visible, the trees green with summer foliage.

It wasn't long before we passed over the Arbuckle Mountains and Turner Falls, which brought back memories from when I was a kid and our family would travel for a few days of camping during the summer. "The waterfalls were something to behold," my mother would say as she would sit there in her one-piece, wearing her white-rimmed sunglasses, smoking a Winston cigarette. One year, it rained so hard that it flooded the campground and we were forced to leave early; but only after losing our pup tents and sleeping bags. Pop was so pissed. But as any true farmer learns how to deal with Mother Nature, he let it go without a word.

The pilot turned left, heading west into the sunset; and then he brought us in on a northern approach to Will Rogers World Airport in Oklahoma City. Turning west allowed us to avoid the air traffic over Tinker Air Force Base, giving us a clear shot at the runway there at Will Rogers. He brought the plane down from altitude, flying over the prairie, green and lush from the summer rains. The grass was tall this year as black cattle dotted the landscape, grazing undisturbed by our presence overhead as we zipped past them, the shadow of the plane following along the ground.

In the terminal, my brother, Clay, was waiting with his brilliant smile, teeth from ear to ear. His blonde hair had turned darker. His blue eyes, as piercing as ever, now showed the signs of age. Crow's feet gave him a mark of distinction, strength, and resilience. His arms reached skyward to gain my attention, and he hugged me around the neck as if we hadn't seen each other for a millennium. He slapped me on the back and said, "Welcome home, brother! Welcome home!"

The emotions I felt at that moment were indescribable, but the tears in my eyes showed my heart as we walked down the terminal to the baggage claim area. Speechless, I walked with my arm around and over his shoulder, listening as he chattered away about anything and everything.

I don't know why I felt so emotional at that moment. It surely wasn't very characteristic of me, but the feelings of love I had for my family had been buried in my heart for so long I had forgotten how powerful the connection I felt with them was. Now it all came streaming out of me; and it took awhile to regain my composure. It took at least ten minutes.

Finally, Clay said, "Come on, you big dummy! Snap out of it!"

I laughed and cried for a moment, smiling, tears running down my face as he looked at me, bewildered, as I tried to choke back the tears.

We found his old truck on the top deck of the parking garage and threw my luggage in the back. It was littered with farm trash: wire, pieces of metal, steel fence posts, a spare tire, and a five-gallon can of hydraulic fluid. His toolbox was dented and rusty, full of tools and parts for the multitude of tractors he used to run the old place. The rear of the truck hung low under the weight of it all as he fired up the diesel engine and I climbed into the passenger seat, the lingering smell of the exhaust following me.

"So, how is Pop, Clay?" I asked, and he looked at me for a moment as he backed the truck out of the parking spot and pulled away.

His eyes seemed to focus on finding the exact words he wanted to use. "Oh, Pop's fine. He doesn't do much work anymore, just sits around, hanging out with his old dogs. He goes down to the diner in Noble most every day and hangs out with the old-timers. And they try to solve the world's problems, but never quite figure it out, so they'll be back the next day, working it out all over again."

I said, "Hey, we should stop for a few beers on the way back, perhaps pick up a six-pack?"

He nodded in agreement as we got out on the interstate and headed south. We headed south through the city, passing by some of my old stomping grounds, and then headed down old Highway 77, turning on Franklin Road, and stopped at Hollywood Corners Grocery.

"I used to buy bait here when I was a kid," I said as we got out of the truck and went inside to retrieve our vice. There was a lady behind the counter who struck me as incredibly familiar. It took me a moment, and then I recognized her and said, "Holly McBride, is that you?"

She replied, "Well it ain't Holly McBride no more. It's Holly Nickel. And who are you?"

I couldn't believe it. She didn't recognize me. "Well, hell, it's me, sweetheart. It's Mike. Don't you remember me?"

She practically jumped over the counter and wrapped her arms around me and gave me a big kiss. Clay just stood there, smiling; and I realized it had been a set up.

With her hands on my chest, she looked up at me and said, "We got big plans for you, honey. I'm so glad you're home!"

I just smiled and hugged her as the other girls working there that night came out of the back to see what was going on. Clay paid for the beer; Holly followed us outside, chatting away like a parakeet, trying to tell me her entire life story in the few short minutes she had before we left. I got into the truck and rolled the window down, and she handed me a card with her phone number on it and said, "Give me a call. We've got a lot of catching up to do."

I leaned out, and she kissed me on the lips, leaving the sweet flavor of her lipstick behind as a reminder.

It was incredible. I looked over at Clay as he pulled out of the parking lot, one hand reaching into the paper bag to retrieve a beer. He had a smile on his face from ear to ear. And then he said, "Here. Have a beer."

I reached over and grabbed it from his hand, and we laughed and laughed. I hadn't laughed so hard in all my life.

Then Clay said, "You know, she has three teenage boys. The oldest is getting ready to join the Army."

"Is that so?"

"Yup. He looks just like you too."

I looked over at him. "No. It couldn't be. It just isn't true, Clay. I know what people said, but it wasn't me. I promise. Holly and I never did go all the way."

"You sure?" he asked.

"Positive!" I knew he didn't believe me, but it was true. The two of us, Holly and I, had agreed that, should we ever, we would wait until we got married. Things just didn't turn out that way, and so I left for the Army and she got married a few months later.

"I haven't seen her since that last night at the Rodeo down in Lexington, that night I rode my last bull. Now you tell me she has a son that looks like me?"

"Yep. Spitting image."

"Well, that is impossible." I shook my head in disbelief as he drove through Norman, past Main Street and the old Central High School, and then passed by the Catholic Church. To my surprise, the Mont, a restaurant that had been there since I could remember, was still there. People sat around umbrella-covered tables and watched the traffic go by. The buildings of the university loomed just over the hill a short distance away. We drove across Lindsey Street, just down the road from the Oklahoma University football stadium. And then we passed the old Spanish Villa apartment complex where we had lived for a short time back in '69, that summer before I had started the eighth grade. I was surprised to see it still there. It had a new name, but the buildings were still there. We polished off a few more beers as we headed out of town, down the old highway through Noble and down to Lexington.

"I'm taking the long way so we can finish these beers," Clay said.

I just nodded in agreement, looking at him, still not believing that folks thought I had gotten Holly pregnant before I had left.

"You know that old quarter horse stud of yours, Ol' Leo, died a few years ago, didn't you, Mike?"

I had heard about it, but I had given that horse to Pop when I left and hadn't thought about him much since then. "Yes, I heard. What happened?" I asked.

"Well, he was almost blind there toward the end. And he got out onto the road, and a truck hit him. It was a terrible sight. We had to put him down."

The news hit me hard. I hadn't realized how terrible his death had been. In my mind's eye, he died of old age out in the pasture somewhere.

But before I could say anything, Clay said, "He sired three colts that last year, one stud and two fillies. The fillies weren't worth much, so we sold them off. But I kept the stud colt. Had him broke last summer. Thought you'd like to take him out for a ride one of these days."

I hadn't ridden a horse since I had left. There had been one trip that I had gone on down to Argentina to attend the Argentine mountain infantry course. We had ridden mules and learned to skin one as a survival technique, but I hadn't ridden a horse just to ride since before I had joined up. "I'd love to go for a ride. Perhaps in the morning we can take a look at him. What did you name him?"

Clay looked at me and laughed. "Little Leo, you fool. Little Leo. What else?"

I joined in the laughter, and we both enjoyed the memory of that old stud horse of mine as we turned off the highway onto what had been a dirt road.

"They paved the road to our house?" I asked.

"No. They paved the road for our farm. We are one of the biggest operations around here now. We own over three thousand acres of bottom land along the South Canadian, and I've leased another twelve thousand acres or so. Hell, the county commissioner practically begged me for my endorsement. So for that and a sizeable donation, I got our road paved."

I couldn't imagine having that much pull around here; but our family had settled on a half section, three hundred and twenty acres along the South Canadian River over, a hundred years ago. My great grandfather had spotted this land while driving cattle up to Kansas out of Texas. He had told my grandfather about this place, and the two of them snuck across the border early the night before the land rush in 1893 in order to stake their claim to a quarter section each, the piece of ground where the old home used to be. Our family was Sooner from the word go; and we had been here ever since, surviving the Dust Bowl, the depression, recessions, and a multitude of floods and tornados over the years. My great-grandfather was one hell of a man. A drover by trade, he settled here to raise a family and started his days as a rancher, a decision that had affected four generations.

Clay and I drove the ten-mile stretch of road, the pavement ending at the driveway to Pop's house. "Well, Mike, you'll stay down by the river at the old fishing cabin next to the big pond. I've got it all set up for you, food in the fridge, bait in the freezer. Let me know if you need anything, and I'll see you in the morning."

I was pretty tired after having a few beers and the long trip and needed to stop moving for a while. We drove past Pop's house, around the barns, and past the cattle pens, following the trail, two lines in the grass created from vehicles traveling the same route over and over, through the pasture until we got to the cabin.

Pulling to a stop, dust swirling in the headlights, Clay said, "Here you go," as I got out and retrieved my luggage.

Slapping the side of the truck with my hand, Clay knew it was okay to pull off; and he did, neither of us saying a word.

There was a light shining on the front porch. *Clay must have had electricity installed in this old place*, I thought to myself as I walked around the side and up onto the porch that faced the pond and to the east. We had built it this way to catch the morning sun.

Years ago, Pop had Clay and I build this cabin after the summer planting season was over. We didn't know why he worked us so hard, but the end result was amazing. Grandfather had built a sawmill on the old place way back when, and Pop wanted us to know how to use the equipment. That fall, he had us cut down a stand of white oak trees and some cedars to build this place.

Clay was probably thirteen, and I was almost fifteen years old when we built this old place. We had milled the logs and the shingles ourselves as we went along. We built our own cabin, a one-room shack really, with a loft large enough for a queen-sized bed and a dresser. We had quarried the stones for the foundation out of the river, large, flat pieces of limestone that had washed downstream onto our land. Lucky for us, we had a tractor with a front-end loader on it, which made things easy. We used a neighbor's backhoe to trench out the foundation and then laid the limestone slabs into it, slowly building the foundation up, using good ole Oklahoma red clay from the bank of the river to seal the slabs and logs together. The foundation was solid, and the old cabin was still as sturdy as it had ever been.

Opening the front door, I noticed that Clay had remodeled the interior. It was now very well decorated in a rustic, cattle-ranch-style. Ceiling fans hung from the ceiling joists, eight-inch beams cut from a large oak tree. There was a modern kitchen with chrome appliances and tile flooring and a half bath with a nice, round shower in it. There was a note on the fridge that said, "Welcome home, son. We'll be over for breakfast. Pop." I smiled, laying the note down on the countertop; and I opened the fridge to find it completely stocked with eggs; bacon; hash browns; sausage; steaks; potato salad, the kind with mustard like I always liked; and a variety of fresh fruits and vegetables. On the bottom shelf, there was a case of ice-cold Budweiser with my name on it. I swear. Reaching in, I retrieved one and popped the top of it off and took a long, slow drink as I walked up the stairs to the loft.

That night, I slept soundly for several hours until a pack of coyotes started yelping just outside the front door. The sound they made alerted everyone and everything to the fact that they had made a kill, a rabbit or a prairie dog perhaps. They never really took anything larger, although at times they would kill newborn calves.

Their yelping reminded me of the times Clay and I would go camping down here by the pond when we were younger. We'd build a small fire and fish for catfish all night. Then we would bring our catch home in the morning and filet them for our mother, who always cooked whatever we caught or killed. That included a poor old armadillo we killed one year. Well, at least we thought it was. She had thrown it out and cooked up an uncured ham she had thawed, telling us it was the armadillo we had shot. She let us believe that we had eaten one for quite some time, Clay and I telling everybody of our exploit, enjoying the look on their faces as we described how she had cooked it up. Finally, the word came back around; she told us the truth and made us promise to never kill another armadillo again and to stop telling everybody that she had cooked it for us.

Unable to continue sleeping, I looked at my watch and realized that it was almost time for the sun to come up; so I retrieved a fishing pole from the wall and found a tackle box on the shelf underneath it. In the tackle box, I found some bullet sinkers and worm hooks, along with a bag of blue and gold plastic worms, about six inches long. I rigged up the pole and walked outside onto the porch to check out the pond as the morning sun prepared to come up over the horizon.

In the Army we called this before morning nautical twilight. Back home, we called it time to go fishing. I noticed that Clay had built a dock directly in front of the cabin, so I walked out to the very end and started casting my worm back toward the bank, pulling it back toward me a few feet; and then I let it drop down, back down to the bottom. I repeated the motion several times before reeling it all the way in.

It didn't take long before I hooked a good-sized largemouth bass. The pole bent sharply under the pressure he put on it as he fought against my effort, splashing out of the water. I was so immersed in the fight that I hadn't noticed Clay and Pop as they rode up on horseback, Little Leo in tow. They had dismounted and tied off to a hitchin' post alongside the cabin and then stood there without saying a word, watching as I fought that monster until I finally got him out of the water, grabbing him by his upper lip as I raised him up over my head to take a look.

"He'll weigh five, six pounds at least," I heard Pop say, drawing my attention back toward them and the cabin.

He was standing there with Clay, both of them grinning from ear to ear. I held the fish up for them to see and walked back down the dock toward them. "He'll make a pretty decent breakfast, won't he?" I said, and they both burst into laughter. I left my pole out on the dock; and as I walked past them with the fish in my hand, I put my arm around Pop and we walked together up the stairs and into the cabin. "Ya'll relax for a bit while I clean this fish and make us some breakfast."

The filets from the fish were large enough to feed a family of four. Washing them off and then drying them with a towel, I put the filets into a bowl, spiced them up, and covered the bowl with plastic wrap and then put it into the fridge for later. We ate our breakfast of eggs, bacon, and toast, sharing the time together, listening to Pop talk about how much trouble we had been as kids. We enjoyed each other's company as Pop sopped up his egg yolks with a piece of toast, his elbow high in the air as he used the toast to wipe the plate clean. Satisfied with his effort he wiped his hands and face with a paper towel and looked up to see Clay and I sitting there, watching him.

Smiling, he said, "Let's go!"

We got onto the horses. Little Leo was actually bigger than I had expected, taller than his sire. He was smooth in his gait, confident in his march as we rode out into the field. He held his head high, fighting against the reins, snorting. He wanted to run, to break out; but he maintained pace with the others. He was a handful, not the type of horse a novice should ride. And although

I had grown up around the rodeo, around horses, I had my hands full. It had been a long time since I had ridden; and he was aware of my uneasiness as we started out riding along in a group, following a trail along the river. We crossed a stream, belly deep. The water came up over my feet as Little Leo leapt through it; jumping over the bank; down into the water; and leaping upward and climbing out on the other side; water draining off his sleek coat. It was exhilarating, the power of this animal, capable and surefooted as he crossed that stream with ease; and I rode upon his back, holding on, hoping I didn't fall off.

Pop laughed at me as he made the crossing, his horse making it easy for him, taking into consideration the rider as he walked up and out without creating such a fuss. *Little Leo is young, and he is a stud, so he's more aggressive than Pop's old gelding,* I told myself. Clay crossed, his hat pulled down tight over his brow. He climbed up and out; and without hesitation, he bolted into a quick gallop and we followed.

We continued the gallop for a few minutes until we reached a gate. Leaning down, Clay released the chain and swung it open with ease. Then we all entered, leaving the gate open. We cleared over a small ridgeline, which revealed to our front a nice herd of cattle. Clay pulled up and stopped; and we sat there in a line, Pop, Clay, then me, looking out over the herd of Polled Herefords to our front.

They were fat, most with calves, as they grazed under the watchful eye of two large bulls. Their hair was short and bright red, except for the white hair on the tip of their tails, their feet, and their faces.

"Well, they are all yours, Mike," said Pop. "We've been building this herd for you since you left the last time you came for a visit."

Then Clay said, "We started with ten cows about six months after you left, and we've built the herd up to a little over a hundred cows over the last few years by using the money from the steers to buy more cows and by keeping the heifers that showed promise."

I was taken off guard by their generosity and their ability to keep a secret for so long. I was completely flabbergasted by their gesture of kindness, knowing full well that I had doubted my place in the family, knowing full well that I had thought that I wouldn't be welcome; and now here they were, showing me how much effort they had gone through to demonstrate the exact opposite of what I had imagined.

Speechless, I sat there for a moment, scanning the scene as Pop said, "This is the old place, and it is yours, the entire section along with the cows, barns, and house. We just want you to come home, son."

This is incredible, I thought to myself as feelings of guilt swept over me, guilt for having been gone for so long, for not writing letters, for not calling. "How could I ever repay you guys for this?" I asked them. "This is just absolutely unbelievable!" I said as I sat there with my mouth open, my eyes filling with tears that I couldn't and didn't dare shed. I just sat there, looking the old place over—as did they—with a feeling of satisfaction, my faith in my family more than restored. I was home.

After a while, I finally commented, "You know, Pop, I've got two more years before I can retire from the Army?"

He nodded, smiling; and then he declared, "You just do what you've gotta do and then come home safe and sound. We'll all be here waiting for you when you do."

Then Clay slapped me on the back and said, "Come on, you big sissy. Let's take a look at the ole place and then call it a day."

I barely kept from choking up with tears as we galloped off, Clay, and then Pop, and then me.

I watched them as they rode, sitting tall in their saddles, scanning the land with their eyes, making comments, pointing out specifics to me as we checked the entire section, all six hundred and forty acres of it. We checked the fences, every post; the barns; the stables; and the cattle pens and working facility. I was surprised to see that they had modernized it with electricity and hydraulic pumps that allowed a man to work cattle day or night with ease and minimal help.

We spent the entire morning looking the old place over and talking about the good old days, grandpa and great-granddad. The decisions they made had affected us all. They had given us everything we needed to survive and thrive for generations. The importance of those decisions hadn't escaped our thought process, and we all hoped to be able to have that same impact on the lives of our own families someday.

I wonder if my efforts overseas had any sort of positive impact on the lives of people there. Had it been worth it? I thought to myself as I dismounted from Little Leo and handed the reins over to Clay.

Without a word, they turned; and I watched them as they rode off over the hill and out of sight.

The days merged into night as we worked together, cutting hay, harvesting wheat, and cooking our meals. We worked from sunup to sundown and then some as the weeks passed. The summer was hot, and dust hung heavily over the fields as we labored; and each day, the sun set through a layered haze extending to the horizon with a rainbow of color that masked its brilliance and produced in me a sense of connection between heaven and earth.

My heart forgot about the troubles of the world. My soul renewed at church every Sunday. Neighbors and old friends made a big deal of my presence. Their hugs embraced my soul, and their praise poured out over me. They were like a summer rain that quenches the earth's thirst and renews the green. They saved my soul, made me feel whole again. I belonged here, and I knew it; but I had to go back. The time would come soon for me to leave.

Holly had been on my mind since that first night, but I had been avoiding her for all the wrong reasons. I guess the timing wasn't right. There was much to be done and other relationships that needed mending. I suppose I should have called her right away; but now that my time at home was nearing its end, I felt the need to contact her, to see her again.

I searched my luggage, my clothing, but couldn't find her number. All morning, I turned everything I owned, the entire cabin, inside out until I just couldn't look anymore. I sat down on the couch; and then, out of the blue, the phone rang. It was the first time it had rang since I had gotten here.

"Hello," I answered, not sure what to expect.

"Hey, you! It's me, Holly! Why haven't you called?"

Pausing for a moment, searching for the perfect words that eluded me, there was no excuse for not having called her; and now I sat there, like a teenager, unable to say anything. It didn't matter though. Holly broke the ice.

"Can I come over this afternoon? And perhaps we can go fishing in that pond of yours."

Immediately, I knew that Clay or Pop had put her up to calling. But that was okay. I was glad she called and I knew that it was time. "You know, Holly, that would be great. I am so glad you called. Would you please come over as soon as you are ready?"

I could hear a sigh of relief at the sound of my voice and the words that I had spoken, but she didn't hesitate and replied, "I'll be over in an hour or so. Please wait for me!"

"I'll be here." I replied.

Then she hung up without saying a word.

Sitting back, I looked up at the ceiling and noticed that I had clothing hanging over the railing of the loft. A quick glance around the room and my heart sank as I realized that I hadn't cleaned the old place up for several days. There were dirty dishes in the sink, clothes scattered everywhere, beer bottles on the coffee table. Frantically, I started picking up the mess, gathering all the clothes and stuffing them into the dirty clothes hamper upstairs, picking up the trash, and washing the dishes. Satisfied with my effort, I scanned the cabin with my eyes, checking to see if I had forgotten anything.

Quickly, I jumped into the shower and then toweled off, spraying a bit of cologne on my neck, and then brushed my teeth. There were clean clothes in my suitcase, so I retrieved a pair of golf shorts; a light blue, cotton T-shirt; and a pair of tennis shoes. All my socks were dirty, so I took the cleanest pair of ankle socks and put them on and slid the shoes over them onto my feet. Standing, I looked into the full-length mirror that hung on the wall outside the bathroom door and thought to myself, *Well, at least I'm comfortable.*

There was a jar of grub worms that I had dug up a few days ago.

The worms wiggled and stretched as I shook the jar, checking to see if they were still alive.

"Perfect bait," I said out loud as I set the jar down on the shelf next to the door and the fishing poles that were ready and waiting.

I turned on the television to see what was on the news and then decided against watching it. The last thing I wanted to do was think of what was going on outside my own world at a moment like this, so I turned the set off and went into the kitchen to retrieve a bottle of wine and a few glasses. I retrieved a bottle of merlot from Mendoza Argentina from the wine rack that hung from the kitchen ceiling.

As I searched for an opener, memories of Mendoza raced through my mind—the mountain climbing, snow skiing, the mules; but mostly the tour we had taken through one of the wineries there. I could still see clearly the vineyards and the irrigation canals filled with clear and very cold runoff from the snow high in the mountains to the west.

Finding the right tool, I opened the bottle and allowed it time to breathe; and then I impatiently poured myself a glass. Enjoying the aroma, I swished the merlot around inside the glass, my eyes closed. The scent of blackberry and oak mixed with the sweetness of grape. I sipped a bit over my tongue and savored the spirit and then enjoyed the dry aftertaste on my tongue and the top of my mouth.

In the fridge, I had some summer sausage, so I cut up a dozen or so slices and then sliced some dry cheddar and placed it all on a small plate with some saltines, the only crackers I had. Satisfied, I placed the bottle and plate of food on the coffee table in the living area and set the glasses down next to each other. There were no candles, so I left it at that. Having already overdone it, I felt a little embarrassed at how much I had put into the thought of impressing Holly. There really was no need but decided it was my way of showing her respect as a woman, as a really good friend, as a person whom I adored. *It doesn't matter how tough women might act. They all want to be treated like a lady from time to time,* I thought to myself. I just hoped she wouldn't laugh at me or perhaps take it wrong and get angry. For a moment, I thought about tossing it all away but didn't. I guess I had laid my cards out on the table and wanted to see what kind of hand she was holding.

Deciding that I had done enough, I went outside and sat on the porch and waited for her to arrive; but it didn't take long before I saw her coming over the hill, down the trail, toward the cabin in her dad's old pickup truck. It was the same truck she drove back when we were dating—a little rusty and dented, but it was still running strong. She had a smile a mile wide on her face. Her hair, as blonde as ever, bounced over her shoulders as she drove down the hill and pulled to a stop in front of the cabin in a cloud of dust.

Jumping out almost before the truck had settled to a stop, she ran up the steps and flew into my arms. Her feet didn't even touch the ground as she wrapped her arms around my neck and kissed me deeply on the lips. She caught me a bit off guard but I settled down and returned the kiss. She had unleashed my desire with her surprising embrace, and we continued to kiss for at least a minute or so before stopping to take a look at each other for the first time really. Her eyes were as clear blue as a cool spring sky. Although time had created a few wrinkles, she was as beautiful as ever.

We stood there, looking into each other's soul for a moment; and then she broke down and started crying. Crystal pools of tears filled her eyes as she slumped away and sat down on the porch. She was overwhelmed with emotion. Bracing her body from the floor with her left hand, she held her face with her right, covering her eyes, looking down. Her shoulders shuttered, signaling the depth of her pain.

I knelt down in front of her. Putting my hands on her upper arm, I tried to pick her up, to put her on her feet; but she resisted. She wasn't able to stand for a moment, not until she had regained her composure. Finally, she let me help her up; and I said, "Come on inside, honey. Let's have a glass of wine and talk about things."

She looked me in the eyes, and asked, "Is my makeup all smeared?"

I laughed and said, "Well, yes, it is a bit, but we can fix that!"

She laughed and sobbed as we walked back into the cabin. I

had her sit down on the couch, poured her a glass of wine, and gestured for her to eat some of the treats I had prepared. Then I went into the bathroom and got her a hand towel to wipe the tears from her eyes.

Walking out of the bathroom, returning with the towel, I stopped for a moment and watched her. As she tasted some of the cheese and sausage, she nodded her head in approval. I walked over to her, handed her the towel, and sat down. I sat next to her, put my arm around her shoulder, and pulled her back and rested her head on my shoulder as she kicked her feet up onto the coffee table, already having removed her shoes.

She just sat there, still sobbing a bit. Quiet, she didn't or couldn't speak; so I did. I started talking, telling her about everything, about the cows that Pop and Clay gave me and everything I had done since I had left for the Army. I talked and talked for hours, recanting stories that I thought were forgotten. I told her about the jungle in Panama, the monkeys, the canal. I told her about the mountains in Argentina and the origins of the wine we were drinking, the desert in Iraq, on and on. I would apologize, saying, "I'm talking too much," and she would say, "No. I like it. Don't stop."

The hours passed, night fell, and I just kept talking. Finally, she started to open up; and she told me about how she had gotten married shortly after I had left, that her ex-husband, Donny, had started working in the oil field, dragging her and the kids all over Texas, Louisiana, and Oklahoma for years and years. He had been abusive, which made me mad as hell; but I knew that God would get his revenge, so I let it go.

She had been having a particularly rough time since the divorce. There wasn't much opportunity for a thirty-seven-year-old divorcée, for anybody really. The economy was bad, and it had affected her entire family. She had taken a second job at the store on Hollywood Corner just to make ends meet, but it was never enough because her boys were all three teenagers and needed more than she could provide.

That's when it hit me; and without giving it another thought, I offered the old place to her. "You can live there as long as you want. All I ask is that your boys help Pop get his chores done and take care of my cows."

She looked at me and smiled in disbelief. Then she said, "Are you sure?"

"Positive!" I replied, and said, "You won't have to worry about anything. Just make sure your boys help Pop take care of those cows and that will take care of rent and utilities. You could even butcher a calf if you'd like, perhaps grow a garden." Then I added, "It's not a handout. There is a lot of work to do in order to get the old place fixed up. All I want is to make sure your boys help Pop out where needed."

She just looked at me, perplexed, not knowing what to do or say; so I stood up, offered my hand, and said, "Do we have a deal?"

She shook my hand, shook it excitedly, giggling a bit. She said, "Deal!"

"Then it's settled. You can move in as soon as you're ready."

She stood and hugged me tight and said, "Thanks, Mike! Thank you so much!"

We spent a few more hours talking about all that needed to be done, all the things she would need to do to move in. I told her not to worry about a truck or help. Clay had some hands and plenty of trucks to move her stuff. I would take care of that. All she had to do was set her schedule and everything would be taken care of. The wine flowed with the conversation until we finally both fell asleep on the couch, laying there with an old blanket for covers. We slept until the sun came up.

She woke up excited and ready to go, so I made her a quick breakfast: a bowl of cheerios and a cup of coffee. She wolfed it down with the enthusiasm of a cheerleader, and then it was time. She had to leave, get everything started. I walked her outside to the truck and opened the door for her, and she jumped in as I closed the door behind her.

She rolled down the window and shouted, "Give me a kiss, you fool!"

Smiling, I obliged, taking my time, enjoying the moment. She drove off, making a circle around the back side of the cabin, honking her horn and waving good-bye as she drove over the hill back toward Pop's house and the road.

It wasn't long before Clay and Pop came down to see what was going on. Curious as cats, they had smiles on their faces that begged to ask the question; and I said, "No, no, no. It wasn't like that, not at all."

They laughed and joked, poking fun at me; and I knew they would never believe me.

That is when I told them about my decision to leave, to leave soon in order to travel around the country for a few weeks before I had to report in, before I had to go back into the Army. They didn't understand why I wanted to leave so soon, but they didn't try to convince me otherwise. They knew how I was, that I was a wayward soul that still hadn't settled. They knew that there was something calling me to be who I had become and that nothing could change that. They knew that I was called to be in the military, that perhaps something greater than any of us wanted me there. They knew that when it was done, once I had done what was being asked of me by perhaps God, then and only then would I come home for good.

I explained to them what had transpired the night before with Holly, and they agreed to work the boys hard, to teach them how to take care of their mom. I really did appreciate their willingness to help. There wasn't a question of why, just how much. They understood how difficult her life had been and how she needed somebody to have her back, to make sure those boys had some sort of leg up on life. They agreed to help in every way possible, and that is when I asked them for one final favor.

I asked, "Pop, if anything should happen to me before I get back, I want you to give those cows to Holly, make sure she has a place to stay, that she is taken care of."

He agreed.

THE MISSION

It was another day on the flat range, a warm September day. In charge of running the advanced marksmanship training for the entire group, I had risen early that day in order to meet the day head on, to get the training done, and to get another group through the training we were providing. We had already conducted four courses, having trained a little over two hundred men; and we could see the progress being made as the students had returned to their units to spread the knowledge around.

The new students were doing much better, and today was only day three of this new course. Still on the flat range, we were running tactical two gun drills, up drills, turning and movement drills. This was the way we would start the new guys off; and then we would work our way up to a stress test that would examine each man's ability to handle his primary and secondary weapons through a variety of obstacles that, when combined with an unknown time limit, induced a certain degree of stress allowing us to evaluate each man to ensure they were ready to move onto more difficult room-clearing and other immediate-action drills. Once they were ready, we would teach them room-clearing techniques with live ammunition along with breaching techniques using explosives and shotguns. This wasn't a typical day at the range, not when you stepped onto the range with this group of instructors. Each man knew that he was going to learn something new or at least improve upon what he had already known.

Still at the training headquarters on main post, I had already launched the men out to the flat range with their weapons and ammunition. Their day had begun, and the rest of the cadre was working on setting up training over the next few weeks. Sitting there at my desk, I was working on an ammunition spreadsheet, a detailed analysis of the requirements to support the next few weeks of training. There was a television set on the wall across from my desk, on the other side of the room, over the top of where the coffee pot and refrigerator were located. The sound was turned down as I peeked up at the set, and I saw a large city with a building on fire. I thought that it was strange, so I picked the remote up and turned up the volume just as the second aircraft crashed into the other tower at the World Trade Center, exploding as it crashed through the building, a fireball exiting the far side.

"What the hell was that?" I shouted as I stood up and walked, unaware of anything else, up to the television hanging there on the wall.

I guess several others heard what I had said and came running in. We stood there, awestruck, as the first tower and then the second collapsed. I ran over to the phone and called the guys at the range and explained to them what had just happened, and they questioned me in disbelief. I gave them instructions to continue training but to keep their eyes peeled because we were under attack and we had no idea who it might be. Hanging up the phone, one of my guys, who was a national guardsman getting ready for a tour of active duty with my team, called me from Newark, New Jersey.

He was a member of the swat team there, actually one of their team leaders. That was why we had recruited him for the training team. I answered the phone; and before I could say much of anything, he shouted, "Mike, I won't be coming out there for awhile. We've been attacked by terrorists. And, well, it's a target-rich environment around here right now!" With that, he hung up, not waiting for me to respond.

The phone continued to ring off the wall throughout the day as the situation developed. The operations center would call and ask me a few questions about the team and the different personnel I had assigned to it.

"Who is HALO qualified on your team, Mike?" the group operations officer asked.

"They all are, sir, except for one guy, the one from New Jersey."

He hung up, and I knew something was going on. I called out to the range and gave my guys a heads-up. I told them to keep training but to get mentally prepared for an alert. But nothing happened that day. We just completed our training and came back to the barracks.

That night, I gathered the entire team around me and talked to them about what had happened. I asked a lot of personal questions: "How is your marriage? Have you set it up so your wife can pay your bills on time?" so forth and so on. We went to bed that evening not knowing what the future might hold. The entire world had been turned upside down.

We started training the next day, not knowing what the events on 9/11 might bring our way at any time in the near future. One thing was for certain that morning. The resolve our men came to work with was very different than it had been the day before. There wasn't as much smoking and joking going on as usual as each and every one of us knew that something big was going to happen. The president couldn't just sit back and let this happen without some sort of reprisal. We had to act, but how? That was the big question.

General Shelton was the chairman of the joint chiefs. An ex-Special Forces warrior, he was the one who would put together the plan that we would execute. Regardless, today, we trained at the flat range, all of us angered, none of us wishing we could go home, all of us ready. We wanted revenge. Every conversation that day hinged upon that very subject. When will we get a shot at whoever did this? That was the question on everybody's mind. We didn't even know who had done it, but the picture was becoming more clear as I watched the team gather its will to fight. As a group, we were more than ready for anything that should come our way. Today, we would train. But in the back of our minds, we were already getting mentally prepared to do whatever it took to get back at those who had done this to our country. It was just a matter of time, just a matter of time.

Later that afternoon, the phone on my desk rang. Quickly, I answered and recognized the voice of my company commander on the other end. "Mike," he said, "I'm sending another team to replace your guys out there on the range. Once they get there, hand everything over to them and get your team over here to the isolation facility as soon as possible."

"No problem, sir. We'll be there as soon as we can." I called the range and told the guys to shut down, pack up, and come on back to the training headquarters. We would turn the students loose for the day and have the other team pick up where we left off the next day. Without question, they executed; and within the hour, we had turned over the training program to another team and were on our way to the isolation facility.

Loaded on a pair of Humvees, we drove across post to the group's isolation facility, a large cinderblock building complex with a chain link fence and razor wire enclosing the compound. This wasn't a training event, and we all knew it as we downloaded our rucksacks and secured our gear and weapons. In a group, we walked through the gate, the guards holding it open for us as we passed by them silently. The front door opened in front of us, and it was the company commander and the sergeant major standing there, holding the doors, as we moved into and down the hallway. There was a young NCO standing in front of a door about two hundred feet down the hall, motioning for us to enter the door where he stood as we walked down the hall, our boots clicking on the shiny cement floor as we passed the unpainted cinderblock walls. We turned right; walked into the room; and found it set up, ready for a briefing.

The sergeant major said, "Men, down your gear in the back room there and come on back in and have a seat. The briefing will start in a few minutes."

We all filed back into the briefing room as the staff started to arrive. One by one, they all came in and took their seats along the outer wall. Mostly officers, they were all wearing a freshly starched set of fatigues. And unlike my team, they all sported fresh high-and-tight haircuts. They were all casualties of being on a staff, their very professional appearance identifying them as such, although I couldn't help but respect them for their intellect and dedication to getting us the support we needed for whatever mission came up. Lately, all we had been doing were training missions—training each other, training our host nation counterparts, doing physical training, getting ready for any eventuality that might present itself.

Today, we would receive a new mission, not that much different than those in the past. But since 9/11, we all knew or at least felt that the time had come. The time had come for us to stand up. We would have to actually do what we had trained for since we all went through training group. Now we would go into the storm, but we didn't know exactly where or how soon.

As the last of the staff filed into the briefing room, the battalion sergeants major called the room to attention; and the battalion and group commanders walked in with two generals. I didn't know either of them, nor did I recognize the unit patches. *They must be from the pentagon,* was all I could imagine. As we took our seats, the group S-2 officer stood up and walked forward; and with a nod to the clerk in the back of the room, his briefing appeared on the projector screen that was centered on the wall directly to our front. Clearing his throat and adjusting his thick glasses, he began his briefing slowly. His Southern drawl hung heavily on every word. His slow rhythm forced our attention as he began.

"The attacks that took place a few days ago were perpetrated by a group on non-state actors, a terrorist organization known as Al-Qaeda. As you know, they attacked the United States by flying commercial jets loaded with innocent civilians into the World Trade Center in New York, the Pentagon in Washington DC, and into the ground in Pennsylvania. The leader of this group is a man known as Osama Bin Laden, a wealthy Islamic radical who is being sheltered by the government of Afghanistan, also known as the Taliban.

"Afghanistan is approximately the size of Texas. It is bordered on the north by Turkmenistan, Uzbekistan, and Tajikistan and then in the extreme northeast by China. It is also bordered on the east and the south by Pakistan and by Iran on the west. The country is split east to west by the Hindu Kush Mountain range, rising in the east to heights of twenty-four thousand feet or seven thousand three hundred and fifteen meters. With the exception of the southwest, most of the country is covered by high snowcapped mountains and is traversed by deep valleys.

"The primary languages spoken in Afghanistan are Dari Persian and Pashtu, both of which are considered official languages. However, there is a large element of those who speak Turkic and other minor languages.

"The Pashtu people make up the largest ethnic group throughout Afghanistan, with forty-two percent of the population, followed by ethnic Tajiks at twenty-seven percent, the Hazaras and Uzbeks at nine percent, and then there are the Aimak, Turkmen, and Baloch that round out the major ethnic groups found throughout the country.

"Conquerors since the time of Alexander the Great have been trying to control Afghanistan, which is also known as the gateway to India from Central Asia. Islamic conquerors first arrived in the seventh century, and Genghis Khan and Temerlane followed in the thirteenth and fourteenth centuries.

"In the nineteenth century, Afghanistan became a battleground in the rivalry between Imperial Britain and Czarist Russia for control of Central Asia. Three Anglo-Afghan wars took place and ended inconclusively. Although, in 1893, Britain was able to establish an unofficial border, the Durand Line, separating Afghanistan from British India. It was then that London granted full independence and Emir Amanullah founded an Afghan monarchy in 1926.

"During the Cold War, the Soviet Union launched a full-scale invasion into Afghanistan and installed their own government. But soon, they were met with fierce resistance. The Soviets and the Soviet-backed Afghan government were quickly immersed in a civil war against a guerrilla group that called themselves the *Mujahideen*. Initially armed with outdated weapons, the *Mujahideen* became the focus of the U.S. Cold War strategy against the Soviet Union. And with Pakistan's help, Washington began funneling sophisticated arms to them. It was during this time that Osama Bin Laden became well-known throughout the Muslim world as one of the most radical leaders within the *Mujahideen*. By the end of the nineteen eighties, the Soviet Union withdrew, leaving behind a pro-Soviet government while various Islamic rebel groups fought one another for control.

"Amid the chaos of competing factions, a group calling itself the Taliban seized control of Kabul and imposed harsh fundamentalist laws, including stoning for adultery and severing hands for theft. Women were prohibited from work and school, and they were required to cover themselves from head to foot while in public. Although Bin Laden did travel to Africa and other parts of the world after the war, he was still one of the staunchest supporters of the Taliban throughout this time period. And they, in turn, have provided him with the sanctuary that he ultimately needed to build his network of Islamic radical terrorists. By the fall of 1998, the Taliban controlled about ninety percent of the country. And with their scorched earth tactics and human rights abuses, they had turned themselves into an international pariah.

"Believing that Bin Laden was involved in the bombings of American embassies in Kenya and Tanzania on August 7th, 1998, both the United States and the United Nations asked for the

Afghan Taliban government to deport him to stand trial for the crimes he had committed, yet they refused, as they have done since the attacks on September 11th. To this day, Bin Laden enjoys the sanctuary provided him by the government in Kabul.

"The United Front for the Salvation of Afghanistan (UIF), also known as the Northern Alliance, is the only real possible opposition group to the Taliban government. A military-political umbrella organization created by the Islamic State of Afghanistan in 1996, it is made up of various Afghan groups that have joined together in an uneasy alliance to fight against the Taliban.

"On September 9th, 2001, the legendary guerrilla leader of the Northern Alliance, Ahmed Shah Massoud, was killed by suspected Saudi Arabian Al-Qaeda agents posing as journalists who used their cover to conduct a suicide bombing attack. Just a few days after his assassination, seemingly a death knell for the anti-Taliban forces, the terrorists attacked New York's World Trade Center towers and the Pentagon, and Bin Laden has emerged as the primary suspect in both tragedies.

Organization and History of the Northern Alliance: "After the Soviet Union withdrew from Afghanistan, the *Mujahideen* fighters who had previously defeated the communist government formed the Islamic State of Afghanistan or ISA, they soon came under attack and, in 1996, lost the capital to the Taliban. It was at this point in time that the *Mujahideen* created the United Islamic Front; primarily because the warlords, such as Rashid Dostum, belonged to various tribes but to no specific political party and they did not want to recognize the Islamic State of Afghanistan as a legal entity. So the defeated government devised a military strategy to utilize these forces while not offending their political sensibilities.

"Although recognized by most foreign nations as the legal government, the Northern Alliance only controls about ten percent of the country. President Burhanduddin Rabbani is the national head of the United Islamic Front. However, the real power on the ground is maintained by the post of Defense Minister, which was held by Ahmed Shah Massoud until his assassination a few days ago. He has now been replaced by Mohammed Fahim. Before the attacks on September 11th, Russia, the Central Asian Nations of the Commonwealth of Independent States, India, Turkey, and Iran were giving aid to the United Islamic Front or the Northern Alliance. However, Pakistan, Saudi Arabia, and the United Arab Emirates were supporting the Taliban. It is our feeling that this is about to change, as they have all condemned the attacks and will likely turn their backs on the Taliban.

"Three ethnic groups dominate the Northern Alliance. The Tajiks make up twenty-seven percent of Afghanistan's population, and they are the second-largest ethnic group in the country. The Hazara and the Uzbeks each make up about nine percent of the population. From the Taliban conquest in 1996 until now, the Northern Alliance had controlled approximately thirty percent of Afghanistan's population in provinces such as Badakhshan, Kapisa, Takhar, and parts of Parwan, Junar, Nuristan, Laghman, Samangan, Qundzu Gory, and Bamiyan all in the north of the country, hence the name Northern Alliance.

"The political leader of the Alliance is President Burhanuddin Rabbani. However, he is little more than a front man for the military commanders. Ahmed Shah Massoud served as the UIF's Minister of Defense and was by far its most visible and powerful figure. He personally commanded around ten thousand of the UIF's estimated forty thousand troops. Massoud's troops are the best trained and equipped within the Northern Alliance. Several other important military leaders controlled different factions within the Alliance, including Abdul Rashid Dostum, General Mohammed Fahim, and Ismail Khan. General Dostum has the right to nominate six ministers, including those of defense and foreign affairs, and is the military commander in northern Afghanistan.

"It has been confirmed that Ahmad Shah Massoud had died following the attack by Al-Qaeda assassins posing as Saudi journalists. The most senior Tajik commander, Mohammed Fahim, has now succeeded Massoud, and the Northern Alliance is poised to receive United States military assistance in order to defeat the Taliban.

"More detailed information pertaining to the personalities and terrain are located in the binder that I have provided for you. If there are any questions, please feel free to ask them after the briefing is concluded or contact me via your secure phone at my office."

It was at this point that the battalion sergeants major recommended that we take a short break to get something to drink and perhaps have a smoke before we continued. Agreeing, the generals stood up along with the other officers and exited the room. This was a bit unusual. Normally, a mission brief didn't take more than an hour; and we had already eaten up about a half hour. This was going to take awhile, and the sergeant major knew it.

As I walked out into and down the hallway toward the water fountain, he grabbed me under my arm, wrapping his fingers around my left bicep, and pulled me back against the wall. He leaned in real close—I could smell his chew—and he said, "Mike this is the real thing. Are your men ready?"

"Sure they are. We couldn't be any more ready, Sergeant Major, and this is what we've been waiting for our entire lives."

"Good. Just so you know, you're on stop loss. Your retirement is on hold. Do you understand?"

"Yes, I do." I knew I only had three months left to my retirement date. Having cashed in my leave for the money instead of going home early, I had postponed my departure for that, and I understood now that I would be stop loss for at least another year.

Then he said, "You guys are leaving here tonight for Germany. This won't be one of those long, drawn-out ordeals like in the Q course. Once you get to Germany, just get your plan together and get your men on the ground and take it from there. Hooah?"

"I understand. Thanks for the heads-up."

He let go of my arm, and we walked in silence down to the water fountain. Finding a coke machine, I put my money in and listened intently as the can followed the chute down into the receiver tray. My thoughts were on the mission at hand: Afghanistan.

We all filed back into the briefing room, having relieved ourselves, each of us carrying a soft drink as we took our seats. *The two generals must be here to observe,* I thought to myself. Perhaps they would go back to Washington and report to the Secretary of Defense or perhaps the President himself about what their impressions were of us.

Once we were all seated, the group operations officer stood up and prepared to give his portion of the briefing. A Japanese American, he was a very large man, standing over six feet tall. Over the years, I had come to know him well. He had earned not only my respect but that of many others. He was perhaps one of the strongest leaders we had. At one point, he had been a company commander who launched his teams downrange with a frequency not matched by any other commander I had known. He would likely become a general someday; he already resembled a squinty-eyed, muscled version of Norman Schwarzkopf, although he couldn't roll up his battle dress uniform shirtsleeves due to the incredible size of not only his forearms but also his biceps.

"Men, your mission is to infiltrate Afghanistan and conduct a linkup with the Northern Alliance and support their effort to topple the Taliban government in Kabul.

"Our intent is to lead them into combat against the Taliban and capture the capital. Our overall objective is to remove the Taliban from power and facilitate the capture of Osama Bin Laden, the leader of the Al-Qaeda network.

"This mission will be conducted in five phases.

"Phase one: Infiltration via military freefall parachute operation.

"Phase two: Link up with the Northern Alliance, facilitated by another government agency already on the ground.

"Phase three: Train, equip, and advise primary elements and prepare them for combat operations.

"Phase four: Lead the Northern Alliance into combat, guiding their efforts while providing close air support as required.

"Phase five: Exfiltration, method and time to be determined.

"You will find the specified tasks to subordinate and supporting units listed in the briefing folder under paragraph three of your mission brief. If you have any questions, please feel free to ask them after the briefing or contact me via your secure phone."

Just like that, he had confirmed what we had all wanted to hear. We all looked around at each other; and somebody slapped me on the back as the room became unsettled as the murmur of low speaking voices filled the air. Looking around, I could see the smiles on the commanders' faces as they looked proudly at the team, nodding their heads as if they were in agreement with the mission statement or as if they were saying, "Yes. These are the men for the job."

Meanwhile, the group logistics officer was preparing for his portion of the briefing. Clearing his throat, he silenced the room; and we all gave him our full attention as he began.

The briefings continued for another hour. Each member of the staff stood up and gave their portion. We listened, but our thoughts were on the fact that we were going to Afghanistan. They briefed, giving words of encouragement and advice. Even the chaplain got up and said a few words. He stood there in silence for a moment, each of us waiting with anticipation and hanging on his every word; and he said, "May we bow our heads in prayer.

"Almighty God, who art the author of liberty and the champion of the oppressed, hear our prayer. We, the men of Special Forces, acknowledge our dependence upon thee in the preservation of human freedom. Go with us as we seek to defend the defenseless and to free the enslaved. May we ever remember that our nation, whose motto is 'In God We Trust,' expects that we shall acquit ourselves with honor, that we may never bring shame upon our faith, our families, or our fellow men. Grant us wisdom from thy mind, courage from thine heart, strength from thine arm, and protection by thine hand. It is for thee that we do battle, and to thee belongs the victor's crown, for thine is the kingdom, and the power, and the glory forever. Amen."

As he finished his prayer, we all raised our heads and opened our eyes to see him smiling from ear to ear. A light in his eyes unlike anything I had ever seen beamed upon us all as we stood there for a moment.

And then the chaplain saluted and said. "It's a great day to be a soldier!"

We stood there in silence for a minute, waiting for somebody to say something; yet no one was willing to break the silence, so I sounded off, "Men, let's go back over to the team room and secure the rest of our equipment and get ready for palletization over at Green Ramp. We are leaving for Germany tonight, so let's get moving and get on the road."

With that, everybody began to move about, milling around as we retrieved our gear and exited the building. We all knew that we couldn't discuss what had just taken place with anybody, so we didn't mention it. The battalion would contact our families in a day or so. Other than that, all we had to do at this moment was make it over to Green Ramp and get our gear ready to fly.

The flight overseas took what seemed like forever. We landed in Dover, Delaware and refueled. This allowed us time to deplane and get some coffee and snacks before the aircrew was ready for takeoff again. The skies over Dover were clear and warm as we arrived, although the feel of autumn coming on was unmistakable. A cool breeze penetrated the warmth from time to time. The stars shined brightly as we moved across the tarmac over to the air mobility command terminal.

As far as the rest of the world was concerned, we were just another group of Army soldiers. Nothing about us drew attention. There was no reason to think we were bound for the destiny that had called our names. We entered the terminal and meandered around thoughtlessly. I found a sandwich machine and put my money in. *A buck fifty for a bologna sandwich. Jesus H Christ!* I thought to myself. I retrieved my sandwiches, selected a coke from the other machine, and took a seat in the lounge where there was a television with Fox News playing. All the pundits had an opinion that they believed was the most important. They continued opining about some subject that really held no true importance to anybody outside of the beltway. I sat there, not speaking, enjoying my stale, white bread; sandwiches; and soda.

Soon, members of the aircrew appeared and let us know that it was time to go; so we all quietly gathered our snacks and meandered back out onto the tarmac. The warm, late night air felt comfortable. Turning, I looked back at the terminal as we approached the plane and took in the view of it and the tarmac and then entered the side door just below and behind the cockpit, leaving the United States behind perhaps for the last time. Finding my seat, I fell asleep before the crew had removed the chocks from beneath the tires of the plane.

The flight over the Atlantic was uneventful, and it did allow me the time I needed to get a little rest, although I couldn't really stay asleep. I knew that I needed to have a plan. I needed to take this time to consider what the team should do as we hit the ground in Germany.

There would be the inevitable unloading of the aircraft and a short trip over to an isolation facility that was being set up for us to finish our mission planning. There wouldn't be that much to do since the battalion had already set a lot of the requirements into motion. We would need to pack our gear and ammunition; get the immediate resupply airdrop bundle packed; and of course, we would have to pack our emergency resupply bundle. We had already gone over and rewritten the team's standard operating procedures for this, so all we really had to do was review the procedure and brainstorm any other requirements this mission might require.

I didn't anticipate a shortage of ammunition or gear, although you could never tell. Communications equipment and medical supplies made up the majority of our needs, although ammunition for the Northern Alliance would be something that we would have to plan for.

I discussed that with my weapons sergeant, asking him to come up with a list of requirements to provide a basic load of Russian ammunition to the Northern Alliance. It would need to be large enough to support a brigade-sized element at least.

We would present that to the battalion as an additional automatic supply requirement that we would expect to receive within seventy-two hours after hitting the ground. The captain and I discussed an operational fund. I figured we would need at least ten thousand dollars. That should cover any immediate requirements unless we were required to pick up the payroll for the troops we would inherit. That was something we would find out once we were on the ground. From what I understood, funding wasn't going to be one of our roles; but we needed to be prepared nonetheless.

One requirement that would have to have extra special attention would be our escape and evasion plan if all went to hell in a hand basket. We would probably be required to move a great deal of distance, so we would need to set that up; and that would take some time and effort. I discussed it with my assistant operations sergeant, and he asked if he could tap some of the other guys on the team to help him out. I agreed that it would be good to get a consensus effort and recommend that he include the medics and commo men. Although the weapons guys would have a huge role to play, their expertise in infantry tactics was an asset we couldn't ignore.

The flight landed in Germany in early afternoon, a nine-hour flight, but we lost about a half day; and the jet lag was settling in, having been awake all night and apparently all day. We were aided by the flight crew as we downloaded our pallet onto a fork lift as the committee of folks there to meet us strangely stood around, watching. They ushered the team off of the aircraft and onto a forty-four-passenger bus and we went directly to a hangar located near the airfield that had been converted into a large isolation facility. They had used makeshift plywood barriers to set up planning areas and sleeping areas. There was a briefing area and a dining facility, to include showers, restrooms, and a gym. I was impressed. Being the first team to occupy one of the several planning areas that had been set up, we were being catered to like rock stars. Our needs were more than met, and that took a lot of the pressure off.

This wasn't like the planning exercises that we had participated in, in the past. This time, we were doing it for real; and those men from battalion and group had gone all out, achieved their objective, and now were putting their plan in place. This was great for all concerned; and it definitely allowed us to focus on our mission planning, which, despite the advantages of having our needs catered to, was still a rigorous twenty-four-hour-a-day process, a relentless process that tested everybody's mettle. There would be no rest until we had completed our mission brief; and then and only then would we get a little sleep, likely just a few hours, before we boarded for the final leg of our journey.

The days went by quickly as we worked toward our objective. We planned for, packed, wrote, and rehearsed every aspect of the mission profile that we could imagine. We were successful in getting one last airborne operation off the ground as part of our rehearsal, although we weren't able to rehearse the pre-breathing operation as I would have liked. We went to the range and worked our weapons, test firing everything and running up drills while getting our physical training in at the same time. Going to the range did a great deal to relieve the stress of being locked down. More than anything else, we rehearsed immediate action drills; patrol base procedures; and, of course, the linkup procedures. The linkup could make or break our mission. One mistake on linkup, and we could all end up dead before we even got our boots dirty.

The men started letting their beards grow. Mine came in dark despite my blonde hair. It was the first time I had ever grown a beard, ever. I didn't like it at all. After a few days, my beard made me look more like I had been on a three-day drinking binge back on Hayes Street than anything else. The whole team looked a bit like the Dirty Dozen from the movie; and quickly, we earned that as a team nickname, although we referred to ourselves as The Outlaws.

We even stood for a picture near the latrine, holding a sign that said, "Welcome to Hell, Signed the Dirty Dozen." If you think about it, we were all somewhat outcasts in our own right. Of course, we weren't hardened criminals; but we sure looked like it. One of the things that the men enjoyed the most was when we were issued sets of customary clothing like the locals wore that we called our hagi-flage, versus camouflage. They gave each of us a set of clothing along with the hats. Now we would be able to dress like our future

Northern Alliance brethren. We packed all of it into our immediate resupply bundle and prepared to give our briefing back to the staff.

Several days had passed. Having sort of lost count, I knew that it had been about five days since we had arrived in Germany. We had advised the staff that we were ready, but they asked us to continue mission planning. They were waiting for execution authority from the national command before we set the wheels into motion, before we prepared to launch. We were to stand by and be on call, ready to provide our briefing at a moment's notice. And then we would immediately load the aircraft and go. My idea was to allow the team time to rest for a while after the brief back; but that wouldn't be my call, so we rested now.

It didn't take long before we got the word: less than twenty-four hours. "The President had displayed a great deal of resolve," our company commander said as he woke the team and brought us together to let us know that the briefing would be held soon.

We all took a shower and dressed, preparing mentally. And then we were summoned to the briefing area. It was going to be transmitted via the teleconferencing system they had set up for an audience back in Washington DC. We couldn't see them, but they could see and hear us.

The brief back went well—nothing extraordinary, just the normal questions from the staff. We fielded the usual questions from staff members who really had no bearing. Perhaps they were only trying to impress others, likely their commanders.

The battalion sergeant major, the senior noncommissioned officer present, rolled his eyes as the young officers asked away. We fielded the questions like machine gunners blasting away, making sure there were no gaps in the line, no gaps in our united front. From time to time, one of my guys would ask permission to field a certain question. This only tended to solidify the fact that as a unit, we were ready.

Without warning, a voice came over the teleconference speaker. It was George Bush. Clearing his throat, he asked, "Men, can you hear me?"

We all responded, "Yes, sir."

"Good. I just want to thank you men for being ready to answer the call to arms. This is a historic moment, and I want to be the first person to wish you luck and to tell you that my prayers are with you. Good luck, men. Remember, dead or alive."

We all responded, "Yes, sir!" My men were smiling.

"Well then give 'em hell, boys!"

With that, the line went silent.

When it was all over, the crowd departed the briefing area, happy with the results of our planning and preparation. And we had been granted execution authority from the man himself, from the President. That meant that this time there would be no turning back. As soon as it got dark, we would move to the airfield and load the aircraft that awaited us.

Our infill platform was an enormous aircraft, a C-17, with its four turbofan jet engines, the new workhorse of the Air Force. It was huge in comparison to its cargo, a single Special Forces team preparing for a high-altitude, low-opening parachute jump. We had the entire aircraft to ourselves, and its overwhelming size was impressive even for my team. We had jumped these planes before, but we had never had one all to ourselves.

Having loaded all of our equipment onto the tailgate, the crew was busy center-loading it all. They were stacking our rucksacks and assault boxes in a line down the center of the aircraft's cargo hull floor; and then they used large, yellow cargo straps to secure it as we stood in line, waiting for the brass to download from the bus they were in.

We stood behind the behemoth plane, looking into it through the open tail section. The sound of the jet-powered generators onboard was deafening; and each of us listened attentively as our company commander congratulated us on our selection for such a prestigious mission as he wished us luck and shook our hands, hugging us all in such a manner that made me feel a bit uncomfortable, not being used to such affection from this man.

We were continuing our journey into combat, into Afghanistan, the first team to get a mission; and this time it was for real. The night air in Germany was chilly in late September, to say the least; but we didn't notice. It had been less than a month since 9/11; and we were the chosen few to be the first as we stood there, shaking hands with the brass, each general and colonel giving us a congratulatory pat on the back as they moved down the line, all of them wishing that they could be on our team.

I didn't have time for this. I had too much on my mind to appreciate it. My team was on its way, having been chosen as the best. For that reason, we had been selected to be the first one to deploy into Afghanistan, to link up with the Northern Alliance, and to take down the Taliban. Others would follow, but we were the first. As the generals lined up to shake our hands, all I could think of was getting onto the aircraft and on with the mission.

The tarmac was well lit, but the fog that surrounded the plane kept the light muffled downward toward the ground as the crew worked feverishly to get the aircraft ready for takeoff. The pilots were walking around, doing their preflight checks, as the load master and crew chief set up the oxygen console along with the oxygen technician, who would supervise the pre-breathing operations as the period of unpressurized flight and subsequent high-altitude jump would require.

A light mist began to soak through our uniforms as the last of the brass had made his way past our formation. I gestured with a final salute, as did the rest of the team; and I signaled for the men to follow me onboard. Behind us, the load master and crew chief began closing up the paratroop doors at the back and on each side of the plane as we moved toward the forward section of the aircraft directly behind and below the cockpit and took our seats.

Our plan was to conduct in-flight rigging of equipment, prebreathe oxygen for an hour, and jump—simple really, nothing to it. We had done it many times in practice, although not recently. As a unit, our mood was somber, not having had much freedom over the last few days.

The rigors of mission planning can really zap your strength,

THE NIGHT EAGLES SOARED

I thought to myself as the sound of the aircraft's engines being cranked up made me feel a bit sleepy. I knew we had a few hours and that it would be best to use the time getting some rest; so I shouted over the roar of the engines, "Get some sleep. I'll wake you up when it's time to put 'em on!"

With that, I sat down and looked at my watch, making a mental note. *It should only take about ten hours 'til we are over target, plenty of time to get some sleep.* The high-pitched winding of the aircraft's jet engines escalated as the crew continued doing their chores, preparing for takeoff. Our equipment, to include the parachutes, was stacked up neatly in a line two feet wide and about waist high in the center of the cargo floor. A bright yellow cargo strap stretched over the line of equipment from end to end, holding it all in place, the weapons box in the middle.

Each member of the team had a basic load of ammunition, and we all relaxed with the comfort of knowing that we had packed a resupply bundle with enough ammunition to keep us in business for some time. I felt comfort in knowing that we had all that we needed. The fact that we had national-level support was also something that made us all feel more confident. I knew that with all of our weapons, with all the ammunition we had, we were a formidable element, especially when you considered our level of training and the fact that we had an Air Force tactical air controller with us. He could call in air strikes—not just fast movers, but the big guys, the B-52's with their massive payloads.

The team, seated, began to relax as the aircraft taxied from its chocked position on the tarmac and headed out under the fog-dampened lights. It rolled out toward the runway. On the flight deck, the pilot, co-pilot, and navigator were completing their pre-flight checks and communicating with the control tower as the crew busily prepared for takeoff, finding their seats and strapping themselves in. The aircraft shook a little as it rolled over the cement and onto the asphalt taxiway.

For me, this was the beginning of the end. I knew that my time in the Army was coming to an end. It was a matter of age, and this was a young man's business. Although this was my pinnacle moment, how had I gotten there? How did it turn out that I would be selected to lead this team at this point in time? *This is an incredible moment,* I thought to myself. *How did I get here?*

It didn't matter after having that thought. When I did try to sleep, I couldn't. It was impossible, as I kept reliving my entire life over and over again, my mind racing. Every time I opened my eyes, something would remind me of something else, of some event or mission I had experienced over the last twenty years. It was as if I was seeing my life pass before my eyes. I had ten hours 'till it would be time to jump, ten hours to prepare myself mentally, ten hours before I would perform the duties as jumpmaster. I tried to occupy my mind with the task at hand, but the minutes and seconds ticked past almost as if time was standing still.

The drone of the C-17's engines continued their high-pitched spinning sound as the aircraft continued on its way, bouncing a bit from left to right on toward the end of the taxiway, turning onto the runway and coming to a halt. The brakes squealed loudly as the weight of the aircraft lifted from the rear toward the front.

The entire aircraft shook violently as the pilot brought the engines up to full power, holding the brakes, preventing the aircraft from moving. Then he released the brakes; and with a sudden jolt, the aircraft leaped forward and began gaining speed as it rambled down the runway. Even with earplugs in, the noise was deafening. But the experience of tactical takeoffs wasn't anything new. This was a common practice, one that the Air Force used regularly to get their large cargo aircraft up into the air as quickly as possible.

Memories raced through my mind as the feelings and emotions of the times swept over me. I could see myself riding in the staff car with that sorry recruiter, the one who smoked constantly and talked about impressing people with his medals. I chuckled to myself as I remembered the Hare Krishnas trying to convert me as I walked off the plane in Saint Louis, my ears and head pounding with pain since I didn't know how to clear the pressure. I felt a warmth come over me as I remembered that first haircut and the NCOs who ran our basic training.

Nothing could compare to jump school, though, and the physical training that they put us through. "Hit the hole pole,man. Hit the hole." Now look at me, sitting here with my team. More than twenty years had gone by; and now look at us, all scruffy, getting ready for the ultimate skydive.

A sudden jolt snapped me out of my daydream as the aircraft bounced from side to side. Rubbing my face, I sat up straight and looked around. Everybody had settled in for the long flight. The captain was reading a book, and the rest had gone to sleep. The sound of the aircraft seemed extraordinarily quiet as I realized that we were just experiencing normal turbulence. I stood up and walked to the back of the aircraft, found one of the windows, and looked out into the night sky.

A full moon lit up the white clouds below with the black night glowing bright. It was comforting; and at the same time, it reminded me of skydiving out in Washington State. When I had first gotten out of HALO school, my team had gone out there; and we spent two weeks doing all different types of military freefall operations in the Yakima training center. We would load the aircraft at McChord Air Force Base in the morning and fly out over the Cascade Mountains. We had conducted night, full-combat-equipment, high-altitude, and high-opening parachute operations with more than a twenty-five mile standoff from the designated drop zone. Mount Saint Helens had been covered in snow that last night; and from altitude, it looked like a pimple ready to pop.

My thoughts drifted as I remembered all the different freefall jumps I had made over the years: night, full-combat equipment operations all over the country and daytime chopper blasts just for fun on Sicily, Normandy, Rhine Luzon, and other drop zones all over Fort Bragg. I had jumped into El Salvador to link up with the troops that we led into combat. Chuckling to myself, I remembered how scared I had been that day at Fort Benning, that day I had made my first jump. I had just finished basic training at Fort

Leonard Wood, Missouri; and then I had been to Fort Gordon for training as a radio operator. That had been the beginning of my career, attending jump school on my way to Fort Bragg and Special Forces qualification. Since then, there had been a lot of water under the bridge. I had come a long way.

The loadmaster stepped up behind me and said, "The weather over the target area is looking good. We should be there just before the sun comes up. You've still got quite a bit of time left before we start the pre-breathing op."

I looked at my watch. The digital timer showed that over four hours had passed since we took off. I couldn't believe it. The time was going by so quickly. It seemed as though we had just taken off, but I guess my mind was so occupied with memories that I had lost track of the time. I walked around a bit, to the back of the aircraft, and checked the location of paratroop lights. Shining red, they waited for the opportunity to let us know it was time to exit the aircraft.

The inside of the aircraft was quiet. The sound of air rushing past the fuselage was steady as the red tactical lighting reminded me of a barroom scene, only there wasn't any smoke or loud music. I stood at the back of the aircraft, watching the loadmaster check out his night-vision goggles as we continued on our journey. The scene of him sitting there reminded me of my first jump after jump school, the jump into Camp Mackall, and the prayer I had said that day. Since that day, I had repeated that prayer many times; and it seemed appropriate at that moment to say it one more time.

Father, give me the courage and strength to do that which I must. And Father, please help us all to make it without getting hurt. Amen.

I had made that jump, my first since getting out of jump school that day, feeling protected through prayer; and although I wasn't a religious man, I did feel as though I had a relationship with God, especially when we were at altitude, getting ready for a jump. I guess this time I needed to say that prayer more than ever before. It is true that the heart of a soldier is the soul of a man, the soul of a man that needed strength and courage to accomplish that which he has been asked to do; and tonight, we all needed that strength. We all needed to believe in something bigger and greater than ourselves. *Was this our destiny?* I thought to myself. *Is this what God had planned for each and every one of us since before we were even conceived?* I didn't know the answers to that question, but I thought that surely those three church ladies Jimmy and I had rescued from the FARC guerillas in Colombia so long ago felt that we were angels sent from heaven.

I had never heard from any of them ever again. I didn't even know what had become of them. I just remembered the looks on their faces that day I left them with Jimmy out there in the jungle. They had an understanding of God that I'm sure I will never know, but the look of fear on their face and willingness to follow our lead was something I would never forget.

Considering how lucky we had been that day, stumbling upon their captors like that, it was almost as if there had been some sort of divine guidance. We had chalked it up to luck. I guess a little soul-searching at a time like this wouldn't hurt anyone. At least it allowed the time to pass by more quickly. Obviously, the chant we had recited that day in the classroom out at Camp Mackall could be chalked up to wide-eyed innocence. It was the chaplain's prayer, the one he had delivered after the initial mission brief, that had been the overall guiding principle that had led us all to success, to be the ones chosen for this mission. We were champions of the oppressed; and this was our chance to bring honor upon ourselves, faith, families, and fellow men. I wondered if folks back home had any idea how precious the freedom we have really is. I didn't think that many did. *They take it for granted,* was my thought. I'm sure that if any of it was ever taken away—and I mean really taken away—they wouldn't take their freedom for granted. How would they feel then?

It was irrelevant though. At this point, our focus must be on the Afghan people and their freedom. I would never forget the outrage I felt as we had studied the Taliban and learned how they had been mistreating women and children. It just wasn't right; and even if we didn't get Bin Laden, at least we could help the people regain their freedom. The old-timers, the Vietnam veterans who were still on active duty by the time I had joined up, had a saying that they were very fond of. I tried to remember it word for word but couldn't. It went something like, "The sweet taste of freedom will have a greatness the protected will never know," and I suppose that brought them a sense of pride in themselves and our country. We all had a great deal of respect for them. All of us who hadn't been there felt as though we could never live up to their achievements as soldiers. I suppose that in some ways, they felt the same about the Korean War and WWII vets. How could anybody ever live up to the sacrifices made by so many? They were truly the greatest generation, the men and women who had fought in WWII.

Before we had departed Germany, we had watched a bit of news on television; and there were some comparisons being made between today's generation of warriors to those of the past. There was some doubt about this generation's ability to stand up against the tyranny that had been thrust upon us, but I knew in my heart that we had what it would take to make this mission and any other mission after that a success. Sure, some of us wouldn't make it. Perhaps I wouldn't. But one thing was for sure. We were ready, and we were meeting this challenge head on.

There hadn't been any such debate about that, at least as far as I could remember, before the Gulf War. I was a young NCO at the time, and we had gone into Iraq without hesitation, without question, knowing our mission was what it was. We had survived without fanfare, and that was the way I preferred it. There was no need for a ticker tape parade through the streets of New York, although there had been one. My only thought was how glad I was that I wasn't forced to endure such a painful march on pavement.

We certainly didn't have a parade after we came back from El Salvador, licking our wounds, trying to reintegrate back into a society that had no clue about what had been going on. I had flashbacks to those days while working with some of the troops from the 82nd Airborne. Many of them were young Latinos or inner-city blacks. If it weren't for the American flag on their uniforms, they could have been part of any of the third-world militaries I had trained and fought with over the years. Our boys weren't much different than any other soldiers. They were, however, Americans; and they all had the mettle within them, the mettle of their forefathers who had fought and sacrificed so much for this country. I have the utmost respect for them all.

Deep down, I had a sense of pride about what I had done in Central America throughout the nineteen eighties, during the Reagan era. We had won the Cold War not only in Europe but right there in our own backyard. The night ambushes; the patrols; the training; the months and months on end deployed to places like Honduras, Guatemala, and El Salvador; the vision of tracer rounds ricocheting off the rocks that first night ambush I had led with the Honduran lieutenant flooded into my memory. The smell of the smoke from the Claymores and machineguns filled my nostrils and my mind; and I could see the faces of the men as they looked up at me from behind the sights of their weapons, mouths half open, as if they were asking, "What next, Sergeant?' The memories and thoughts flooded into my mind without restraint, each one beckoning another until I felt almost overwhelmed.

The loadmaster stood up from his seat on the tailgate and tapped me on the shoulder. He pointed at his watch, and so I looked at mine. We were getting closer. Eight hours had passed since we took off, and it was time to start rigging for the jump. I walked back up to the front of the aircraft and stood in the middle of the floor with our equipment to my back, the team and the oxygen set up to my front. Stomping my right foot on the floor really hard, I woke the team up. As they cleared the sleep from their eyes, yawning and stretching, I shouted out, "Let's get it on!"

With that, they all stood up, knowingly understanding exactly what we had to do.

I turned around and motioned for the crew to undo the straps on our gear so we could get to the parachutes and equipment we needed. We all started helping each other don our parachutes. The younger guys on my team had never jumped anything other than the square canopies on a freefall jump before. I was the only one who had jumped the old MC-3 Para-commando round canopies that had been left over since the Vietnam War. They didn't look at these new rigs with the pride I felt in them.

I would always tell them, "You should be thankful you have these rigs. No, they aren't as fast or sexy as the civilian gear you jump on weekends, but you should try jumping with the old MC-3 like I used to."

They would just look at each other and say, "There he goes again."

I would just smile knowingly.

Tonight, however, they were all serious. I watched with pride as the men went about their business, gearing up, getting ready. The captain and I worked together, helping each other out. He put his gear on first, and then I gave him a jumpmaster pre-jump inspection. All was good, so he helped me put my gear on. Since I was the only jumpmaster, I had to ultimately check my own gear out; but I had taught the captain how to do most of the checks, so I felt comfortable knowing that he had kitted me up. In addition to my regular gear, I had an extra bailout bottle, which I would use to continue my pre-breathing while doing my duties as jumpmaster. I would disconnect it though prior to the jump and work off my own bottle just prior to exiting the aircraft.

One by one, the men completed putting their gear on. We had so much stuff strapped to us: rifles, oxygen bottles, load-bearing equipment, rucksacks, and our helmets. What a sight we must have been. One of the crew had a camera, and they were snapping photos as we worked.

Inspecting each of the men, I checked everything, sometimes twice. *There is no replaceable man on this team,* I thought to myself. *Each and every one of these men is an integral part of this mission, so there is no room for error here.*

The men must have taken that same attitude. Of course, none of them thought that he was mere cannon fodder. These were experts in their field, and they were very proficient at this mission. We had rehearsed it many times in the past, jumping at night from extreme altitude with full combat equipment into mountainous terrain. The jump into a country like Afghanistan was somewhat different though. It was as if we were trying to land on a small valley in the Rocky Mountains. We had never tried to do that before.

Perhaps, I thought, *I should write up a training concept when we get back and we could practice base jumping.*

Smiling to myself, I continued the inspections. Not finding one gig on any single soldier, I finished, stood erect, and patted the last man on the shoulder. I gave him two thumbs-up and looked to see the entire team seated, ready, and waiting for the next command.

I looked at my watch and saw that we still had about thirty minutes until time to start on oxygen, so I stomped my foot on the floor and shouted, "Relax for the moment! We still have time!" With that, I sat down, taking my place back on the paratroop strapped seat, and put my seatbelt on.

Over and over again, I tried to focus on the task at hand; but time stood still as I sat there, going over my pre-mission notes pertaining to the jump. We were flying at over thirty thousand feet above sea level. We would have to drop some altitude. Although the mountains around the drop zone rose to over twenty thousand feet, the drop zone itself sat at a nice eight thousand feet above sea level. We had already adjusted our altimeters to give us a true reading for our altitude above the drop zone, but that didn't help matters much if my spot was off just in the slightest amount. We could end up out over a mountaintop. The entire team would be in danger. This time there was not much room for error, and we all knew it.

I felt a bit nervous in the pit of my stomach as the oxygen technician got up and walked over to me, pointing at his watch, indicating that it was time. We all reached for our oxygen masks and pulled the hoses so that they would reach our faces. Attaching the masks to our helmets, we all looked at each other. I tried to show a smile through my eyes, but to no avail. It really didn't matter. Now each of us was locked into our own thoughts, unable to speak, and we just looked at each other and made hand gestures. I waved at the team, getting their attention; and I pointed at my watch and then raised a finger in the air to indicate one hour. They all nodded understandingly as I looked each of them in the eye. We were all excited, a little nervous; and the anticipation was building. After this long flight, we were all ready to get our feet back on the ground.

The oxygen tech walked past each man, stepping over the lines, checking the status of each man's mask, making sure they were on correctly and that the console was working at each position. He kept a close eye on us as the aircrew connected to the oxygen system of the aircraft. Once everybody was hooked up, the pilots depressurized the aircraft. Pressure built in our ears as we rose higher and higher in altitude. The men and I started to do the Valsalva maneuver in order to reduce the pressure building in our middle ear. We held our nostrils and kept our mouths shut, squeezing on the outside of the mask, and tried to push air out through our nostrils in a way that would release the pressure. It worked, but some of the guys would bang the side of their helmet to release the last bit. We all understood that at this altitude, flying unpressurized, if any one of us had a problem with his oxygen he could pass out almost immediately; so we kept a close eye on not only ourselves but the aircrew as well.

It wasn't long before the crew chief came over to me and let me know we were about twenty minutes out. I reached over, flipped on my extra bailout bottle, and disconnected from the oxygen console. Standing up, I walked over to the center of the aircraft, turned, and faced the team. Standing at the position of attention, something not that easily achieved with all that equipment on, I stomped the floor with my right foot and thrust my arms forward twice. My fingers spread on each hand; I gave the signal, "Twenty minutes," but without actually saying the words. There was no need. I had an oxygen mask on. The men, in unison, undid their seatbelts and waited.

I turned toward the back of the plane and moved toward the tailgate as the crew chief started opening up the aircraft. The sound of the hydraulic pumps reported their function over the sound of the aircraft's engines and the sound of the air rushing past the fuselage. There was a distinct releasing jerk as the seal was broken and the ramp forced its way downward into the open air. This had a tendency to slow the aircraft, so the pilot increased power as he started bringing us down to jump altitude, twenty five thousand feet above sea level but only seventeen thousand feet above the drop zone. The floor of the aircraft dropped down away from my back as the crew chief continued to work the hydraulics, opening the tailgate, cold air rushing in, so cold it stung as it brushed against my brow, the only part of my body that was exposed to the elements. Once the ramp was opened, and to a level position, level with the rest of the floor, he wiped his gloved hands on his pants for some reason. Then he turned to me and pointed with his entire hand, fingers together as if to say, "Your aircraft Army!" Signaling with my right hand, I gave the sign for okay; and I walked out onto the ramp, keeping a handhold on the superstructure of the frame for balance.

The back of the plane floated back and forth slightly as the pilot leveled off. I checked my altimeter, and it was correct. We were at jump altitude. One of the crew tapped my shoulder and gave me the signal for ten minutes, so I walked back toward the team and let them know. I had them stand up and move more toward the rear of the plane, and then I returned to the tailgate and started trying to spot the drop zone.

I walked back as far as I could and still kept a handhold and stood there, facing to the rear, looking down under my right arm, checking to see if I could see anything. The night was crystal clear; I could make out the tops of the mountains. But I couldn't see the drop zone. So I turned, facing the team, and had them move closer to the hinge and stopped them there. Kneeling down, positioning my gear so that it wouldn't be in my way, I held on while I protruded my body as far out of the aircraft as I could.

Obviously, the pilots had picked up on the flashing strobe several miles ahead. It was the only light to be seen, except for the lights of some large city that was off in the distance to our rear—probably Mazar-e Sharif. They had picked up on the strobe and were heading straight for it. I imagined that their navigation system was also letting them know that they were on track. I picked up on the mountain ranges on both sides of the valley, although I had to lean way out to see the far side. We were on track, perhaps slightly off to the left; so I came back inside the aircraft and signaled to the crew chief, "Five degrees right." The aircraft started turning as he relayed the information; and as it did, the drop zone came into clear view.

I put my right hand on the floor, the fat side of my fist down; and I raised my hand in the air and gave thumbs-up, indicating three minutes. I looked back out to check the drop zone, finding the strobe light blinking all alone. Although there were a few small villages along the valley floor that were dimly lit, their yellow light circled by dust that hung in the air.

The pilots maintained their heading, smooth and steady, as smooth as I had ever seen. There appeared to be some campfires burning along and on top of several of the mountainsides. Later, I would learn that these were Taliban positions; but for the moment, they didn't seem to represent any threat. We were way too high for their anti-aircraft guns.

As we approached the release point, I pulled back inside. Sitting on my knees, I checked the paratroop lights. They were on, green, ready to go. I had discussed it with the pilots beforehand and had asked them to give me a green light at one minute out as long as we had a safe jump condition. He had remembered, and they were on; and we were good to go. I gave a quick glimpse out the side of the aircraft, checking one last time, and could see that we were getting close, so I gave the team the signal for, "Ten seconds," by holding my right hand up and making a pinching motion with my thumb and index finger. In unison, they moved forward of the hinge, almost to the edge of the ramp.

As I stood, the prayer I had said earlier came to mind. *Father, give me the courage and strength to do that which I must. And, Father, please help us all make it out of this situation without getting hurt. Amen.* Turning, still holding onto the side of the aircraft, I faced outward, toward the rear of the plane, and watched the strobe light from under my right arm as the aircraft rapidly covered the remainder of the ground between us and the release point.

I used the edge of the ramp as a guide and waited until the strobe light was lined up with the back of my right heel. Letting go of the aircraft, I looked over my left shoulder at the men and waved my left arm over my head, pointing toward the open space, the command for, "Follow me."

Without looking back, I dove over the edge of the ramp, into the darkness of the Afghan night. The morning sun and the hope of a nation were arriving from far off in the distance. It was the night eagles soared and the dawn of a new horizon.